MIRROR
IMAGES

Books by Linda Gray Sexton

MIRROR IMAGES
RITUALS
BETWEEN TWO WORLDS: YOUNG WOMEN IN CRISIS
ANNE SEXTON: A SELF-PORTRAIT IN LETTERS

LINDA GRAY SEXTON

MIRROR IMAGES

Doubleday & Company, Inc.
Garden City, New York
1985

From *The Oedipus Rex of Sophocles,* translated by Dudley Fitts and
Robert Fitzgerald, copyright © 1949 by Harcourt Brace Jovanovich,
Inc.; renewed in 1977 by Cornelia Fitts and Robert Fitzgerald. Re-
printed by permission of the publisher.

The lines from "Diving into the Wreck" are reprinted from *Diving into
the Wreck: Poems 1971–1972,* by Adrienne Rich, by permission of the
author and W. W. Norton & Company, Inc. Copyright © 1973 by
W. W. Norton & Company, Inc.

Library of Congress Cataloging in Publication Data
Sexton, Linda Gray, 1953–
Mirror images.
I. Title
PS3537.E92M5 1985   813'.54
ISBN: 0-385-18372-0
Library of Congress Catalog Card Number: 84-13515

AUTHOR'S NOTE

I would like to thank:
> Kate Medina, my editor, for her faith and persistence
> Hazel McCarthy McDonald, for loving Alexander so well
> that I could leave him to do my work
> Dr. Steven Sandler, for helping me through three miscar-
> riages
> Dr. Eleanor Hannah, for telling me to start writing again
> Drs. Frank Silverman and John Quagliarello, for having
> patience

and, of course, John, who stayed

To Alexander and his dancing face

Can you use
birdflight or any art of divination
to purify yourself, and Thebes, and me
from the contagion?

> Oedipus to Teiresias
> Scene I
> *Oedipus Rex*

I came to explore the wreck.
The words are purposes.
The words are maps.
I came to see the damage that was done
and the treasures that prevail.

> Adrienne Rich
> *Diving into the Wreck*

MIRROR
IMAGES

1

1

SHE WOKE. Her body tingled—an electric shock. In the dark the nightmare pressed down on her. She saw the baby's face and reached for her belly, for the reassurance of a kick, for the comfort of her size.

Her hands found her hipbones. A flat line. It was not a dream; she was living the dream; this dream was memory.

On the other side of the bed her husband curled into his own animal world of sleep. She was alone in the blackness: 3 A.M. Four months ago, contractions had snapped her awake at this hour. Then the hospital: blurred walls, faces, sheets, examining tables, stirrups cold against the soles of her naked feet. Machines taking pictures, listening for a fetal heartbeat. The doctor's mouth delivered words. She could not allow herself to feel.

Since then she had waked every night at this hour, pinned under an anguish that refused to stop or be reasoned with, an anguish that had a life of its own, inexorable and measured— the animus of pain. The panic of that night in December had become the panic of every night; now it was fear that woke her and made her struggle to sit up, to get away from the pictures in her head.

She knew she had to stop fighting the dream and the memory or they'd never go away. Trapped on her back in the dark, she tried to let them in, tried to give herself to the pain in order to heal—as a diver enters the sea in a black dawn, sinking under the chop to some silent cave where there exists neither movement nor vegetation, but only undiscovered life. She forced herself to see it all once again: *the baby is dead,* she said silently. She underlined the last word in her mind. *A son. Six months old. Curled inside me, with a heart and fingernails, eyelids, nerves, and a smile. He was already a person. His name would've been Evan. Each day he was more real.*

Pain ignited inside her body in tiny bursts of fire; she drew back from it; she forced herself to go on: she touched her breasts, her belly. Her body had supported that fragile tree of veins and arteries, her body had conceived and held tight, her body was empty now. It had given up on life for a second time —for a second time had miscarried in a rush of pain, and blood, and betrayal.

She made herself imagine her son, a mystery, moored there inside her, dreaming unborn dreams, forming unknown ideas. He had trusted and then been cut loose. Her body had simply undone the knot to set him free, baptized him into premature death.

She wanted to cry and wash herself of the heavy black sorrow, but there was no relief. Even as she wanted it she could feel her body stiffen, refuse, withdraw. To cry would release the pain. To release the pain would release him. She couldn't let it go; she couldn't let him go. She slid from the bed. Without using a light she found a pair of Peter's ragg ski socks, glad that a stack of magazines now hid the clock and its terrible reminders. She wanted to float in space and stop thinking, stop being—just wait until the pain went away.

Eve groped her way through the dark, down the uneven staircase to the second floor. In the foyer she turned on the brass lamp to light her way into the kitchen, but stopped short at her reflection in the mirror: red and gray striped knee socks;

a baggy flannel nightgown that did a good job at hiding the body she didn't want to confront; a washed-out, slender face; a red nose. Her eyes were a dull brown—even her hair looked depressed, she thought, trying to perk up the flat auburn waves with her fingers. *You look like a sad clown,* she said aloud, forcing a grin at her image as she wiped her nose on her hankie. *Straighten up. Forget it.*

The kitchen was dim and comforting: the smell of pot roast, red wine, and garlic lingered from dinner. Plants hung above the windows and herbs grew on the sill in bright red boxes. The room faced south. Eve waited in the rocking chair for the water to boil, subduing her thoughts with the rhythm of the rocking. When the kettle whistled she set a tray for herself: the teapot snug under its cozy, a plate of Freihofer's chocolate chips and her favorite mug—familiarity to push back nightmare.

She smiled. The cookies made her think of her mother, her mother's face, creased by years of laughter. Other women earned their fame with brisket or blueberry pie, but laughter was her mother's specialty. When Eve or any of her three sisters fell and skinned their knees, messed up an audition, or lost a boyfriend, Rachel's remedy was to "laugh and make it better." As Eve left the room now, she could hear her mother urging her to eat those buttery cookies—"eat and make it better"—while at the same time making her feel guilty about the calories. When Eve thought of her mother, she thought of the old-fashioned word "ample." Ample in hip and bust and heart. But Eve could eat anything from french fries to strudel and never gain a pound. She'd kept her sweet tooth a secret for all her years at home: her mother had never had the satisfaction of seeing her indulge.

Her parents still lived just outside Boston's city lines, in the big old house where Eve had grown up, the second daughter among four. It wasn't such a different house from this one, she thought, as she carried the tray down the flight of stairs from the kitchen to her study. She'd been surprised to find that, after all the years of high-rise apartment living while she was a student at Columbia, what she'd really wanted when she finished her psychiatric residency was a tumble-down house with lots of room—the space to play and the warmth she'd grown up with, the space and warmth she'd always intended to provide for her own children.

When Eve and Peter decided to buy a house out of which she could run her psychiatric practice, they'd looked on New York's West Side because the streets here seemed more like her old Boston neighborhood. On West Seventy-fifth between Amsterdam and Columbus there wasn't a single apartment building, not a doorman in sight, and Bloomingdale's was the whole park away. Trees grew up out of the concrete and spread their roots through the small rectangles of dirt the city allowed them; last spring she and Peter had planted two small hedges of lilac on either side of the front door. It was a neighborhood of young professionals, people who wanted more space for less money, less pretense than the East Side, and who weren't intimidated by the more dimly lit streets.

Peter and Eve had done most of the renovations on the brownstone themselves, after using all of their savings and her inheritance from her grandfather for the down payment. Her study was on the bottom floor, her favorite room in the house. Under the kitchen, it caught the sun in the day and had a fireplace for nighttime—a fireplace whose original brass had been discovered by Peter and restored after three weeks of scraping and sanding blue paint. In this room she saw her patients: a mass of books, papers, and journals buried the battered desk that stretched the length of one entire wall, and plants sprouted wildly from all corners and sills because she never remembered to pinch them back.

She sat down in one of the old leather chairs that faced the fireplace, glad to be away from the bedroom. This was where she sat with her patients: Eve didn't believe in talking around a desk, especially since everyone she treated was either a child or adolescent. *They needed to see all of you, you needed to see each other,* she thought, as she picked up a file folder and crossed her feet on the ottoman.

Since finishing her psychiatric residency at New York Hospital a year ago, Eve had been doing consulting work for the Breton School. The private coed school on East Eighty-fourth had been looking for someone who would be more than a guidance counselor but less than a full-time therapist. When the offer had first come in, she'd nearly turned it down. "It'll take too much time," she'd protested. "I ought to be setting up my own practice." Having specialized in child psychiatry, Eve was eager to begin practice, to help others dig into their lives, to feel their emotions brush her face. It put her own life into perspective: it diluted her pain. Especially now. She thought of each patient's life as an unconducted orchestra—the tubas out of time with the oboes, the violins straining against the piano —and she wanted to lift the baton, bring balance, order, harmony, light. But Peter had been practical. "First novels don't pay the bills," he'd said darkly, referring to the small sum Farrar Straus had advanced him against earnings on his first novel. "Take it. For now." And it had turned out that Breton had many kinds of children with many kinds of problems. Most of them also had one thing in common: money. A family's economic well-being did not guarantee its stability, Eve had discovered; it guaranteed only that they could pay for help. She began to find the work even more absorbing than she'd thought possible.

The folder on her lap contained the school's history on Miranda May Webster, an eighth-grader known as Mira who had been referred to Eve by Marie Scott, Breton's guidance counselor. Mira's grades, which had been extraordinary for her first seven years at the school, had fallen sharply in the last three quarters. Eve flipped through copies of Mira's report cards and teachers' summaries. Her homeroom teacher's most recent comment read that Mira was now more withdrawn than shy and seemed to be cutting herself off from her friends.

Yesterday had been Eve's first appointment with Mira and she thought back on it now. She had seen the girl in the office she used at Breton—a room originally bare and blank, softened by the reds and blues of a print of Matisse's *La Danse* and a scatter rug Eve had bought while she was a med student at Columbia. Mira had knocked on the open door and stood there, uncertain, twitching the long straight fall of brown hair back from her shoulders. She didn't come in until Eve moved from behind her desk and pointed at the chair, and even then she walked tentatively, hesitating, poised on the balls of her feet, shoulders tilted forward just a little—as if she did not want to commit herself to any particular direction, as if she might pivot and run if anyone moved too fast. She was thin, fragile almost, in her brown velveteen jeans and cream-colored sweater. Her hazel eyes took up most of her face, which was too narrow to be pretty, just as her arms and legs were still too long, too out of proportion, to be graceful. Her breasts were small, her hipline nearly straight; despite the eyeshadow and mascara and lipstick, she was not a woman. Yet.

Mira sat down in the chair, holding tightly to the wooden arms.

"Physical science is giving you trouble this year, isn't it?" Eve had said.

Mira sat back a bit and her face loosened; Eve thought she looked relieved.

"I hate it," she said. "All those formulas and equations are just, you know, hard to get." The girl looked down at the floor. "I want to do better. I try. But . . ." A shrug.

"But what?"

"I guess it's just too hard for me."

"Have you talked with Mr. Harding? Gone in for special help?"

"It wouldn't make any difference." She turned her face to the window.

"Why do you say that?" She'd shut herself off, Eve saw, pulled back. *It's safe to talk about grades because something else is what's really bothering her.*

"Are you kidding? I couldn't talk to *him*—*he* wouldn't understand." Her voice was angry, but still subdued; she was trying to control the anger with casual words.

"Understand what?" Eve was looking for a wedge, anything that might get her past Mira's guard.

"What it's like. To have trouble in your courses. To have other things on your mind."

"Is that why you've dropped choir? Because you've got other things on your mind?"

She shrugged and answered with an edge. "Like I said. I'm just really, really bored."

Eve waited a minute, allowing a silence to come between them, a vacuum in which Mira would have room to talk. The tension built: she hoped the pressure would encourage Mira to reveal herself more. But Mira only stared at the hedges in the back garden with an impassive expression. Eve had just about decided that she would not respond when Mira shifted suddenly in her seat.

"What do you think about abortion?" Mira asked, picking at the cuticle of her thumbnail. Her face looked pinched and small.

Eve looked away, trying to cover her startled reaction with a bland expression. "That depends on a lot of things, I guess," she said, buying time. "Who's having it, and why." Her mouth had a funny metallic taste; she wished she could leave to get a drink of water. "Are you pregnant?"

Mira looked at her for a minute, then nodded slowly, as if Eve were forcing her to admit it against her will. "Third month." She bit her lip and looked away again. "I keep wondering if it's a baby yet."

She makes it sound like a casual question, as if she's wondering whether the Rangers will win the cup, Eve thought, pausing to wait and sense what kind of response Mira was looking for. "Does it seem like a baby to you?" she asked after a while.

"My mother says it isn't. But I went to the library and looked at one of those books with pictures. Did you know that it already has a heart, and eyes, and even hands?" She lifted her head to look straight at Eve, and her eyes were filled with tears, her eyebrows made a tense arrow across her forehead. "My mother says not to be scared." She cleared her throat.

There are an awful lot of things going on here, Eve said to herself. *Fear of the procedure, fear of what she's doing, fear of her mother. Slow it down, take it apart.* She reached out and took Mira's hand. "You don't have to have an abortion if you don't want to." She tried to sound pragmatic. "You have to decide what *you* want to do."

Mira shook her head and pulled her hand back into her lap. "My mother made an appointment for me next week. She says I have to go before it's too late."

Eve had felt the small bones of Mira's fingers before she'd moved away. *That was a mistake. She doesn't want to be touched,* Eve thought. "What does your father think?"

Mira started. "My father's dead," she said, looking up at Eve with a curious expression. "Didn't they tell you?"

Eve flinched. She couldn't help it. "I'm sorry. They just gave me your file this morning, it's probably in here somewhere."

"He died last March," Mira said, her face sympathetic at Eve's embarrassment. "Maybe they don't put that sort of stuff in your record."

"Last March?" Eve repeated. She picked up the file and quickly flipped through to the computer printout of Mira's grades. "Do you see any connection, Mira, between that and your grades?"

"Sure," she said easily. "Like I said, I can't concentrate. I'm depressed. I just can't do anything about it."

"Maybe there are some feelings you need to work out," Eve suggested gently. "Maybe then you'd be able to concentrate again." She offered up the standard advice almost without hearing herself speak; she was thinking about Mira's pregnancy: *was it a way of making life after a death, a way of cheating death? Or, even more, a retaliation, an angry answer to being left by her father? A way of asking for help, a way of putting out a public and unavoidable distress signal?*

"But what about the baby?" Mira asked.

She was avoiding confrontation, Eve decided; it was easier for her to keep this discussion on a philosophical, practical level. She waited, giving Mira a chance to move in the silence.

"Will it feel anything?" She looked at the floor again. "Do you think it will know what I'm doing to it?"

Eve wasn't used to questions like these from a pregnant student. "I don't know." She'd counseled a lot of pregnant girls during her medical training, but few seemed to wonder very much about what they were doing. It seemed unusual, almost odd, for someone so young to consider the life budding inside her as something more than an inconvenience, or to think of abortion as anything other than extended birth control. *They're too damned young to consider much more than that,* she said to herself.

The irony made her want to laugh out loud: to deal with a pregnant student was the last thing she needed right now. After two miscarriages, just *talking* about a conscious termination of life brought her sharp, irrational pain. Until two years ago, Eve had believed that ending a pregnancy was a woman's

choice. That was the modern viewpoint, and everyone she
knew agreed with it; she'd never really thought about it all
that much. When she'd counseled pregnant women seeking
abortions, she'd seen the issue as a legal definition. Most of
those who came in were just relieved that they lived in an age
where safe abortion was available; few considered what they
didn't want to know. It was quick, easy, neat. But now Eve
was not so sure. She could only feel the injustice: what was an
unwanted burden to one woman was an unattainable gift to
another. All she could think of was the babies she had lost. All
she could think of were the long months she and Peter had
spent waiting to conceive after the first miscarriage, the expensive fertility pills, the endless routine with thermometer and
basal body temperature charts—love reduced to a clinical
event. Sitting there looking at Mira she felt envy, anger, and
finally, incredulity: other people conceived by accident. She
fought to control her face and recenter her thoughts. What she
was feeling had no place here.

"What about your boyfriend—what does he say?"

"I don't have a *boyfriend.* You know," Mira flipped her hair
over her shoulder again in a nervous gesture, "not like you
mean."

Eve looked confused.

Mira sighed. "My mother says it's important to see lots of
different guys. That I'm not old enough to have just one *boyfriend.*"

She uses her mother to answer my questions, Eve thought.
"Do you sleep with most of the boys you see?"

Mira shrugged.

Eve lifted an eyebrow. She wondered what the girl's motiva-
tion could be. "And do you enjoy it?"

Mira blushed and looked at the floor. "I guess. Doesn't everyone?"

"Do you use birth control?"

"My mother helped me get the pill last year. But some mornings I forget to take it."

"How many mornings?"

"I don't know," Mira said, beginning to sound discouraged. "When I do I just take extra, you know, double up. Maybe a couple times a week."

"Being so sexually active, didn't you think you might get pregnant if you weren't more careful?"

Mira looked up in mild surprise. *As though it's never occurred to her that sex and pregnancy might be linked,* Eve thought.

"Not really," she said.

Eve looked at her watch. "Would you be willing to come in and see me with your mother? I think the three of us should have a chance to talk together." She stood. "I'll call her and make an appointment for tomorrow or the next day."

Mira seemed nonplussed. "Well, sure. I guess. But I don't think Vivian could come over here. She's awfully busy."

Vivian. Not Mother or Mom. "You let me worry about that," Eve said, opening the door. She watched as Mira moved down the corridor with that floating, hesitating stride; then she shut the door to the office quietly and sank back down into the chair. She let the emotions she'd been fighting overwhelm her for a minute.

She wanted to take the baby from Mira's body and transplant it into her own—to hold that warmth in her arms, smile into a small face, give the shelter of her breast. Again she felt the uselessness of an empty body, and again she tried to put these thoughts aside. This was what she'd never been able to get straight in training—how to keep her world, her self, from interfering in her patient's therapy.

She forced herself to reconsider what she'd just heard, and it struck her again that the girl never answered for herself: *my mother says, my mother thinks, my mother my mother. Subli-*

mation. Why was the girl so apathetic? If she had the pill why was she so careless? And so detached from her sexuality that she'd let the pregnancy occur? Psychiatry allowed for very few accidents; Mira's child did not seem like an accident to Eve. And there was the atrophy of her relationships and her lack of interest in extracurricular activities as well. *Is it all just a reaction to her father's death? Or is there more?* The questions flipped up in Eve's mind like the fruit in a slot machine, as yet unmatched.

A car trying to gain traction on the ice just beyond her window brought Eve back to this night, the dusky room, the empty fireplace. She realized then that she was cold, and lifted the cozy from the teapot to pour the last of the tea. From a chest in the corner she took an afghan and draped it over her knees. She looked at her watch. Five-thirty. Time went so quickly when she was working. In half an hour she would not be alone anymore: the world would begin its routine clamor, she would make eggs and coffee with Peter. By eight o'clock she would be at work in her office at Breton. These were the things that enabled her to go on, to continue. *And later this afternoon,* she thought to herself, *I'll meet Mira Webster's mother.* She had the sense of unease that always came when a case was about to get complicated, and yet she was looking forward to working this puzzle out. She wondered how it would solve itself.

She couldn't get warm and suddenly liked the idea of curling around Peter for a few minutes before they had to gear themselves up for the day. The nightmare was gone; she'd put it behind her. It was safe to go back to bed. She padded up the two flights of stairs to their room. Peter had moved to her side of the bed, and she climbed in and put her cheek against his back. He did not wake. The room grew light. It was almost six.

The whistling started. Persistent. Irritating. Like a cat in heat, Mira thought, like the pentatonic scales in music theory. A metallic dissonance blown staccato by the army of Park Avenue doormen in black coats and caps as they tried to flag down cabs. Just like always, it began a little after six, when the winter streets were beginning to get brighter. From Seventy-fourth Street, the building's back entrance, Mira heard the garbage truck crunching up what the city didn't want—dog food cans and broken toys, wire coat hangers and empty bottles, orange peels and the fat rinds of steak. She opened her eyes.

She'd learned to wake up quickly, as her bedroom shifted from black to pale gray. The pulse of New York snapped her awake with no lazy lapses back into dream. She stretched under her quilt and thought about the city, how it woke up every morning at this time. The tall buildings of glass and steel were empty now, waiting for the secretaries and lawyers, for the businessmen with briefcases and wing tips, but in an hour lines would form in front of lobby elevators and everyone would complain. The department stores had wide aisles now, but at ten o'clock they would be narrow with women in fur coats, loud voices would clamor across the counters. Sidewalk trash baskets were stuffed full with a whole night's new treasure, just waiting to be raided by the old women with their paper sacks. A yellow river of taxis would surge down the streets and through the white clouds of steam that came from the city's secret underground. The traffic would snake around the towers of concrete and gold, pull against the high-rise vertical vacuum that made standing on the sidewalk seem almost dangerous—as if both the pavement and the people could be sucked upward and out of this world, like Mary Poppins with her umbrella.

From her bed Mira could feel that pull, the city's pace. It was her alarm clock. She turned over, slowly, getting ready to throw the covers back, trying not to start up the pain in her back. Last spring she'd cracked a vertebra in a fall from her horse, and it still made getting up hard. When she moved pressure began, a pain sharp against her spine. She lay there for one more minute, luxury, thinking about the English paper she hadn't finished last night, about whether Bill Phillips would ask her to that party next Saturday, about whether to wear her new silk shirt today. And then, surfacing up, although she hadn't wanted it to, a worry. The baby.

She slid from the sheets, went into the bathroom without turning on the light, and sat down on the marble floor. When the doctor had taken her brace off two months ago, he'd given her an ultimatum if she wanted to start riding again—a morning set of stretching exercises. They hurt. She hated doing them. She kept the light off so that she could pretend she was somewhere else. Her muscles pushed out against the pain, the marble was smooth and cold against her back. The ache began to ease up. She wondered when she'd be okay again—these exercises were as bad as having to wear a retainer.

She finished and snapped on the light. Without meaning to, she turned sideways to check her profile in the mirror over the tub. In the mornings the baby seemed the most real, maybe because this was the one time she was really alone, with all the silence, with nobody and nothing to interfere. Or maybe it was just seeing her body naked. Every day the baby was growing inside of her, and even though she tried hard not to notice, there were just too many changes to pretend everything was the same. For one thing, she had some cleavage for the first time ever. And her stomach seemed maybe just a little bit rounder. She couldn't stand the idea of hurting it. She thought a lot about what it would be like to hold the baby, soft as a puppy, and she was sure, positive really, that it was a girl. Someone to cuddle and talk to. How good she would smell after a bath. How soft her hair would be against your cheek.

How could she go through with an abortion? This was the worst thing that had ever happened to her. She felt tears coming again, but she knew she wasn't supposed to care so much. She tried to squash the feeling down. She tried not to think about next week's appointment, next week—when her life would just stop. "Hey—Daddy?" she said aloud, calling to him through the mirror. It seemed as likely that he could hear her through a bathroom mirror as through a church spire. Her parents had had a bad argument when Vivian had tried to get Mira the pill two years ago, and Mira thought that maybe her father understood how she felt about the baby now. Vivian sure didn't. Her father had been pretty straight. He probably wouldn't have even let her get an abortion. "I don't want to do it, Daddy. Why doesn't she understand?" She leaned her forehead against the cold glass of the mirror and her breath steamed a small O of moisture on her reflection. Tears wet her face. She missed him so much—if he'd been here, somehow they'd have fixed this. He'd have been on her side.

He'd have been mad, a small voice inside of her contradicted. Quickly she pushed herself back from the mirror, wiped the tears from her cheeks, and started to brush her teeth, hard. She spit, wiped her mouth on the towel, and quickly dabbed a little Clearasil on the red spot near her nose. It was getting late and she'd been dawdling again. Mornings brought her biggest responsibilities, and she shouldn't be wasting a lot of time being down. She was good at forgetting emotions. She'd learned to hide them in a closet in her head. She could stack depression, anger, and despair as neatly as pillowcases and sheets. Grabbing her wool robe off the hook on the door, she went through the dark bedroom to the kitchen.

The signs of last night's party had disappeared. The staff knew that if they didn't clean up every glass, crumb, and cigarette butt—even if the last guest didn't leave until 3 A.M.— Vivian would give them trouble. As Mira went by the living room her nose picked up the lingering smell of cigar smoke. She closed her eyes and saw a room full of people once again. It had been a good party. When she'd opened the door to greet the guests and take their coats a warm wave of affection had spilled over her. Her mother's friends liked her. She remembered everyone's name, what they did, how to talk to them. It was like a game. It made Mira happy to feel grown up. She liked being efficient, well organized, responsible—she was an expert.

The kitchen was a great big room done in white and chrome, and the bright fluorescent lights made her blink. Every morning she brought her mother the same breakfast on a tray. Breakfast was a chance to be together before the day really started, a chance to share some time in a world where time was tight. Even when her father was alive they had done it like this—the maid had brought his tray to his bedroom. He didn't like to have to talk to people so early in the day. Her parents had started sleeping in separate rooms when Mira was twelve.

She liked moving through the silence, following her routine exactly. She put the water on to boil and found the orange juice—already poured into glasses and covered with plastic wrap in the refrigerator—and put it on the tray with two croissants, butter, and raspberry jam. She dripped a china pot of French-roast coffee. The steam floated up onto her face. She liked the smell, it would always make her think of dark rooms, privacy, cold mornings.

Her mother's studio call was for eight o'clock, but she was half an hour late almost every day. Unlike most other soaps, ABC's "Megan's World" was still broadcast live, and Vivian had to be at the studio early enough to rehearse before airtime. The set was farther east than the apartment—on Eighty-second and First—and it was Mira's job to make sure Vivian got there reasonably close to eight. She needed at least an hour to wake her mother and get her up and going, then she would rush to dress and make it to school before the eight-thirty bell for homeroom.

She was proud to be a part of her mother's TV career—a partner, sort of. At restaurants people recognized Vivian and asked for her autograph. And sometimes even Mira's. When they shopped in Saks or went to the theater, people often stopped to stare and whisper. At home Vivian played the role of Mira's mother. In public Vivian was Megan O'Neal, the wily, beautiful woman who spent all her time on screen scheming to get what she wanted. Audiences loved her. Mira kept track of the ratings and read *Variety* every week—anxious to be reassured that her mother was still the favorite in America's number-one soap. Her mother depended on her a lot, and she liked that. She liked sharing her mother's life. She liked being needed, feeling loved.

Balancing the breakfast tray, Mira headed back through the dark apartment to turn on Vivian's bath. Maybe she'll show me a new way to do my hair, she thought. I wish Bill would ask me to that party.

Her mother's breathing sounded uneven, her sleep sticky and drugged. Vivian's room was a place apart from time—heavy drapes blocked out the light, no clock counted the hours. Here, Mira was the watchman.

She hesitated before waking her mother, sat on the edge of the bed, and studied her face, which was lost in dream. Without makeup she looked so helpless, defenseless. Reaching over, she stroked her mother's cheek with a finger, once, lightly, tracing a line, a wish. It was easy to touch Vivian when she was asleep—then it was nothing but a touch, an impulse of love.

With a sigh, she shook her mother twice, and called her name, but Vivian just rolled over, away from her hand. She didn't wake up the way Mira did, suddenly and sharply, to the noises of the avenue. She slept like a baby, Mira thought, and wondered what secrets, what fantasies her mother dreamed about. She worried that Vivian didn't get enough rest—being tired on the set might lower her ratings. But she had to wake her up.

She reached over and shook her one more time before going to the bathroom to turn the hot water tap on full. Steam began to fog the room. It would help clear Vivian's morning head. Mira sat for a moment on the edge of the tub, feeling queasy. Last night's party had been exciting, but she was tired. No wonder it was hard for her mother to wake up. She turned off the light and went back into the bedroom.

"Hey," she said in a soft voice, "it's nearly seven."

"Christ." Her mother's voice was husky. She opened one eye and her hand groped under the blankets. "Coffee."

Mira poured a mug and helped her mother sit up. Vivian couldn't make do with less than two cups and a bath in the dark before facing the day. She hated the morning. Morning was the enemy.

While her mother wrestled with waking up, Mira turned off the taps in the tub and added oil to the water.

When she called again, Vivian appeared at the door, dropped her nightgown, and submerged herself in the tub. "Time?"

"Ten minutes till makeup." She handed her mother a re-filled mug and two aspirins, then went back to the bedroom. The curtains now had to be pulled open just enough to let in a sliver of light. At her mother's dressing table, Mira lined everything up within reach. Highlighter, shadow, rouge, mascara. She'd need more cotton balls and the eyeliner pencil had to be sharpened. Mira rummaged through the top drawer, seeing that she needed to reorganize again. Vivian got stuff into a snarl faster than anyone. A stack of hankies scattered, spare pots of rouge, linty now without their tops, a ton of loose change, the small pistol Vivian kept "in case of burglars" at the front of the drawer instead of at the back, and a torn package of Winstons shredding tobacco over everything—all of it made Mira smile. Maybe it was the dusty smell of the face powder, a smell that reminded her of the time when she was a little girl and just sat and watched her mother make up every morning, a smell that carried emotions—love, worship, the rich safety of being little. How magical this drawer had seemed then. It had been forbidden, off limits. It had held the essence of her mother. Now this drawer was as much hers as Vivian's.

She picked up the hairbrush and, running a comb length-wise through its bristles, cleaned out the stray hairs left from yesterday. She rolled them into a ball between her fingers. It was so soft. She sat down on the bed and drank her juice, and waited.

The first thing Vivian was aware of was the hot water: she was steeping in water so hot her skin tightened against her bones in defense. It would steam-clean her fresh and wrinkle-free. She put the wet washcloth over her eyes and felt sleep fade slowly as the dream slid away from her into the water. This particular dream came often now, a nightmare whose specifics she could never remember. Each morning she woke with just a picture in her mind: an old woman, alone in a bed, slumped into wrinkled sheets. Her face was familiar—a face Vivian had known when it was younger, and beautiful. The bones were signposts; the skin hung under the throat like the wattles on a turkey. Maybe, she thought, maybe it was her mother, in her bed at the nursing home the year she died, senile before her time with Alzheimer's disease. Her hands were the only thing left alive then; they were still large—still life-size and all bone. But it was not her mother, it was not her mother's face, and each morning in the tub, as she thought of the dream, her heart beat at an uneasy pace, like an engine that idles unevenly, out of tune.

She picked up the nubbled handbrush specially designed to banish cellulite and twisted in the tub so her hip was above the waterline; the drumming of hard plastic soothed her. She had to work at beauty now, where before it had all been so easy. Now she dieted and massaged and saunaed, and soon she would add surgery to the list. Last night David had said how great her body was—for someone her age. For an instant she'd felt anguish, humiliation, despair, and then fury: she'd almost told him the truth about himself—that he looked like a duck when he was naked.

She rolled in the water to switch hips, thinking that she had a good body, period. The hell with what some young jerk said. She could hear Mira moving around in the other room, pulling the drapes, clinking the glass jars on the mirrored top of her dressing table. The familiar noises made Vivian smile. She'd seen a perfect dress for Mira in the window of Bergdorf's yesterday: she'd get it today, as a surprise, for that party Mira was going to this weekend. Or hoped to go to. Vivian's brow creased. Bill Phillips should've asked her by now—Vivian liked Bill, liked his brash style, not like that shy Michael Mira sometimes hung around with—and she wondered if something was wrong between the two of them. If she bought the dress and Mira didn't get a date—she cut herself off in midthought. She'd just buy the dress as a silent vote of confidence. She visualized it again: a soft green, Mira's green, in a silky textured fabric. It would be perfect. Mira was so good she deserved a treat. Vivian scrubbed her toenails with a brush, hard, wishing once again that Mira hadn't gotten herself knocked up. She just couldn't understand it.

She'd argued with Stewart before he'd died to get Mira those pills: he'd been scandalized—Mira was only thirteen, he'd said, a "nice girl" her age wouldn't need pills. Vivian had accused him of being more old-fashioned than her own father. Then they'd really fought. That night Mira had turned the stereo in her room up loud, so that she wouldn't have to hear them, and Vivian remembered how angry she'd felt at the gesture.

But she hadn't won that night; only after Stewart died had she been able to give Mira the prize—freedom, no fear, no restrictions, and the chance to choose her own way. When Vivian was a teenager she hadn't even been allowed to date until she was sixteen.

And despite all this, Mira had still gotten herself pregnant. To Vivian it seemed a betrayal: Mira hadn't kept the bargain modern women made with their bodies. Vivian caught her sometimes, looking sideways in a mirror or plate glass window, studying her reflection for change. She didn't act panicked by the pregnancy at all, but seemed to bask in it. She just doesn't know, Vivian thought, soaping her armpits and the mound of dark curly pubic hair; she just doesn't understand what being pregnant really means. In the first few months you could ignore it, but then it took over: it invaded your body; it possessed you in a way no man ever could.

When she'd found she was pregnant with Mira she'd wanted to have an abortion: she was only twenty-four, her first bit part on a soap had just come through, and pregnancy meant ruin. She'd gotten started on "The Secret Storm" simply by being persistent as a girl Friday—if you laid end to end all the miles she'd walked for other people's coffee, they would circle the globe at least twice—and the part was her start, her chance at all she wanted. But Stewart had refused to give her an escape clause. He wanted the baby. She'd damned the day she'd married a man ten years older than she was—she had been so naive when she was nineteen—a man whose values were so different from her own.

When they'd first met at a party of mutual friends, she was

still a drama student at City University and he was already famous, a young genius in cancer research, his first discovery making the science page in *Newsweek.* Vivian had seen immediately how desirably different they were. She'd grown up surrounded by the highways and oil tanks of Elizabeth, New Jersey, on a small city street of two-family, double-decker houses packed shoulder to shoulder, a Monopoly board of pastel green, blue, and pink. It was a Catholic neighborhood, where the smell of broiled mackerel never seemed to die, but renewed itself each Friday night.

Stewart was from North Carolina. Even the name of his hometown, Chapel Hill, was refined. He was a Southern gentleman, with pale red-gold hair and a slight accent, with his talk of classy hobbies like chess, duck hunting, or fly-fishing for trout and land-locked salmon. Nothing with any sweat to it. And his parents' "home" was just as she'd imagined it—a sturdy white three-bedroom Colonial set back on a square one-acre lot of neat trees and grass. Respectable. His father, Stewart Senior, had been the town's general practitioner before he'd run into a tree on a house call one night when Stewart Junior was ten years old. His mother Vivian had seen as gallant: Charlotte Webster raised her boy on a widow's budget and still kept her hands smooth. She liked to invent variations on the New England specialties of her hometown, Boston: thick chowders full of Southern fish, and gleaming loaves of yellow cheddar cheese cornbread. Vivian had admired her red hair, her quick temper, her lively expressions, her full-bodied laugh. She'd stood up to life's difficulties undaunted. The first time Stewart took Vivian home she fell in love with his mother.

Her own mother had worked the cash register at the drugstore the family owned, the side of her palm tough from punching the long total key. Oscar and Edna Carson—straight up the line, hard-working, routine people. "Ox" was a pharmacist, his square shoulders straining the seams of his white jacket. Edna obeyed: she tagged the merchandise with the prices he gave her, she let him dictate the budget, Saturday night's movie choice, even the meatloaf recipe—corn flakes instead of breadcrumbs. Edna's profile was a dull brown blur, but Ox had sharp dangerous edges. His strict discipline ruled: bedtime at nine, homework before dinner, no roughhousing in the living room.

Vivian thought her parents were as ordinary as the plate glass window with "Carson's Drug" lettered in tall green script, as boring as the shelves of greeting cards, bubble gum, hairnets, and enema bags. She was the next-to-last in a line of ten—six boys, four girls—and always fighting to keep from being lost in the shuffle. Drama was a way of distinguishing herself: she directed neighborhood plays in which she was the heroine, while at home she was always in trouble. But Stewart didn't need these devices: he was an only child, the object of his mother's full attention. Vivian married him because his life had been so different.

And they were happy until she got pregnant. Stewart had loved her pregnant, kept reaching out to touch her. Swollen with his child, she was a reflection of him then, of his power and control, of what he could accomplish. She felt like a rat in one of his experiments: observed, weighed, and measured daily. He made her stand in front of the mirror while he admired his handiwork, while he stroked her belly. She'd closed her eyes. She hadn't wanted to see it. She'd hated him for it.

He wanted to make love every night, but she'd felt sickened by the idea; it was the only time in her life she hadn't wanted sex. At night when the baby kicked she slid from their bed and sneaked into the kitchen for a cigarette. Sometimes she smacked it back with her closed fist, but it just kept kicking— laughing at her. She moved from room to room in the dark, trying to get away from it, but it had her trapped from within. No escape.

She'd cried all the time. She'd lost control of her body and her life. The stretch marks lengthened, her belly button popped inside out, her breasts drooped with weight. She was being forced to share herself, a hostage to what they had created. And when Mira was born, Stewart had insisted Vivian nurse her, although it was not fashionable then; he talked about antibodies, the immunities in mother's milk. But when she'd seen how it was changing her breasts, how the nipples were being pulled outward by the baby's greedy mouth, like teats on the udder of a cow, she'd lost her milk, and as hard as Stewart argued with her, it never came back.

It was only when she went back to work, when Mira was a year old, that Vivian really began to love her daughter. It was only when she wasn't a slave to endless diapering, feeding, burping, and loving that she could feel the stirrings of pride in what she'd created. And then she'd wanted to sit for hours and just look at her, or watch the way she got graham crackers in her hair. There was a peculiar pleasure in overriding the nurse's authority to bathe that smooth skin herself, soaping each crease and fold of fat leg and arm. She spent hours comparing her own baby pictures with the changeable face in front of her, and soon she realized that she wanted to be with Mira more than she wanted to be with Stewart: she resented the time he took away from this perfect creature, this small model of herself.

She'd seen then how it would be different with her daughter than it had been with her mother: she'd be warm, loving, not cold like Edna. She'd never let Stewart get between them, never let him dictate what would be for Mira. And so there were new arguments, arguments over who knew best, a rivalry, a silent contest to win their daughter. It hadn't really ended until the day he died, and then Mira had belonged, entirely, to Vivian.

She still had her stretch marks; now she covered them with

lotions and creams, and in the summer, with makeup, so they wouldn't show above her bikini. Vivian stood and stripped the excess water from her body with the flat of her hand. Mira just didn't know what she was getting into, she thought as she stepped from the tub. Mira was romantic about being pregnant —all she saw was golden curls, and soft skin, and need disguised as love. And that was only half the story. Vivian toweled herself off. How much more she wanted for Mira—the opportunities that only time could bring: time to grow, to fall into love with a wonderful, sensitive man, to go to college, to find a career, to be whatever she might decide to be. That was why Vivian had never even asked who the father was: she didn't want this pregnancy to seem like a baby to Mira. Mira was just beginning. Nothing would happen for her without an abortion.

Dry now, she flipped on the harsh overhead light for inspection, moving in close to the mirror. She noted the lines in her forehead: could the camera on the set see them? The producers kept her on edge, hiring eighteen-year-old girls with skin as translucent as bone china. Vivian always wondered which one of them would replace her eventually. Still, her jaw line was firm, her breasts high and hard. She took care of herself and it paid off. But how much time could really be left? And after she lost the battle—what would she do then?

Mira was sitting on the bed, thinking about the baby again. She was sure it was turning inside her, swimming around like a little fish, and she'd put her hand on her stomach when Vivian came out of the bathroom, awake now, and in her usual morning rush. She sat down at the dressing table and started on her face.

Mira loved watching her mother make up, liked to see the lines drawn and smudged in, layers of base applied and then shaded with rich color. It was an intricate procedure, and Mira laid out each ingredient in exactly the same place on the table every day so Vivian could reach without thinking. As the makeup went on, Vivian's beauty sharpened. The green eyes grew clearer and more almond-shaped, a deeper emerald. The bones of her face stood out more prominently, her mouth arched fuller and redder.

As she brushed her black hair with long strokes from root to tip, she smiled at Mira for the first time. "A great party last night." She began to coil the hair back into a chignon: at the studio her hairdresser would rearrange it into whatever style today's episode required. "As usual, you were better than any manager or agent," she said, talking around the hairpins she held in the corner of her mouth.

"But I don't really *do* anything." Mira came to the dressing table and began to brush the snarls from her own hair with her mother's brush. She wished her hair were her mother's dark color, that her eyes were a deeper green. Most of the time she felt she was only a pale, washed-out imitation of Vivian. She made a face at herself in the mirror over her mother's head.

"You're *there*, sweetie, and that's what counts." Vivian stopped for a second and put her arm around Mira's hip in a hug. "I'd never remember anybody's name without you. Besides, everyone loves you—they're always impressed with my smart daughter."

It was Mira's job to remember names, to make charming conversation, to fill in where needed, and she liked moving through rooms full of adults, refilling their drinks and laughing at their jokes. She liked being a part of their world. But when she looked back in the mirror she felt unhappy again. She was still so young. The way her face fit together displeased her. She sighed, and tried pulling her hair to one side in a twist.

"We'll have to try something new for your party this weekend," Vivian said, swiveling on the stool. "Here, bend down."

Mira knelt in front of her mother. "I haven't even been invited yet." She looked at the floor, but Vivian could see her lip quiver.

"You will be," she said. "Give Bill a chance."

"I saw him yesterday with Marta Geiss. Maybe he's going with her."

"If he is, someone else will ask you," Vivian said, keeping her voice steady and sure. She pulled Mira's hair back off her forehead and piled it on top of her head. "No," she decided. "It should be more casual." She dropped Mira's hair and gave her another hug. "Someone will ask you—you'll see. And I promise we'll find a special way to do your hair. Okay?"

Mira looked at herself in the mirror and poked at her skin nervously. "Anything'll help. By then I'll probably have *five* zits," she said morosely.

"Miranda May, will you quit worrying!" Vivian gave her a playful jab in the ribs and Mira laughed, a little. Vivian started to do her eyes, lining and shadowing the lids. "Did you catch Joyce Hanson's dress last night?" Vivian smiled and leaned into the mirror. Mira knew that her mother enjoyed doing a postmortem on her guests almost as much as she did the actual party. "Why she came with that creep Ed Powers is beyond me."

Mira looked blank.

"You know who I mean—the assistant producer over at NBC," her mother said as she primed her lashes with the first coat of mascara.

"Oh," Mira nodded. "You mean *Les Towers.*"

"Whatever. Anyway, he tried to strong-arm me into bed." She gestured her disgust with her mascara wand. "I was pretty high, but not that high. He's just *repulsive.*" She drew the word out, as if she were looking at a snake.

"I saw you arguing with him," Mira said, keeping her face impassive. Details about sex made her feel vaguely nauseated. She didn't want to picture Vivian with men other than her father. That her mother'd had affairs when her father was alive had hurt Mira, shamed her, but she'd accepted it because she'd been able to ignore it. Now Vivian was so open about her sex life, she liked to share it all, and it meant only one thing to Mira—her father was dead.

Still, at the same time, she wanted to be grown up and she wanted her mother to trust her. She didn't want to be left out just because she was young. She guarded Vivian's intimacies jealously so that no one would be closer than she was. Sometimes she just liked to sit and think of the things Vivian had confided, stacking the incidents in her mind like the net bags of gold foil-covered chocolate coins you get at Christmas. The confidences were her insurance. Her mother loved her too much. She would never be left again. Mira smiled. "I think he's *gross.*"

"Mira, I got a call yesterday afternoon from school"—Vivian was working on her mouth now, outlining the shape with a pencil and then layering on lip gloss with a brush,—"but I didn't want to talk about it in front of everyone else last night. A Dr. Strauss wants me to come in for an appointment today." Her voice was serious, all playfulness gone.

Mira felt a pulse of anxiety; she'd wished Dr. Strauss would forget. "It's nothing," Mira said, keeping her voice casual, and moving over to sit on the edge of the bed. "She wants to talk about my grades or something."

"Something's wrong with your grades?"

"They're just down a little. No big deal."

"Miranda honey, I'm getting worried about you. Are you in *more* trouble?" She sighed and looked at Mira with exasperation and a little bit of hurt. "I mean, I wish you'd told me before. I don't like hearing all this from a stranger." She surveyed her image in the mirror and tried on a smile. She looked over at Mira and their eyes met in the glass. "Well, we'll go see her. But you buckle down. That's not so hard for you."

"Sure," Mira said, in a voice so low it just scratched the surface of the tension in the room. It hurt to disappoint Vivian. She wanted to be perfect. She wanted her mother to be proud of her. It used to be easy.

Finished at the dressing table, Vivian grabbed a croissant on her way to the closet and dropped her robe. She doesn't look thirty-eight—she looks too young for sure to have a fourteen-year-old daughter, Mira thought. She watched Vivian pause at the mirror to inspect her figure, turning this way and that. Mira never understood why her mother seemed to expect that something would have changed overnight. She averted her eyes and looked at the floor. It was embarrassing to see Vivian naked.

Pulling on her blouse, Vivian came over to put her arms around her daughter. "Don't you worry, sweetie—I'll handle this Dr. Strauss thing. Now what's the time?"

"Eight-ten," Mira answered, using this as an excuse to slip away from her mother. "I'll get dressed and call a cab."

Back in her bathroom Mira brushed her teeth hard. She was angry with Dr. Strauss. Why couldn't she have left Vivian out of this? Nothing would be changed by talking. She would still do what she had to do. She pulled on a pair of corduroys and a sweater, and then went to the mirror in her bathroom. With a deep green pencil she outlined her eyes, green like Vivian's eyes, but not as good a green as Vivian's eyes. The rouge went over cheekbones not nearly as high, the lipstick and gloss over lips less red, less full. Less, less, less, she thought. When will I look like her? She peered at herself with an immense sense of dissatisfaction and made a face, pulling her lips back across her teeth to make sure she'd gotten all the croissant out of the cracks with her toothbrush. "Oh yuk," she said, sticking her tongue out at her reflection as she zipped her makeup pouch shut with a rasp. She ran to buzz the doorman for a cab.

2

HALF AN HOUR later Mira came out of the building's dark foyer into startling sunlight. It was raw enough that even the sun didn't warm her face, and as she began to walk up Park Avenue to school her muscles tightened under her coat, and her skin pricked up in goosebumps. She put her shoulders back into the March wind. It was a clear day—last night's sleet had turned to rain and rinsed the city clean.

On Park Avenue the sun seemed to shine as it did on no other street in Manhattan. It unrolled itself down the broad avenue at a voluptuous slant, draped itself across the shrubs and trees on the center island in a bath of gold. It took its time, Mira thought, not like the quick way it fell on the narrow side streets. On Park the sun spread out—luxurious, rich, abandoned. Mira thought of it as a royal carpet, running up the aisle of the avenue to a great queen's throne.

The pedestrians who passed her huddled against the wind, down into their wool melton or mink or suede, without looking around them, intent on their destinations. Mira, on the other hand, had been walking this route every morning for eight years now—ever since Vivian had gotten her role on "Megan's World" and they'd left the small apartment in Chelsea to come uptown—and she'd never even been tempted to try Fifth or Madison. Park was her avenue. She knew its traffic patterns, its gray face and clean-washed pavement glistening under the streetlamps on rainy days. She never took its luxury for granted—the small crooked streets of lower Manhattan had too often smelled of garbage and dogs.

It made her happy to nod to the doormen each morning, block after block, the same faces, year after year. It seemed to her that doormen never grew old or got promoted. Mira had known their doorman George since she was seven, had said hi every morning, depended on him for taxis and packages and safety, but she'd never once heard his last name.

She liked watching the same old ladies emerge from their nests—like the chickadees on the farm Grandma Charlotte had moved to when she left North Carolina, Mira thought. Some of them had grown humped around the shoulders in the last few years, their hair more silver-blue, but they always walked their manicured poodles and Pekingese at just the same time she was on her way to school. On her way home there were black nurses pushing babies in fancy Italian carriages, and it made Mira feel good that in a city where most people were strangers, where most passed on the sidewalk without looking each other in the eye, she had neighbors of a sort—people who greeted her with a nod or a smile as she skipped across the curbs.

Until last year, this morning walk had always been shared with her father. The faint smell of his Right Guard had clung to him in the cold air, and she'd matched her short stride to his clipped steps, looking up at his face from the corner of her eye as they walked. He was always hurrying, even though he was never late. By seven-thirty, his mind was already immersed in his latest work at the lab. Mira pictured his brain as a series of tickertapes and digital readouts, a sophisticated microcomputer that kept on calculating new formulas of velocity, mass, number.

She was not good at science, and her father's work was a

puzzle. When he tried to explain it to her, smiling with enthusiasm, it was too technical and scary. The ideas were a dense wall her mind couldn't climb over or get around. She knew that recently things hadn't been going too well, that there was some kind of trouble at the institute that pressured him. But he never talked about that. She just intuited it from overheard conversations and the discouraged look on his face when he came through the front door at night. In fact, they hardly spoke at all as they walked. He didn't know what to say or ask a daughter, Mira thought, he didn't know the right questions. She'd grown satisfied just to read his mood by his expressions. He was a tall slender man, with hair a crinkled gray, his brown eyes sometimes happy, but he always seemed to be somewhere else. Mira imagined him far away, in a land where mathematical language was the native tongue and street signs were painted in scientific formula.

Even so, when he kissed her goodbye he always looked into her face and smiled. In the mornings he was never angry, his sharp edges were hidden by the start, the promise, of a new day. When he came home at night he was not so much weary as tense, ground down. That was when he and her mother fought. Especially after he read the evening newspaper. They could argue over nuclear disarmament, political candidates, war in the Middle East, or just corruption in the New York Police Department. Mira never read the newspaper—it was too full of dangerous topics—or joined the political clubs at school. And her father didn't like living in their big apartment, either—didn't like her mother's salary paying the mortgage and the maintenance. Mira never knew what to expect in the evenings—she played her stereo loud a lot—but mornings were always different. In the mornings they were by themselves.

Now she walked up the street alone. She missed him. She wondered if her mother ever thought of him at all anymore.

Vivian's life just seemed to roll on, unchanged. How could her mother forget him? It hurt.

She turned the corner, off Park onto Eighty-fourth. The Breton School had once been a mansion, owned by one of America's richest men. Now it was a school where affluent, slightly liberal parents sent their sons and daughters because the administration worked to keep a racial and ethnic balance.

It was a building of smooth granite, stretching the entire width of the block. An ornate wrought-iron fence—topped with sharp spikes—testified that the property was private. The windows were elegantly spaced, their curved panes reflected the early sun. On either side of the front entrance shrubs grew in profusion, defying the city's soot, and the oak door with brass boar's head for a knocker was waxed and polished each day. Mira joined the other students crowding through the door and ran up the central staircase. She opened her locker, hung up her coat, and went back into the hall. In front of a large mirror she stopped to fiddle with the collar of her shirt. Without turning around, she could see Bill Phillips as he leaned against the bannister, flirting with Marta Geiss. Bill was a junior, with hazel eyes and a compact, muscular body. Mira liked being seen with him, liked the way he put his arm around her in front of other people, liked the musky odor that clung to his shirts, and she felt jealous of Marta. She was sure they were going to the party together. She hadn't bothered to tell him she was pregnant, but now, studying him as he smiled down at Marta, she wondered if he were the father. Would the baby have his blond hair? Or maybe Mark Rizzo's dark eyes? Mark cuffed her shoulder as he stopped to adjust his sweater in the mirror. "Hey, Mira," he said. "Got a date for the party Saturday?"

Mira shook her head. "Not yet," she said with a confidence she didn't feel.

"How about it?" He smiled. "I'm still free."

"Okay," she said slowly, still wishing it could be Bill. "I'd like that." Better to go with Mark than stay at home.

"Pick you up at eight."

It was stupid even to think about the baby having a father, Mira decided, as she watched Mark cross the hall to his locker and spin the dial. She turned back to checking her hair and makeup in the mirror. Michael Ross leaned over her shoulder into the glass and made a face at her. "Get the English paper done?"

She smiled. Michael was one of her best friends, and they met here most mornings before class. He was tall, already six feet, and skinny, with hair and eyes the same shade of light brown. His grin grew in a lopsided curve from one side of his face to the other. He was different from the other boys in her class. He talked about different sorts of things. Best of all, he demanded nothing.

Their friendship had started in the lunchroom a year before, two months after Mira's father had died. Alexander Ross had been killed in a car accident when Michael was eleven. Talking to Michael had made Mira feel better. Her other friends— mostly girls her own age—didn't want to hear about her unhappiness anymore. For them her father's death was finished, the drama worn off. After a month of feeling sorry for her, they'd gone back to more routine worries—like grades, boys, and parents—and they expected her to pick up where she'd left off.

But Michael had still been willing to listen. He knew how long it took to mourn. Now they talked about everything. He was the only one who understood how she felt about the baby. In fact, he had brought her the book from the library that explained how an embryo develops.

"The paper?" she said, shaking her head. "Nope. Guess it'll be another lunch-time quickie."

"Boy, Mira." He wagged his finger at her disapprovingly. "You'd better get it together."

She was going to say how tired she was, but stopped short. Michael thought it was unfair of Vivian to ask so much of her on weeknights and so she made up her mind not to mention last night's party. He didn't understand the glamor or the excitement. He didn't see how much she liked to help Vivian. Her father never would have allowed her to stay up so late. He would have liked Michael, who came from another world. Michael didn't know people like her mother and her mother's friends. *His* mother was an attorney with a New York firm that did mostly copyright law, and their family was quiet and ordinary. Mira thought of the Rosses as a normal family. Dull. Mrs. Ross was in most nights with her two boys. They ate supper at seven and then cleaned up the dishes together. Schoolnights were for studying, and Michael's grades showed it. He was at the top of the class and Mira called him for help a lot when she got stuck on her science homework. The Rosses spent summers in a cottage on Long Island and Mira had gone with them for a few weekends last year. She liked Mrs. Ross— she was almost as easy to talk to as Michael was.

"Give me a break, will you?" Mira asked, sliding her arm around his waist. "Just help me figure out a topic!"

"That's all?" He smiled. *"Just* a topic?"

At the door of homeroom they hurried to take their seats before the bell. Michael sat behind her, one row over. He leaned across to whisper. "What happened with Strauss yesterday?"

Mira turned her thumb down. "Vivian and I have to go this afternoon. Talk about *nervous!"*

"Everybody says she's real understanding."

Mira made a face. "Who's everybody?"

"Well, Penny for one." Michael nodded at the heavyset blond girl sitting on the other side of the room.

"She never said anything!" Mira said, hurt. Penny Saunders was one of her best friends.

"Probably embarrassed." Michael shrugged. "It was about her weight. She told me she really liked Dr. Strauss. Check it out."

Mira sighed. "No matter what anyone says, Michael, I'll still be uptight."

"So what's the worst that can happen?"

Mira pushed her hair out of her face as the bell rang and cut off their conversation. "I don't know. Something tells me my mother and Strauss just're not going to get along."

Mira knew her instinct had been right as soon as she saw Vivian and Dr. Strauss together—they did not get along at all. Her mother resented Dr. Strauss. It was three o'clock, just when Vivian usually started rehearsing her lines for tomorrow's shoot. Mira cringed when she saw Vivian's polite face. Her mother was always irritated when she got interrupted during these hours, and this appointment was even worse—having to drag herself all the way over here.

They were already talking when Mira came into the room. "I'm just not sure I understand, Dr. Strauss," her mother was saying. "I thought this had something to do with Mira's schoolwork."

Dr. Strauss ran her fingers through her wavy auburn hair and asked Mira to sit down beside her mother. She was prettier than Mira remembered from the other appointment: a pale cashmere sweater contrasted with her hair and eyes. Mira especially liked her eyes. They were a nice warm color.

"It does. What I'm trying to explain to your Mom, Mira, is that your teachers here see a continuing problem. Your grades have been falling consistently since last spring, which, I understand, is also when your Dad died."

"Stewart died last March," Vivian said, opening her bag and taking out a pack of cigarettes and a lighter. "But Mira didn't miss any school, and I just don't see why Breton is making such a fuss over a few low grades." She leaned into the flame, inhaled hard, and then shut her purse with a snap. She didn't like the whole tone of the discussion. It made her nervous. What did this doctor want anyway, she wondered. "Mira's handled her father's death very well," Vivian went on. "I made sure of it—by being there to help her. She's lucky. When my mother died, my father wasn't there for me at all. Not a bit."

"Mrs. Webster, when a student's record shows a consistent drop in all courses, we look into it. Always." Dr. Strauss put her elbows on the desk and smiled. "That's our job."

"Well, I never made the honor roll in school, and it never hurt me any, but I'm sure Mira will promise to work a bit harder," Vivian said, reaching over to take Mira's hand. "Won't you?"

Mira nodded, seeing that her mother was trying to end the appointment. The grip on her hand hurt. Vivian's diamond ring dug into her palm, and for a minute Mira thought of the thin gold wedding band her mother never wore anymore. It made her feel like a little girl, sitting there with her mother holding her hand. Her palm got sticky. She forced herself not to pull her hand away, and watched her mother give Dr. Strauss her most disarming smile.

"I'm sorry, but I don't think that's the answer." Dr. Strauss shifted in her chair and turned to Mira. "How do you feel about all this?"

Vivian dropped Mira's hand and leaned forward in her chair. "What do you mean, 'not the answer'?" She didn't like being cut off like that. After all, she was Mira's *mother*.

Vivian's voice had an edge to it now, and Mira tensed. She knew what kind of anger came after that tone—her parents always fought when the harsh sound came into her mother's voice. She closed her eyes for a second and rubbed the place on her hand where Vivian's ring had pinched her.

"Let me draw you a picture," Dr. Strauss suggested. "Mira's father dies, her grades drop radically, she withdraws from extracurricular activities, gets pregnant—*and* feels disturbed enough about the possibility of an abortion to speak to me—a total stranger—about it. We are not talking about a simple problem here."

Vivian turned abruptly to Mira, feeling betrayed. That had been *their* secret. "You told *her* you were pregnant?"

Mira didn't answer, shrinking back into her chair.

"That was a matter just between us, Mira," Vivian said, leaning back and forcing herself to stay calm under the doctor's scrutiny. "I thought we had an understanding—you *cannot* have a baby just because you are too sentimental to get an abortion."

"I'm sorry." Mira's voice was a whisper. She looked over at Dr. Strauss, her eyes begging to be let out of this impossible situation. She couldn't bear it when her mother was angry with her. "I got upset, it just leaked out."

"Mrs. Webster, I think the important thing here is that Mira is disturbed about things," Dr. Strauss cut in, leaning across her desk. "It's important to hear her out."

"Frankly, I fail to see where any of this is getting us." Vivian stubbed out her cigarette and picked up her purse. "This is a family matter." She held onto her bag tightly so that her hands wouldn't shake.

"Sometimes family matters cannot be solved by families."

"This one will be. Next week. In my gynecologist's office." She made her voice as final as she knew how. She would stand for no more interference.

Dr. Strauss was quiet for a moment. "I'd like to see Mira again," she said. "If she has the abortion, she's going to need to talk about how she feels and work that out. This is not an easy time for her. Her feelings shouldn't be taken lightly."

Mira could see Dr. Strauss was fighting for some kind of control. Her emotions showed on her face so quickly—unlike Vivian, who used emotions, hid or displayed them, when it was to her advantage. To Mira's surprise, she sort of liked the idea of seeing Dr. Strauss again. She felt so confused all the time—maybe it would help. "I think I'd"—

—"In that case," Vivian interrupted, standing to put on her coat, "she can talk to *me.*" She shrugged and put her hand on her daughter's shoulder, in control again. The situation was hers. "You've got to understand that Mira and I are good friends. More really, than the normal mother and child." She smiled down at Mira, and felt her love radiate out through that smile. "It's *my job* to worry about her—after all, she's *my* daughter." She had spoken the truth, only the truth, and that truth was her best defense. Why would her daughter need to talk to someone else when she had a best friend in her mother?

A funny look crossed Dr. Strauss's face—for a minute Mira thought she'd looked hurt. Then she straightened up, stood behind her desk, and offered Vivian her hand. "That's true, Mrs. Webster. Still," she turned to Mira, "if I can ever be of help, I hope you'll stop by." Mira could feel her dark eyes continuing to ask questions, trying to make contact. Mira opened her mouth to say something and then looked away.

"Certainly, Dr. Strauss," Vivian answered, turning to Mira. "Is it okay if I drop you home on my way back to the studio?" she asked as they went out the door. "Or do you want to come down there with me?"

As they left the room, her mother's arm tight around her waist, Mira pushed away her feelings of depression. She hadn't thought she'd want to talk more to Dr. Strauss, but Michael was right—she was nice. Now the abortion waited for her next week like a wolf in the dark and the one grown-up who seemed to understand how she felt was off limits. Even if Vivian hadn't said so right out, Mira knew it was true. As her mother swept her into the cab Mira told herself she should have known better. Things would be what they would be. There was never a way to change them.

"That woman is so incredibly *obstinate!*" Eve said, getting angry all over again. She and Peter were in the living room, having a glass of wine before dinner. "I hate it when a parent won't listen to what her own kid's saying." She stared down into her glass. "Vivian Webster doesn't see her daughter as a person."

"Come on, Evie—how many parents do?"

"This is more than just the normal my-kid-is-still-a-kid stuff."

"Why?"

"The way all the trouble begins right after her father dies. Getting pregnant. Her attitudes. Her anxiety. Her defensiveness about her mother. Her *anger* with her mother." Eve sipped her wine, taking her time to think it out. "I don't know —it's a tension, an undercurrent, I picked up. Her lack of self-esteem. Her lack of identity."

"I admit she sounds troubled—but not more than a lot of the other stories you bring home."

"I think she's different." Eve ran her finger around the lip of her glass. "But I can't say why."

Peter got up from his chair, took her glass, and crossed to the cabinet they used as a bar. "Are you sure you're not over-reacting? I mean—you're so worked up about this." He poured the wine with an impatient gesture. "You got home an hour ago and this is all we've talked about."

She took the glass but did not speak. Ordinarily their eve-ning ritual in the living room was the most relaxed part of her day. She used it to shed her working worries like a snake's skin. This was where Eve the psychiatrist stopped and Eve the wife began. By grouping the sofas and chairs in small clusters, she'd designed the room so that two people could feel as comfortable as fifteen. In the summer she and Peter sat on the long bench of the window seat and watched the city fade into darkness. In winter they sat in two big armchairs before the fireplace, took off their shoes, and warmed their feet.

But tonight she couldn't seem to get settled: her mind was restless, pacing back and forth over the appointment with the Websters. Once again she felt depression constrict the back of her throat, and she wanted to cry, for no reason at all.

But she wouldn't. Instead, she looked over at Peter as he stared into the fire. His dark hair curled up against the edge of his neck, and she had a sudden urge to press her face against him there. She hadn't even given him a chance to tell her about his day, she'd just burst in full of her own news. Writing was lonely and she usually made an effort to give him the time and space to talk when she came home. It was his one chance to connect with the world.

He turned toward her and she could feel his eyes trying to undo the twine she had twisted around her feelings, trying to undo all those neat boxes of sadness and despair; he wanted to undress her emotions, strip her bare. For an instant, against her will, she remembered: over a year ago now, how bitter that January had seemed against her face as she left the hospital; that time it had been a girl, lost in the fifth month, the small milk-white lamb of a girl they'd already named Rose.

Peter reached over and brought her onto his lap. "Are you thinking about *our* little girl?"

She rubbed her cheek against his, hard, looking for the bone, looking for the sureness of his face. He was scratchy, he hadn't shaved yet today. A novelist didn't need to shave every day, he always said. She didn't answer, but just sat there, his thighs pressing warmth into her. He felt so solid.

"Is that why you're this upset about the Websters?" he asked finally.

"It's just that it's damned ironic."

"What is?"

"Here we are, losing two babies when we'd be *good* parents, and then I see these other people who don't really care, don't even want to know what their kids need . . ." She stopped short and sighed. "Some people see the whole world as a big reflecting glass, reflecting back themselves." She stood and warmed her backside against the fire, feeling the relaxation begin, the sensation of unwinding that came from talking things out with Peter. "But hell no. It's more than that. There's something *odd* about Vivian Webster, something weird. The way she held Mira's hand. She seemed to think she"—Eve paused, hunting for the right word,—*"owns* her." She looked at Peter, triumphant to have at last defined her suspicions with a word. "Mira *wants* to see me!"

Peter sighed, resigned to the discussion, but still skeptical. "Are you sure you aren't making a big mystery out of this because you want to get involved and you've been told to butt out?"

"Look," she said, irritated. "I'll admit that I'm overanxious about this girl—maybe because she seems so needy, and that appeals to me. And because she's pregnant. And because," she paused and swallowed hard, "of Evan. And Rose. But even with all that, I still say Mira Webster's stretched too thin!" Eve sat down in her chair again and leaned forward, elbows on knees. "I'm telling you—there's something more going on than just a few bad grades and a pregnancy. It's not my imagination."

"Instinct—right?"

She looked over at him, starting to feel angry and defensive at the humor in his tone. He smiled and then she suddenly couldn't help it, laughter was bubbling up inside her. She started to laugh: at herself, at the whole absurd, unfair trick life was playing on them. Sometimes all you could do was laugh. The pain was too great, the tragedy too enormous, to assimilate. The last bit of tension she'd felt drained away. It was a game they had learned early on—to make each other laugh when they were getting too serious for their own good.

"Absolutely," she said with a grin. "Instinct—the same kind that tells *you* when a character is real or not, when a word is right or wrong. It's like hunting something gone bad in the refrigerator—you go from shelf to shelf wiggling your nose, and then finally you find a mungy old lemon wedged behind something else, covered with gore. You can smell it— but you can't see it, can't even find it sometimes. You just *know.*"

"Okay, Sherlock."

Eve smiled over at him, and sipped her wine again, remembering their first laugh together. It was when they'd met— almost six years ago. Before Peter, she'd never dated anyone longer than a few months. Med school was demanding: few men understood the pressure or the total absence of free time. When Peter Seidel interviewed her for an article on women in medicine for the Sunday New York *Times Magazine,* he'd asked exactly the right kind of questions, questions that showed he knew something about the work she faced every day. Maybe part of it was that he'd been struggling to make a living too, writing free-lance articles—unlike the other men she knew who were already embarked on profitable law or business careers. His apartment was a one room walk-up in the Village, not an elevator building midtown.

It was spring then, her first year as a resident at New York Hospital's Payne Whitney Clinic. They'd sat outside on a stone bench overlooking the circular drive: when she needed a break from the pressure of the clinic, Eve often went to sit on that particular bench and watch the people come and go over the cobblestones. Behind them the building rose, massive in gray granite, with wide arched entrances and a curved branch-like design woven into its stone face.

"How do they treat you, the men in your program?" Peter had seemed very serious, intent on his subject.

"I heard two residents talking the other day," she said, holding back a smile. "One of them asked the other if he'd heard the old saw about the days when men were men—and the women were grateful?"

Peter made an appropriately scornful face.

"The other guy laughed and said, 'Well, have you heard the one about the days when men were men—and the sheep were nervous?' " Eve paused. Peter's pencil went scratch, scratch against the pad. "Anyway, the first guy looked at the second and said, 'But the best is the one about Payne Whitney— where the men are men and the women . . . are men.' "

Peter looked at her, not sure whether she was kidding or not, not sure whether he was allowed to laugh.

"That about sums it up, wouldn't you say?" Eve crinkled her nose and grinned. "Sexist as hell, but I think it's a howl."

They'd both started to laugh. It didn't seem in the least bit strange that they were laughing at something that shouldn't have been funny, something that should have been an affront. But Eve always allowed herself to laugh at jokes about Polacks, Wops, WASPS, women's libbers, and JAPS: life was too complicated to be taken seriously. They were quick to discover the other things they had in common—he too had been a Columbia undergraduate, although three years earlier than she— and went on to talk careers, politics, hobbies, books, family. She found him more and more attractive as the hour went by, even though he was a good two inches shorter than she: there was something about the way he was built—lean, supple, and taut—that conveyed an impression of stature. He wore a corduroy jacket and soft old jeans that fit him well. His eyes were almost black. They softened and shone as he spoke; her mother would have called them bedroom eyes: they transcended his body.

"Why did you choose a soft field, a woman's field, like psychiatry?" he'd asked, returning to the interview.

Because psychiatry has no formaldehyde, no smell of decay, she thought, *because the mind needs only clean dissections.* "Because my mother wanted me to be a doctor, and I didn't like doing rectal exams," she said, and they both laughed.

"Seriously," she went on, "I really wanted to be a writer, but Mom had a better idea: fantasize all you want and get paid for it—be a shrink."

"And this schedule you have, of every third night on call, what's that do to your love life?"

"Makes it lousy." They both laughed again; suddenly the air felt good on her face and she smiled. "On the other hand, tonight's my night off."

He smiled back but didn't pick up on it.

"I like your questions." She decided to be aggressive. "In fact, I like you. Want to go around the corner for Chinese?"

He hadn't hesitated then, nor did he hesitate to let her move in with him a year later either. In the last year of her residency, she suggested they get married, and he'd accepted.

Now Peter stood and stretched. "Suppertime." He headed for the kitchen. "In five minutes."

Eve nodded and leaned her head against the back of the chair. This was one of the nicest parts of the day: wine, a warm fire, and Peter in the kitchen. He loved to cook; he was, she admitted, a better cook than she. She'd hated cooking from the time she was ten: every edible known to humankind seemed to be her mother's specialty. Working at home all day gave Peter the opportunity to play; most nights when Eve walked through the door she could smell bread in the oven, or roast lamb and rosemary in the air, or the sweet caramel of an evil dessert. It was part of their arrangement: weeknights he cooked; weekends she did; dinner parties they did together.

Reluctantly she got up and left the fire; she felt a little guilty about letting him go by himself. Her mother's warm kitchen was always busy, crowded with activity at this hour: Rachel at the chopping block, her knife reducing mounds of vegetables into salad; Eve and her sisters setting the table, washing dishes, stirring the pots; her father in his chair at the head of the table, contributing conversation while he waited for the meal. At least she could keep Peter company as her father had once done for her mother.

She settled into the rocker, put her head back, and pictured that kitchen, that house. Until she came to college in New York City, she had lived her whole life in Brookline, a Boston suburb that might just as well have been city. Twenty Feller Street was a ramshackle but neat white frame house with a front porch, a small backyard, and a big oak tree out front that spawned an acre of acorns in the fall. At the intersection of Harvard and Beacon Streets, where the trolleys labored up the incline, was Coolidge Corner: the kosher butcher and baker, the bagel shop, the deli, and the Viennese chocolate man. A combination of aromas hung over the street at that corner—garlic pickle, sesame seed, dark sweets, and the acrid exhaust of traffic. The fishmonger's next door had its own pure smell: each salmon, whiting, or cod stacked neatly in the window on crushed ice, glistening in clean, gutted death, its one eye fresh and clear.

The bookstore Eve's father owned was there on that corner too: dark and small with shelves from floor to ceiling, it drew an intellectual clientele, and he still prided himself on refusing to stock either Harold Robbins or Judith Krantz. He was a man who took depression seriously, and so featured in his front window writers who did justice to the bleak ironies of modern life—Kafka, Beckett, Borges, Lowry. When she was little Eve used to like to stop in on her way home from school and help him arrange new displays. Over a cookie and cream soda she told him funny stories about Mrs. Wadsworth and Frankie Pughe: nothing made her feel as happy as getting her father to laugh.

Feller Street was lined with elms and streetlights, and in the summer dusk children left the supper table early for keepaway, run-the-bases, kick-the-can, and ally-ally-in-free. Eve was always the captain of the Strauss team, being a whiz with bat, ball, and bike from the time she was five. The neighborhood was mixed: the Strauss family were not the only Jews, but the street was not only Jewish either. And though bagels and lox were on the Strauss Sunday brunch table along with the New York *Times,* the Strausses belonged only to the invisible temple of American assimilation.

Eve had loved her years on that street and had gone off to college with reluctance, finding it hard to relinquish her distinction as the family's practical joker. She even missed her mother's stern voice calling "Elizabeth Eve Strauss"—Rachel had decided when Eve was eighteen months old that she looked more like an Eve than a Liz—as the marshmallow fluff in the toe of Ruth's shoes was discovered. It was a good time, an easy time.

Not like now, she thought, as she pushed the rocking chair back and forth and watched Peter at the stove, sautéing the vegetables for pasta primavera. Now everything was complicated, tangled—even their food, she thought with a frown. Angel-hair pasta, topped with a julienne of red bell peppers, carrots, snowpeas. A sauce of white wine, shallots, and cream. Fresh Italian Parmesan was already on the table with a bottle of cabernet sauvignon and salad. Peter tasted the sauce. "The best *ever,*" he said, smacking his lips as he turned to her.

Eve's mouth watered despite herself. She still needed to take off five pounds from the last pregnancy, but it was worth feeling a little guilty for one of Peter's meals. "Fat city here we come."

"I was going to do hay and straw, but you should have seen what they wanted for prosciutto at Zabar's. And their green noodle looked lousy."

He'd learned to cook from his father; his mother, a semi-invalid, couldn't manage the kitchen, and so the two men had taken it over and made it their domain. Once he had talked a lot about cooking for their family, how he looked forward to baking bread and making big pots of spaghetti for their kids. One of their first "married" arguments had been over how many children they would have: he had been an only child and he wanted to be surrounded now, buffeted by voices, starved for space, crowded with love, but Eve had always wondered where they would find the time to raise more than two. After the first miscarriage they had consoled one another, tossing the rationalizations back and forth between them: it was a fluke; it could happen to anyone; it meant nothing for the future. But after the second they were silent, seeing only the doctor's uncertain face. Life went on around them: other people had babies, made marriages, advanced their careers; little by little their pain became ingrown and stood between them. They did not share it. Eve was tired of the distance. She wanted to put it behind them.

"So," she said as they sat down at the small round kitchen table. "Tell me about your day."

"Not much to tell. Your Mom called."

"What's up?"

"She just wanted to shmoos. You know, her oldest grandson gets an A in science and she calls the whole world. That kind of stuff."

"What else?"

"They saw *Sophie's Choice* and loved it and why haven't we gone? She says I'm not getting you out enough."

"More like I'm not getting you out enough," Eve said, sipping more wine. "Your pot's boiling."

Peter got up and dumped the pasta into the water. "Will you take a look at that philodendron in the hall before you go to bed? Something's hideous and insidious on the backside of its leaves."

Eve nodded. Peter poured the pasta through the colander. She got up and helped him put it onto the flat white china.

"And let's see," he said, grinding pepper onto his plate, "I'm still stuck in that same chapter."

"Really stuck?"

He nodded.

"Do you know what's wrong?" she asked, twisting the noodles around her fork. "Have you written anything at all?"

"Sure, but it's lousy." He sighed. "I just feel frozen. It won't flow."

"What's it about?"

He took a sip of his wine, and put his head back against his chair. "The death of Masello's wife."

"How can you write about something like that? It's so depressing and, thank God"—she smiled at her own joke—"you've never even gone through it."

He looked up at her. He didn't smile, refusing to be drawn in. "Give me a break. I lost my parents." He paused. "I lost two babies." He sighed again and picked at his pasta. "Maybe that's the problem—maybe I'm trying to use something that's too recent, too immediate."

Eve was silent. She was tired of this rut. She didn't want to talk about it anymore. *If I'd wanted to marry a depressednik I could've stayed home with Daddy.*

"It doesn't bother you at all, does it?" he said, his voice bitter. "You're just fine."

Again she said nothing, but her hand tightened around the wineglass.

"Don't you ever think about him?"

"I still wake up every night," she answered in a rigid voice. "At least *you* can sleep." Her own sarcasm made her wince.

His head came up sharply, and he looked at her directly for the first time. "And what about the days?"

With a start she saw the fury in his eyes.

"*I* have to walk by that damned room every day, with its crib, and rabbit wallpaper," he said. "When I go to the supermarket I have to walk down the aisles full of baby food and Pampers, I have to watch ungrateful mothers screaming at their two-year-olds. And then I come home, alone, all day long, every day." He stood, anger and tears distorting his face. The anger was making him say things he meant but hadn't dared to say. "You're not here—what do you know?"

"You make it sound like I don't care, like it didn't hurt me!" *How dare he say he hurts more than I do? Was it his body, his blood? Evan was mine.* She was shouting suddenly. "This isn't a contest to see whose pain is worse!"

"You're the one who got right up and went back to work the next week—not me." He wiped his face with the back of his hand quickly, as if to pretend he had not cried.

Eve sat wordless, stunned. He made it sound like she was a machine. "What did you want me to do? Sit shiva for eight days? I went back to work to get my mind off it. I went back to help somebody else."

"You're always helping someone else! When are you going to help us!" He stood up abruptly and took his plate to the sink. With a quick motion he turned the spout on full and let water spray the food down the drain. "Maybe you were just ambivalent about having the baby altogether!" He spun to face her.

Eve was back in that nightmare of December—only now he

was saying what she'd known he'd felt all along, what she most dreaded hearing, what he had most denied. He thought it was somehow her fault. He blamed her. The pain his words caused was beating on her ribcage, struggling to get out, to make her scream or cry or vomit, but she locked it down, she held it back. She concentrated on looking at him: her eyes were as hard and cold as dry ice; she hoped it burned him to look into them. "You think I lost him *on purpose?*"

"Well, you read about stuff like that."

She would not cry. She would not. She looked at the cracks in the linoleum and thought of her mother. She wished she were with her mother now. Her mother would sort all this out. Her mother would make a joke and they would all laugh and the pain would stop.

"I'm sorry." Peter's voice was miserable. "I know it wasn't your fault."

"You never said you blamed me for Evan." She finished her wine in one gulp. "But I knew it anyway." She didn't care that he'd said he was sorry. She wished she could hurt him back the way he'd just hurt her.

"I was ashamed of feeling that way."

"It was *nobody's* fault." She spoke through her teeth.

"That just makes it even harder." He looked up at her. "I'm sorry. I love you."

"You shut me out. I minded that more than I minded the anger." She was desperate to make him see, to make him feel all the pain that she had felt. "All that unspoken anger left me alone. It was a wall. I hated you for that wall." Anger, anger, all the world's anger spinning itself out, a tornado, in her head. Why had she ever thought anger could be controlled?

"I didn't want to hurt you. I knew my being angry wasn't fair."

"It was worse to be alone." The aloneness engulfed her. She didn't want to remember it, to relive it, but here it was: all those nightmares while he slept on safe in the dark. "I *still* hate you for it."

He was quiet. He let her anger drum down on them.

"Don't you think I was angry too?" Her voice was shaking. She couldn't stop now. "Don't you think *I* blamed *you?*"

"Me?"

"It could've been some kind of defect from the sperm instead of the egg! Why does everyone assume it's the *woman's* problem? You never know for sure!"

Words bounced around in her memory, kind expressions of concern about getting better medical care for her "condition" —what condition? she'd wanted to ask—or making sure she reduced her workload next time. Friends, relatives, strangers —they all thought she had been to blame through negligence or some physical defect. Her rage then had been muted by bewilderment, but now it was a thick vein heavy with pure, unadulterated ore. "I wanted it to be your fault instead of mine! If I'd failed as a woman then I wanted you to have failed as a man! If I wasn't a woman anymore then it wasn't *fair* you should still be a man!" She tried to hold on to her breath but it was escaping with her anger out into the air. She heard what she said with a sense of distance, of shock. She hadn't even known she thought such things. "Why couldn't you yell at me and get it over with! Why couldn't you stop being Mr. Nice Guy and just come back to me!" She banged her wine glass down on the table and the stem shattered under the force of her hand. Red wine dripped down on to the floor.

Peter stared at her. She got up and went to the sink for a cloth, checked her hand for glass and then began to mop up the mess. *The anger is real now,* she thought, as she pushed the rag back and forth through the red wine, *it's out in the open.* She sat down again. They didn't speak for a while. He played with his fork. She stared at the floor. They stood at the edge of a cliff; they were deciding whether or not to jump.

Eve weighed her anger in her hands, like a butcher weighs pounds of suet, balancing left and then right, and suddenly she didn't care, she was sick of it; she just didn't want to be alone anymore. She was broken inside, needy. Anger cost. Somehow they had to forgive each other.

After a while she got up and knelt in front of him. She put her arms around his waist. She didn't want to touch him but she made herself. She didn't want to hear their silence anymore; she couldn't stand the threat. She held him fast against her. They didn't move, both remembering what had been, what was no more. There had been no funeral for the son they'd wanted to name Evan Seidel. *This is as close as we'll get to that,* she thought. *But I still can't cry, it hurts too much.* She didn't know what they were going to do.

"We could try to make another," she said, her voice muffled as she turned her face into his sweater.

"Oh, Evie." He sighed. "It's too soon."

"It's been three months. Dr. Rosenthal says we can start trying again."

"You won't let Evan be real, will you?" he asked, pushing her back so he could look into her face. "You won't really feel the pain—you think getting pregnant again will fix everything."

"I need you," Eve said, burrowing again, rubbing her cheek hard against his chest. "I need to feel you. I need to get warm."

He bent his head to kiss her, and, for a minute, touch extinguished memory.

3

ARIELLA CORTEZ always made sure she was the last to
arrive at and the last to leave a party. From the other side of
the room Mira watched her as she gave her coat to the maid
and kissed Vivian on both cheeks. Mira was sure that, deep
inside, Ariella pictured herself as the heroine she had created
for "Megan's World."

Even though Mira loved the cast parties they gave for her
mother's show, when she'd watched Vivian doing up the guest
list last week she kept hoping that her mother wouldn't put
down Ariella. She didn't think she could ever like anybody
who'd changed her name from Aurelia Collins to Ariella Cortez. It was like getting a nose job—but in reverse.

She buried herself in the conversations around her. Since
last year, when Ariella had very nearly gotten her mother
fired, Mira'd hated the show's head writer and she didn't care
if it was rude for her not to go over now and say hello. She
stared into her glass of diet soda. She pretended to be fascinated by the producer beside her who was talking about cost
overruns. She smiled. She laughed. But she looked up, just
once, quickly, to see Ariella standing with Vivian, and her
mother's angry, silent signal from the other side of the room.
And so, with a sigh, she began to squeeze through tight pockets of people and conversations.

But several times she stopped, in defiance, and dipped into the words around her like an artist into paint. She liked the way TV people scrunched themselves into small circles. There was always something interesting to gossip about.

Vivian was still standing in the corner, listening to Ariella with her head cocked to one side.

"As usual, a superlative party, Vivs," Ariella was saying. She was the only one who had ever given Vivian a nickname. "How clever to combine our tenth anniversary with your birthday." She sipped a whiskey sour.

Ariella wore a black silk suit that snagged at her hips in a wrinkle, with black stockings and high black mules. Her black hair—too black to be natural, Vivian always said—was pulled back in a tight twist, her glasses rimmed with black. Even the hands holding the V-shaped glass were tipped in shiny black polish. She looked like a witch, Mira thought, trying not to scowl as she came up. Ariella'd probably read the March issue of *Vogue,* which said black was chic for spring, and that hemlines could show the knee—but not if your knees were as pudgy as Ariella's, Mira decided, pushing down a giggle.

Vivian was draped against the wall. The batwing sleeves of her white silk caftan floated around her as she moved her hands, gesturing. She was doing a pretty good job of looking interested in what Ariella was saying, Mira thought, but she turned to her daughter as you'd stretch to a fireman in a burning building—desperate, relieved.

Mira smiled and moved into the conversation. It was like stepping into a spotlight on a dark stage. "Hello, Mrs. Cortez."

"Mira, you make me feel old." Ariella sighed. "No one calls me Mrs. Cortez." She sipped her drink and eyed them as they stood side by side. "Speaking of age, maybe you'll tell me how old your mother is today—she's being very mysterious about it."

Vivian didn't move, didn't flinch, but as Mira opened her mouth to say proudly, "Thirty-nine," some instinct made her stop short. It was a trap. "By now?" She shook her head and made a sad face. "At least fifty-five." She struggled to keep from giggling again. "Ready to retire."

Her mother threw back her head and laughed, a clear tinkle of enjoyment. She'd scored a point. Mira felt a flush of relief. Being flip—or fresh, as her father would've said—was scary sometimes. Go too far and you got yourself into trouble.

"Cagey," Ariella said, tapping her fingernail against her glass, her mouth set in a tight red line. She didn't like being thwarted. "And for one so young."

"Thank you," Mira said with a smile, deciding she'd better pretend the comment was a compliment. "How's Hernando?" Ariella had a small black dog shaped like a sausage whom she led around Saks, or the studio, or Gristede's, on a suede leash.

"How should he be?" Ariella sniffed and flashed an angry look at Vivian. "Lonely, probably."

Vivian hated 'Nando's beady black eyes and the way he scratched himself against the underside of all the furniture, and she'd asked Ariella to leave him at home tonight. Now she sighed. "That dog's just conquered your heart, Ariella."

Mira stifled another laugh, but her grin had already escaped.

"And speaking of young," Ariella went on in an irritated tone, seeing Mira's expression, and continuing as though the subject had never been changed, "shouldn't you be in bed by now?"

Mira's face reddened. Pow—that was how it happened. It only took one remark to put you where you belonged, to make you feel silly and out of place, and Ariella was good at it—she knew just how to find your weak spots.

"She'd better not be," Vivian said stoutly, putting her arm around Mira's waist. "Without Mira this party'd be dead. In fact, sweetie," she gestured toward a small group on the far side of the room, "I think Dee could use a refill and a rescue."

Mira turned around and scanned the room for Dee Cavanaugh, the show's popular ingenue, who was cornered against the piano by Sumner Stapleton. She was glad to get away from Ariella and from her mother—she didn't like it when Vivian put her arm around her in public. It made her feel about two years old. She went to the bar to get another glass of champagne for Dee and then elbowed her way back across the long room to the Steinway, searching the room for Chris Light, who didn't seem to be here yet. She wondered whether she should check her hair—done up like her mother's—and touched her hand to the back of her head nervously, hoping it hadn't come loose.

"Of course she's a preposterous character," Dee was hissing in a low voice. She shrugged. "That's the whole point." She was petite, blond, and had the sort of cleavage Mira dreamed about as she exercised in front of the mirror each night with her Mark Eden Bust Developer. Sumner never stopped trying to pick Dee up, and Dee never stopped trying to insult him.

"*Hardly* the point," Sumner said, tucking his thumb into the watch pocket of his vest. With his pot belly and patrician drawl he seemed more like a banker than an actor. "I cannot stand the turn the show has taken. It's vulgar." Sumner rolled the word on his tongue as though it were spelled with three *l*'s instead of one. "Marlene herself is vulgar." He sipped his Scotch and patted his red, round mouth with a cocktail napkin.

"But Sumner," Mira said as she handed Dee her drink, trying to keep a straight face, "don't you think her Day-Glo stretch pants add a little pizzazz?" Marlene Dubois had just come onto the show, and she played the part of a local hooker. Mira had met Marlene when she'd been on the set helping

Vivian earlier in the week, and had liked the character, with her wide mouth and wide hips.

"When a soap has superior talent like Dee and your mother —and me"—he was talking with his hands now, in eloquent, sweeping gestures—"it doesn't need pizzazz. When I did Othello, when I did Lear, did I need pizzazz? Emphatically not!"

Dee hid her laugh in a sip of champagne, and rolled her eyes at Mira—you didn't need much pizzazz to do summer stock in Akron, Ohio, Mira thought, looking at the floor so she wouldn't giggle.

"That woman"—he turned to send a withering glance at Marlene's back—"is a blight upon the face of 'Megan's World' and I cannot fathom why your mother has not lodged a complaint with Ariella." He reminded Mira of the speech teacher they'd had in seventh grade, with his perfect, well-enunciated consonants and vowels. She imagined him practicing in front of the mirror, exercising his lips like a fish.

"When they add a character Vivian's always glad—someone else off the street and working." Mira made her eyes round and innocent. "And it's better than one of you getting fired, anyday."

Sumner put his glass down on the piano and made a fuss about straightening his tie. The scalp beneath the thinning frizz on the top of his head had turned red. "I think I should go over and greet Ariella or she'll think me terribly rude."

"Good idea," Mira said, trying to sound absolutely sincere.

As soon as he strutted off she and Dee collapsed against each other with laughter. Tears made Dee's gray eyes shiny. "Fired! Never use the word 'fired' around Sumner!" she squeezed out. When she laughed her voice had a hoarse, throaty sound. "He's waiting to get killed off."

"He's awful!" Mira wiped her eyes with the back of her hand.

"Maybe Ariella'll do him in. His fan mail alone is a death sentence."

Mira nodded. "Too bad, too. Marcus Warren could be a good character—if someone else were playing him."

"I like your caftan," Dee said, reaching over to touch the red silk.

"Vivian had it made as a present." Mira ran her hand over the material with pride. "It's like the one she's wearing." The caftan was special to her—it made her feel glamorous and grown-up. It took away some of her awkward edges, she thought. "Of course, hers is a designer original, but still . . ."

"Still," Dee agreed. "She does stuff like that for you a lot, doesn't she?"

Mira nodded. "She likes to surprise me."

"So, how's school, how's your horse, and which boy is it now?" She took Mira's hand and drew her into the alcove on the far side of the piano.

"Terrible, fine, and what a mess." Mira sat down on the love seat with a sigh. "In that order. It couldn't be worse."

"It could always be worse," Dee observed dryly. "What's up?"

"Mostly I keep botching stuff." Mira studied the design of the carpet between her feet. "Exams, friends—I don't know." She hesitated.

"And?" Dee said, watching her closely.

Mira looked up, her eyes filled with the unhappiness she'd been pushing down for weeks.

"What did you decide to do about the baby?"

"Vivian made me an appointment with her doctor."

"For when?"

"Tomorrow."

Dee's face softened with sympathy. "You must feel lousy."

Mira blinked against the tears. "Awful."

"I know." Dee put her arm around Mira's shoulders. "There's something damned incredible about being pregnant."

"Like magic." Mira let her hand touch her tummy. "But Vivian says other things are more important."

"I had three suctions before getting my tubes tied."

"You had your tubes tied?" Mira echoed. "That's so *final.*"

"I wanted it final." Dee shrugged. "Babies aren't exactly part of my game plan." She looked wistful for a minute. "I wish they could be, sometimes."

Mira nodded, as if she knew what Dee meant, but secretly she wondered why. There was a lot about Dee she didn't understand. "I'm not sure I can go through with tomorrow. I'm afraid—" She stopped herself and shrugged. "Oh, let's talk about something else."

Dee's face took on an odd, penetrating expression. "Maybe you *should* talk about it. It might help."

"No—it'll just make it harder." Mira edged her shoulders out from under the weight of Dee's arm. "Look at Sumner going after Ariella," she said, pointing across the room. "They're arguing."

"Probably line changes—he's always trying to rewrite his script."

"Bet I can guess who you're gossiping about." Toni Sommers came up and propped her elbows on the piano.

"Why do you keep him?" Dee asked, getting up to lean against the piano again and keeping her voice low.

Toni shrugged. She was the co-writer for the show and had to work under Ariella every day. Mira felt sorry for her. "It's not my decision," Toni said.

Mira smiled. Toni was a quiet black woman in her early thirties, with a mop of curly dark hair and eyes that shone like the smooth black stones at the bottom of a brook. She paid little or no attention to her clothes, wore no makeup, and obviously wanted to blend into the background, but she was one of the most handsome women Mira had ever seen.

"Well then, why does *Ariella* keep him?"

Toni smiled. "This kid's on top of it all," she said to Dee. She looked at Mira thoughtfully. "Ariella thinks the show needs him for balance."

"More like dead weight," Dee said with a snort.

Toni smiled over at Dee, an insider's smile. There was something going on that Mira didn't understand, and she felt a familiar frustration. "What? Why are you guys smiling like that?" They didn't answer and Mira felt shut out, rebuffed.

"Well, I'll go on the record in favor of Marlene," she said, covering up their silence. "I think she's super."

"Camp," Dee supplied.

"Whose idea was she, anyway?"

"In a good collaboration you don't remember whose idea is whose," Toni answered easily. "What happened to those stuffed birds and animals?" she asked, pointing to the empty wall above the fireplace.

"My father's trophies?" Mira turned to look, distracted. "Vivian took them down right after he died. She always hated them." Mira pushed away the memory of an argument, her father's face blotched red with anger and Vivian's triumphant smile.

"Watch out," Dee interrupted. "Here comes God's gift to the universe."

Mira looked up to see Chris walking across the room, and her face got hot and red. Her hand moved to her hair. He had blue eyes the color of a Hawaiian reef fish, and the contrast with his black hair was jolting. Just nineteen, he was the youngest cast member, idolized by fans across the country. Mira was no exception. She kept a photo of him stashed in a hardcover copy of *Gone with the Wind,* on the bookshelf above her bed. Mark and Bill and all the boys her own age seemed stupid and immature next to Chris.

He slipped his arm around Mira's waist, and she could feel the lean cord of bicep press into her back. "I've been looking all over for you," he said.

Dee rolled her eyes at Toni but Mira didn't care. She was afraid to look up at him. She knew she was blushing and she was afraid she would say or do something stupid. So she just stood there, wishing she knew how to flirt with him.

"I've got a knockout surprise for Vivian." He ran a tanned hand through his shining hair.

"I hope it's not another one of your stupid practical jokes." Dee stood up straight to stare at Chris with a sharp and critical eye.

"Keep your pants on, Dee—this guy's probably not even your type." He grinned. "Maybe no guy is."

Dee's face flushed. Mira knew that Dee lived by herself, but she still couldn't understand why she never brought anyone with her to these parties, why she was always alone.

"You're obnoxious." She swept her blond hair back from her face as she picked up her glass from the piano and headed over to the bar.

"Want to grab some food?" Chris asked Mira, just as though Toni weren't standing there.

Mira turned to the far end of the room and saw the doors to the dining room had been opened. His arm around her, they walked to the buffet line, where Chris filled his plate only with vegetables and Mira chose zucchini and tomatoes and ignored the warm smell of beef. She wasn't really hungry anyway—she was too excited by the idea of sharing dinner with him. Most of the cast had weird diets and there were no two alike: high protein or high carbohydrate, vegetarian or low cholesterol. Working out the menu for this kind of party was one of Mira's favorite games, like a puzzle. Tonight there was everything from filet mignon to seviche.

Vivian watched Mira and Chris shop their way down the long buffet table, picking out this and that as they talked. She didn't like the way he was handling her daughter. He kept putting his arm around her. He was too sophisticated for Mira, and the last thing she wanted was for her daughter to be hurt by a mover like Chris. He was over her Mira's head—way over. She went to where they were picking up glasses of wine.

"Mira sweet, I need a favor."

Mira looked up, distracted.

"Someone has to keep Herbie company over dinner."

"Forget it, Vivian," Chris interjected with a smile. "I've got Mira all booked up."

Vivian saw suddenly, and for the first time really, how handsome he was. His eyes were not his most startling feature. It was his mouth, as full-lipped as a woman's, the color of lush, ripe berries, curving over teeth of perfect oblong shape. She remembered then a little boy in her neighborhood when she was eight: he'd had a beautiful, tender mouth—even at eight she'd wanted to kiss it—and he'd also had the fastest roller skates on the block. She'd hated him for their gleaming silver motion, the glide of their slick ball bearings. One summer afternoon she'd stolen the skates off his back stoop. She buried them in her side yard, never to use or enjoy them: just to have taken them was enough.

She looked down now and saw her daughter's plate with its piles of vegetables—Mira, who loved steak almost as much as riding horses—and she wanted to laugh, reminded of being fifteen, in love with the senior who was the leader of the jazz ensemble. Every afternoon had been spent in the library, listening to each jazz record on the shelves and taking notes—just so she could impress him if they happened to bump heads over the water cooler. Nothing was wrong with Mira's eating dinner with Chris—it was only an adolescent crush. He would get bored with a fourteen-year-old before the night was out. "All right," she said to Chris, "she's yours. But watch yourself," she motioned to Mira. "Just one glass of wine for you." Vivian picked up a plate for herself, thinking maybe she'd join them.

Mira just looked at her mother. She was numb with embarrassment. She wanted to run and hide in her bedroom closet. How could Vivian have said that to her in front of Chris? As if she were some kind of baby. Without thinking, she turned and walked away to the couch. Chris sat down beside her.

Vivian watched her daughter walk away abruptly and wondered what she'd done now. It seemed so easy to set Mira off these days—you never knew when you'd make a benign remark and a second later Mira's lower lip would tremble and she'd be ready to cry.

"They make a cute couple, don't they?" Ariella's voice had a faint, mocking tone and interrupted Vivian's train of thought. "She's a little young for Chris," she said, picking up silverware, "but better too young than too old."

Vivian ignored the remark and helped Ariella to a big pile of potato salad. It fell from the spoon to her crowded plate with a plop. "That's not too much, is it?"

"Bring yours and come sit with me." Ariella turned her back and Vivian was forced to follow her or be rude. They sat on the love seat facing Ariella's husband and Vivian's agent.

"I'm worried," Ariella said.

"About what?" Vivian pushed a slice of steak around on her plate, making a pattern of red swirls on the ivory china.

"About you." Ariella sighed and waved her fork in the air as she chewed for a minute. "And Megan. Megan's having a *crisis.* Her husband's left her, her company's being taken over by a bastard corporation. Worse, she's just turned thirty—

can't you remember back to when you were about to be thirty?"

"Just what is your complaint?" Vivian set her plate down on the table in front of her with precision.

"If you don't eat you'll look haggard," Ariella advised, loading up another forkful. The mayonnaise from the potato salad collected in the corners of her lipsticked mouth and stretched into thin bands as she spoke. Vivian kept staring at her fat red lips pushing around the words and the food. If she fixed her attention on Ariella's mouth the panic would stay in control. "You need to think *young,* Vivs—that's the key!" She punctuated her sentence with her knife. "You transport yourself back. Try to remember how difficult it was to turn thirty."

"I see. Perhaps"—she broke away from Ariella's mouth to cast a glance around the crowded room, in hopes of spotting their director,—"maybe we should ask Marty to join us for this little critique. I'd be curious to know if he agrees with you." She stood up. Her body seemed rusted shut. She was afraid she would creak like the Tin Man if she tried to walk. "He's right over there. I'll just go get him."

"No, no," Ariella said, putting her fork down. "This was just between you and me."

Vivian looked over at Herbie Cortez, who was listening attentively to her agent; Herbie hadn't an idea of his own in his egg-shaped head. "Should we ask Herbie?" She paused, feeling a small measure of control return. "His opinions are always so *thought-provoking.*"

Ariella flushed.

"I'll just go get a refill," Vivian went on. "Would you like more wine?"

Ariella shook her head and Vivian crossed the room to the bar. "Another Tanqueray Gibson." While the bartender mixed a fresh pitcher she went back into her bedroom to regroup. As she stood in front of the mirror with her lipstick, her hands started to shake and the cerise-colored grease smeared over the edge of her upper lip. "Damn!" She wiped it off with a Kleenex and started again. How dare Ariella make those insinuations, how dare she criticize. It all reminded Vivian of last year, how she'd had to call in all her cards, all the favors owed, imposing on old friendships in order to stave off Ariella's attack and the bright new face she'd found to replace Vivian with. Sheilah McLaughlin. But the producers had seen how inane the scheme was: they knew the ratings stayed up because the fans loved Vivian. Still, the girl had been breathtaking, a gossamer wisp barely twenty years old, and Vivian had been forced to compromise by promising to get a face lift any time Marty or the producers felt her age was showing. It was as galling as being a high-priced whore. She'd been clever enough to take care of Sheilah permanently, though; by sleeping with one of the producers on "Loving," Vivian had made sure Sheilah was considered seriously for the new young ingenue they were casting. When Sheilah had called with the news that she was going to work for their competitors, Ariella had been livid: she wasn't sure how, but she'd known Vivian had engineered it. Still, even as Marty had reassured Vivian, telling her there was nothing to worry about, even after Sheilah was no longer a threat, there still had been an edge there, the knowledge that they would one day replace her. And what would she do then? Who would she be? Even now the question made her stomach cramp: living with the knowledge of her age was like being an illegal alien, always on the watch. This party was an elaborate ruse: by celebrating her thirty-ninth birthday so openly, so self-confidently—she had let the number drop "in secret" to the few people she could be certain would repeat it—she had made sure that no one realized she'd hit forty last year. Not even Mira knew the truth.

She leaned against her dresser and forced herself to convert her panic to anger. Ariella was a bitch, she told herself; it just upset her more tonight because she was so worried about Mira. Mira, she thought, pausing to finger the tiny sag under her left eye. She hoped she was right about the abortion. She snapped out the light and waited in the dark for a minute, remembering how frightened she'd been the day she'd had her first abortion, when she was sixteen. It had been right for Vivian then; surely it was right for Mira now. Frank Scranton. He'd been married, in his early forties, he'd smelled of paint and furniture polish. He'd gotten Vivian pregnant on the couch at the back of the hardware store he and his wife owned on the other end of the block from Carson's Drug. He knew how angry Ox would be if he found out. He was afraid of Ox. So he'd gotten the money together and driven her to a place where she could get it done. While Frank waited in the car, she went up those wooden stairs to the second story of the frame house, clutching her black vinyl pocketbook with its four one-hundred-dollar bills, crisp and green, wishing only that she could be using the money for something else, for the emerald silk dress she'd seen in the window of Saks Fifth Avenue the day Frank had taken her to meet his cousin, a talent agent in a dusty office in New York City. Abortion was illegal then: a med student, but a clean one; a kitchen table, but sterile. It hadn't been so bad, no worse than having a tooth pulled; after it was over, the med student had given her coffee and a pain-killer and she'd gone home and pretended she just had a really bad period. Her parents never figured it out and there was something powerful, almost titillating, about having fooled them.

But it wouldn't be like that for Mira. Mira would have a clean antiseptic office with no strings of emotion, no cash in a plastic purse. For Mira it would be easy. And she'd have her mother with her the whole time, supportive, loving, just like a best friend, even better than a best friend. One day Mira would thank her.

Vivian checked the back of her hair by touching it in the dark with her hand and then headed toward the living room, blinking against the shift from dark to light. When she found Marty she drew him aside.

"It's been suggested," Vivian said, drawing lightly on the cool dry gin of her Gibson, "that I'm not quite up to par on Megan's 'life crisis.' I just wondered"—she allowed her voice to dip slightly—"if you thought I was doing a good job? I mean, it wasn't long ago that I turned thirty myself, and I'd thought that was apparent in the way I handled the character, but . . ."

"Ariella said all this, didn't she?" He flicked his cigarette into his empty glass with his thumbnail.

Vivian shrugged.

Marty put his arm around her; she could smell his flowery aftershave. "Come on," he crooned. "That old black bat gets off on making you miserable." He kissed her cheek with moist lips. "I *love* what you do with the part."

"Really?"

"Really."

"I guess I just see Megan as stronger than she does."

"Who knows?" He threw his arms up in the air. "Who cares what she thinks." He looked around the room till he spotted Ariella. "Think I'll have a little heart-to-heart with her."

"Marty." She put her hand on his arm to restrain him for a moment.

"Not to worry—I wouldn't dream of mentioning that you brought it up."

As he elbowed his way across the room, Vivian leaned back on the bar. She liked to handle things. And the party, with its bright noises and colors and laughter, made her feel young. They only needed balloons and a pony. When Mira was six, Vivian had given her a party like that in Central Park. She looked through the crowd to see her daughter sitting with

Chris on the couch. They were still together. He was smiling down at her, and Vivian didn't like that smile at all. He was charming Mira—like a snake luring a mouse into its hole. She frowned. If she tried to tell Mira about Chris's reputation, Mira would resent it; she'd be even more stubborn and determined to have him. Vivian sighed with exasperation. Maybe if she did the reverse—just ignored the situation—Mira would see him flirting with someone else and get over her infatuation. She decided to do nothing, for now, anyway.

Mira was concentrating on trying not to spill anything down the front of her caftan. She wanted to seem elegant and poised, but her hands felt big and clumsy, the plate threatened to tip, and her feet were long thin boats in her sandals. She couldn't think of a thing to say.

She looked across the room at Suzannah Farrar, her mother's agent, sitting on the love seat with Herbie Cortez. "She's really strange." She motioned with her fork.

"Your mother's lucky to have her—Farrar owns this town." Chris ran his eyes over Suzannah. "But a real ugly duck," he said, buttering a piece of bread. Suzannah's severe blue dress outlined her stumpy figure, and Mira thought the gigantic red satin rose pinned to her shoulder was gross.

"Doesn't Herbie remind you of a cartoon strip?" Mira started to giggle as she sipped her wine. He had a long thin face and a bald head that came to a point; she always imagined the bones under his scalp grinding up against each other. "He's so . . . angular."

"Built along the bevel," Chris supplied, looking pleased with himself.

"Faulkner," Mira said with surprise, happy that she'd caught his allusion. Freshman English was one of the few subjects for which she'd kept up with the reading.

"Who and where?" he challenged.

"Cash?" she said uncertainly, hoping she was right. *"As I*

Lay Dying?" She felt a flush of success when he nodded and gave her an admiring smile, but her happiness quickly evaporated into nervousness. Don't let him ask anything else, she prayed—it was the only Faulkner she'd read. "I wonder why Herbie changed his name to Cortez," she said, changing the subject as she speared a mushroom.

Chris snorted. "Ariella told him to, that's why—he does everything she says." He crunched a mouthful of snow peas. "Must beat working for a living."

"I thought he was a poet."

"If sitting at home all day and never getting published is being a poet then I guess he's a poet."

"I wonder what they're talking about."

They strained to eavesdrop. Words like self-actualization and vital creation and intimate destiny were floating out of Suzannah's mouth like helium balloons. "She's probably off on that *I and Thou* kick again," Chris said. "Or some other load of B.S. But look at him nod."

Mira giggled. Herbie, with his long wobbly neck, looked like a baby who was learning to hold his head up. "I never know what to say to her," Mira confessed, wiping her mouth. "She talks in such big words." She flushed—why did everything she say to him come out sounding so young and silly?

"Really?" He was looking at her with a serious expression. "Seems to me you always know just what to say to everyone. You're so put together it's practically intimidating." He smiled. He was teasing her now, she saw, and she blushed.

"What's the surprise present you've got for Vivian?" Mira asked, turning the subject off herself.

He smiled and checked his watch. "It should be here any minute."

"Did I hear my name?"

Mira looked up to see her mother standing in front of them with three glasses and a bottle of champagne. "It's almost midnight," Vivian said, "and I thought we could have a toast to celebrate my birthday's being *over.*" She handed him a glass. "Here, sweetie," she said, giving Mira one, too. "We can't do this without you."

"Not quite over," Chris said with a smile, patting the sofa beside him.

Vivian hesitated in midair before floating down onto the cushion. "You better not have something tacky planned." She frowned for emphasis.

"Tacky? On your birthday?" He reached over and took her hand. "Only the most original present you'll ever get." He raised his glass. "To Vivian."

Vivian acknowledged the compliment with a nod.

"I hear there's a shake-up over at NBC," he said, settling into the comfortable routine of talking shop. "D'you know yet who they've fired?"

Vivian shook her head. "Just that it was all a salary dispute —or that's what they're saying. More likely an argument over control."

"Why d'you say that?"

"Don't be naive. Look at our own problems—everything boils down to control."

Mira began to feel angry. She and Chris had been having a good time, a really good time, till her mother came along and horned in. He was so much more a part of Vivian's world. Would she ever have her mother's gift for talk, the way she tilted her head to one side as she listened, or touched his shoulder lightly, with just one finger? A bubble of envy formed in Mira's chest.

She was glad when the maid interrupted them, showing in a tall blond young man.

"I'm here to deliver a birthday gift. For Vivian," he said, standing in front of the sofa. He set down a radio/cassette player as large as a briefcase on the coffee table.

"I'm Vivian. What is it? Who's it from?" Strangers made her mother nervous—even when they looked as clean-cut as this one.

He bent down and slipped a cassette into the radio. Loud music with a rhythmic beat poured into the room, and from all corners people stopped talking to turn and stare.

"Happy Birthday from the cast," he said. His hips began to rock to the music, his eyes closed, his body swayed. Everyone came over to watch, leaving enough space in the middle of the room so that he could work the floor.

The contrast between his conservative appearance and the steamy music was definitely weird, Mira decided. And why would someone send Vivian a dancer as a birthday present? As the music mellowed from a frenetic pace to a strong slow rhythm, he shrugged his way out of his suit jacket as casually as if he were at a sweaty disco. Then he unknotted his tie, swung it around his head like a lasso and let it fly off into the crowd. A young techie at the back of the room caught it with a whoop and draped it around her neck. The buttons on his shirt were next, one by one he undid them, and then it fell to the floor where he kicked it behind him. He danced on, never losing a moment of the rhythm, hips pumping to the loud tune, sweat making his chest gleam under the light as if his body had been oiled. His muscles rippled. Mira stared.

With an expert kick he slid his shoes off his feet without missing a beat. People on both sides of the room began to cheer and clap. He was smiling. He enjoyed all this. And her mother was smiling too. There was an air of expectancy in the room. He unbuckled his belt with a flourish and tossed it over his head into the crowd. With a clean sensual motion he unzipped his pants and worked them down over his hips. He wore only a pair of very tight nylon bikinis. Mira looked down at his naked feet. She could feel Chris sitting beside her, and she wished she were someplace else—anywhere but here. They were watching a strange man get undressed as nonchalantly as if they were at the movies. She forced her eyes straight ahead. She was afraid to look at Chris.

The dancer hooked his thumbs under the waistband of the pants, and, moving to the rhythmic clapping of the crowd, stripped them off. Mira's cheeks were so hot they stung. Every part of him was swinging to the rhythm. She wanted so badly to close her eyes. She couldn't help it, he reminded her of Hernando waddling across the floor. She'd never seen a man naked this way before, out in the light. When she'd been with Mark and Bill they'd always used the dark as a blanket. This was so bald, so wrinkly, so red. She felt sick. In desperation she looked around, concentrating on faces, and saw that everyone was smiling—except Dee, who looked annoyed.

The music stopped, the young man bowed and stooped to scoop up his clothes. Naked, he walked through the crowd to dress in the bathroom.

Everyone was suddenly laughing and talking. Chris had his arm around Vivian. "He was great!" she said, kissing his cheek in thanks.

He whispered something in her ear and Vivian laughed. Mira turned quickly to look for Dee in the crowd.

It was late and people began to leave, one by one, kissing Vivian and Mira both and telling them what a great party it had been. Mira and Dee went into the bedroom to look for Dee's coat.

"Good luck tomorrow." Dee smiled at her and put her arm around Mira. "If you need to talk, I'll be home."

Her words snapped Mira out of this night, and shoved her forward, into tomorrow. She and Vivian were due at the doctor's office at ten. She nodded at Dee, but her throat felt so tight she couldn't get a word out. She sat down on the bed.

Dee came back into the room and sank down beside her. "If you're this upset, why not wait?" she urged.

"I can't," Mira said, starting at last to cry.

"Why not? Another week won't hurt. You're not out of the third month yet."

"Vivian says I have to go."

"Mira, this is *your* choice."

"But she's right—she's always right."

"It's not up to her."

"I haven't got a choice. I don't even know who the father is." Her voice rose in a wail. Tears fell, spotting the silk of her caftan.

"You don't have to marry the guy, for Chrissakes," Dee said. "What about adoption? Did you think about that?" She put her hands on either side of Mira's face and forced her to look into her eyes. "There are tons of people out there these days, desperate for babies. You could put the baby up for adoption—that's a choice, a good choice."

"Vivian wouldn't let me."

"Mira, listen to yourself—you're talking about this as if it's *her* baby."

"I'm her daughter. In some ways it's her kid too."

"That's dumb."

"Well, it's how I feel," Mira said, drawing away and wiping her eyes on the back of her hand. "I'll go tomorrow and get it over with and that'll be the end of it, just like Vivian says."

Dee stood with a resigned expression. "Would you at least like me to come with you to the doctor's?"

"That's real nice of you." Mira sniffed hard because she didn't have a tissue. "But Vivian's taking me."

"Sure." Dee put her cape over her arm and headed out the door of the bedroom. She hesitated and then turned back toward Mira. "But don't shut yourself off. When you get home tomorrow call me and we'll talk."

"I'll be okay."

Vivian put her head around the corner of the door. "What

are you two doing in here?" Her face looked strained. "C'mon, Mira, I need you to help me do the goodbyes." She disappeared back into the hall and for a second Mira wanted to shout at her, wanted to say leave me alone for once, I'm hurting, I don't want to stand there being polite. But she didn't. She just gritted her teeth and stared at the rug.

Dee put her hand on her shoulder. "Don't be such a hero. Everybody needs someone who understands for things like this. It's not meant to be easy." She hesitated for a minute, drawing on the sleeves of her jacket. "There's something else I wanted to say, but maybe now's not such a good time."

"That's okay, I'm really fine," Mira said, sniffing again and clearing her throat. "What?"

"Try not to have too big a crush on a guy like Chris. He's a lightweight."

Mira looked at her, puzzled. "Why do you say that?"

"The voice of experience. I've watched him play with too many people. Trust me." She waved goodbye without saying anything more, and then went through the door, down the hall, and out of the apartment. Mira didn't get up even though she knew Vivian needed her. She couldn't understand why Dee said those things about Chris. How could you criticize someone handsome, smart, *and* nice. Mira was pretty sure from the way he'd looked at her tonight that he thought she was cute. If she could only get him alone the next time she was on the set he might even ask her out—if Vivian didn't interfere. She looked down at the creases in her red caftan. She'd have to send it to the cleaners in the morning, she thought. She smoothed it out with the palm of her hand and went into the bathroom to fix her makeup. She rubbed away the smeared mascara and eyeliner and did a quick fix. She didn't want Vivian to know she'd been crying.

Out in the hall, she pushed everything out of her mind except the names of the people who were leaving. When Chris kissed her cheek she inhaled the smell of his aftershave and tried not to let her smile waver. Standing side by side, mother and daughter accepted thanks the way actors accept applause. But Vivian looked tired. She closed the door and leaned against it with a sigh. "I survived another birthday."

Even with fatigue drawing lines across her face, she looked beautiful, as precious as a porcelain figurine. Mira forgot her earlier anger, she folded it up like a fragile origami bird and stored it away. "I love you," she said shyly instead, as though she were making an offering.

Vivian's face softened into a smile. "You're the best present I've had all day." She drew Mira to her and hugged her, hard. "I love you too."

She straightened up then, locked the door, and turned out the light. "What about that strip-a-gram anyway?"

"Weird," Mira said, as they headed toward their bedrooms. "Do you want to talk?" she asked, propping herself against the doorjamb of her room.

"You're tired. We can talk in the morning." Vivian stroked the side of her face with her palm. "How about a cuddle though—want to sleep in my room?"

"It's pretty late," Mira said reluctantly.

"C'mon," Vivian urged. "I know you're probably scared about tomorrow." Her voice was soft and sympathetic. She ran to Mira's closet and pulled out her nightie. "I'll even give you a backrub," she said as she closed the closet door. Her mother's arm around her, Mira walked into the master bedroom, squinting at her watch in the half-light. The hands were in a black line straight across the twelve and the six. Tomorrow was already here.

4

MIRA HUNCHED FORWARD in the stiff chair, sick to her stomach. Her mother turned the pages of a back issue of *Vogue*. In the room were three other women, each in the last stages of pregnancy, all doing a different kind of waiting. The soft rock of a radio station flowed down into the monochromatic, chic waiting room, and Vivian's leather boot marked time.

Mira couldn't read. On the wall across from her the doctors had made a photographic bulletin board of their latest snub-nosed arrivals. Something made her think of the fish specimens in the bio lab at school, how they floated in formaldehyde in the giant jars, how they would wait there forever. She closed her eyes—she just wished the whole thing would be over.

"Are you okay, sweetie?" Vivian whispered in her ear. "Your color's terrible."

Mira leaned her head back against the chair. "I'm all right."

"It's just nerves," Vivian said, reaching over to squeeze her hand. "But it won't take long and at least it's legal now. No more kitchen tables."

Mira swallowed. She wished her mother hadn't said that—it made her think of knitting needles and blood.

Vivian held the glossy magazine open on her lap, and pointed to a picture of Princess Diana. "I wonder what she sleeps in at night." She turned to Mira with a naughty grin. "I bet it's not the raw."

Mira made an effort to smile. Her mother was trying so hard to help. "I can't see her in anything but a ballgown or her riding britches."

Vivian laughed, a clear noise that flew from one end of the waiting room to the other. She dropped her voice, looking like a child who's been caught giggling in church. "And they're always holding hands," she whispered, pointing to another photo of Diana and Charles. "They probably even hold hands in bed." She began flipping the pages again, giving Mira an acid rundown of the short leather skirts, the sequined sweaters, the snakeskin accessories. Vivian hated excessive clothes. She wanted clean, sensual lines that didn't force her to compete with the designer for attention. Her idea of a compliment was not "what a beautiful dress," but rather "what a beautiful woman."

The pregnant women sat like big birds on a fence. Mira leaned her head back and closed her eyes again, her arms wrapped around her body for safety. She wished Vivian would be quiet. All these details about shoes and bags and belts were irritating—it made it hard to think or stay calm. She should have come alone. If she'd been by herself she would've only had herself to think about, she could have somehow pulled herself together. It would have been good to talk to Dr. Strauss yesterday, or at least to come today with Penny— Penny, who was a calm person and didn't mind Mira's silences. Penny'd offered, but Mira didn't want to hurt her mother's feelings.

Vivian had taken the morning off from work just to bring her over here, and Mira knew she ought to feel grateful. She slumped forward, wishing she could just melt down into the pattern of the carpet. Tears welled up again and she fought them back, barely in control.

She looked over at her mother's face and it hit her again that it didn't matter to Vivian the way it mattered to her. The abortion was just another piece of business to be taken care of —like waiting in line at the bank. Anger shot up inside her, a geiser, and she wanted to reach out and shake her mother by the shoulders. She wanted to yell, "It's *my* baby, not *yours!*" But she didn't. It wasn't fair of her to be angry when her mother was trying so hard to be understanding, like a sister. Mira sat in her chair and fought the anger down, capped it, compressed the steam. And in her mind, small intricate bubbles formed, one on top of the other—guilt, glistening and percolating up to pock the surface of her heart like gas escaping through mud.

She closed her eyes and wondered how all of this could be happening to her—she didn't even really like sex. It was just something you did because it was expected, the way you shook hands or stood up when an older person entered the room. She'd never understood the way her mother always wanted to talk about it. Some of the things she asked about Mira's boyfriends were sort of embarrassing. Mira tried hard not to mind talking about the details because she knew it was her mother's way of being close. After all, most of the girls at school told that kind of stuff to their best friends.

When she'd first gotten her period two years ago, just after her twelfth birthday, Vivian took her to lunch at Perigord Park to celebrate.

"You're a woman!" she'd said, raising her glass of champagne in a toast. "Let's have lobsters and I'll give you a sip of bubbly as a special treat."

It'd been better than a birthday party. Before lunch they'd gone to get her a new hairstyle at her mother's salon on Madison Avenue, and Mira shook her new bangs and felt them dance against her forehead. It was so much fun to do stuff like this with her mother.

"Soon you'll be off to college," Vivian had said a bit sadly, somewhere near the end of the bottle of Moët et Chandon. "And then it'll be boys, boys, boys." She wagged a finger at Mira. "Just remember that nothing two people do together is ever wrong—the only thing that's wrong is if you get caught short."

Mira frowned. She didn't understand what Vivian was getting at.

"Never let yourself get pregnant till you mean to," Vivian'd said, blotting her mouth with her napkin.

Mira blushed. The whole idea was embarrassing. Boys embarrassed her. Boys were grody. She wished Vivian would keep her voice down. She was sure other people were staring at them. "You don't need to worry about *that!*"

"Every mother worries about it, Mira." Vivian paused. "I was only sixteen when I had my first abortion. I don't want that for you."

Mira stared at her mother, surprised. She didn't know what to say.

"Don't be shocked"—Vivian said—"be careful. I've arranged for everything you'll need with Dr. Fieldston. All you have to do is go in and ask. Whenever you're ready."

She sounds like she's talking about buying a pair of shoes, Mira thought. It's creepy. She couldn't imagine needing birth control because she couldn't imagine wanting a boy to do that to her. Still, it seemed almost as if Vivian expected her to take care of it right away.

When her father found out about Vivian's arrangement he was so furious that he left the apartment. An hour later he'd come back home and then they'd argued. He'd backed Vivian against the wall with his voice, she remembered, had pinned her there like a butterfly on wax. Mira hid in her room. She hated it when they fought, especially over her, but her father's anger had protected her then. After he died, though, Vivian assumed Mira would be eager to see Dr. Fieldston and, because it was expected of her, she went. She remembered in sharp detail the day she'd come home with the bag from the drug store. Vivian had been so excited and pleased that it had seemed worth it after all. On that day Mira had weathered the initiation rites and passed into a select, sophisticated club.

But getting the pill hadn't made it any easier to give in. Vivian kept waiting. Mira could feel it. It made her think there was something wrong with her—she didn't want to do the one thing the rest of the world spent so much time talking about and running after. She couldn't confide in her friends either—both Janet and Crystal had been having sex with their boyfriends for a year by then, and Penny wanted a boyfriend so much she'd never see it the way Mira did. In the end it had been easier just to get it over with. And so, one night when Vivian was out, she'd let Bill into her body—in her own bed, side by side with the stuffed animals and the riding trophies. She hadn't bled, or felt much at all—just a sharp stretch as the girl in her moved over to make room for the woman.

But it was hard to remember that little yellow clock of a dispenser and she hadn't been very careful. There was so much to do in the mornings, and sometimes she'd just forgotten to take the miniature magic with her juice.

Now the door to the inner suite opened and the nurse called her name. Vivian squeezed her hand again. "Do you want me to come with you?" she asked, giving her a reassuring smile, but looking worried anyway.

Mira shook her head and stood up. She followed the nurse. They took her blood pressure, pricked her finger for a blood sample and asked a bunch of questions. Then the nurse bent down and patted her arm. She asked if Mira wanted to talk about the procedure. Mira wanted to say yes but her mouth was too numb, like at the dentist's after the novocaine. She didn't even start to cry again. They led her to an examining room and told her to take off everything from the waist down.

She undressed, climbed on the table and pulled the paper sheet up over her. The room seemed awfully cold. The ceiling was a flat white plane, interrupted only by a dangling red and blue mobile above her head. The nurse laid out the instruments: a metal speculum that she recognized from her appointment a year ago, some stainless steel curved rods in graduated sizes, a tweezer, a long metal stick with a thick loop of wire at its tip. Mira didn't know what most of the things were. In the corner there was a machine—a big white metal box with a glass bottle turned upside down on its hood. She stared and then looked away. She didn't want to know.

The doctor came in. He was stiff and polite in his white coat, and she smiled at him, wondering as her mouth creased upward why she was smiling. She really wanted to get up and run away, she wanted to shout at him to stop. He sat on a stool between her uplifted knees, and moved them apart. He pressed on her abdomen with his hand inside her. What was he doing, she wondered, could he feel the baby already? She closed her eyes.

He told her that what came next would be cold. It was, cold and hard. Then he explained that he was about to do something to her cervix. He held up the needle to show her, and even though she hated shots she didn't move, she just looked at him with a calm expression. She was frozen on her back, like a tipped-over turtle on a beach, out in the open, vulnerable. Her other pelvic exam had been quick and she'd still been embarrassed. This was worse—a million times worse. No one had ever sat for this long between her legs.

Once again she heard his voice explaining something to her, and she tried to pay attention. But it felt as if her ears were stuffed with the cotton Vivian used to put in when she had an earache. He took the smallest rod from the instrument tray and pushed it into her. In a minute he took the next size up, and then the next. Cramps began. Mira bit her lip against them. She was determined not to cry. Only a child would cry. The cold steel slid in and out of her, her body opened under the invasion of her most private space. She wanted to tell the doctor to get out of her, but she was too scared. For a minute, even though she was hurting, it seemed almost funny that those same hands would go from this room of ending to a room where life had just begun. She lay there and watched him enter her body, and thought of her mother, outside in the waiting room, with her magazine and her modern words.

As the doctor inserted the last and largest dilator, the nurse switched on the machine in the corner. It began to hum. Mira began to tremble. Her thighs quivered and the paper sheet rattled. The nurse came and held her hand. She said it was okay, but it wasn't, not at all. The doctor inserted the tube. The machine began to vacuum out the rich lining of her uterus, and she could see the clear plastic filling in a long red line. That was her blood. That was her baby. The machine was sucking her dry. It was taking from her the life she had loved illegally. She began to cry.

When he'd finished, the nurse went to the machine to examine the jar. Mira closed her eyes. She saw it, a fish under glass in formaldehyde now. Tears rolled out from under her eyelids and slid down into her ears. The doctor left. The nurse told her to lie still for a while, then closed the door behind her as she carried the jar from the room. It was done. Mira was finally alone.

The Atmos clock on her mother's dresser blurred in and out of focus as she grew drowsy from the Valium that Vivian had given her. When they'd gotten home from the doctor's office that afternoon, her mother had brought her into the master bedroom and tucked her into her father's side of the big bed. Since he'd died, Vivian sometimes had Mira spend the night with her—to keep Mira from being lonely, she said. Even when her father was alive, if he were away, or if he and her mother had been fighting, Mira sometimes slept here with Vivian.

Vivian had made her have supper in bed—even though the doctor said there was nothing the matter with her and that she could move around—but Mira wanted to throw up. Just the smell of food made her feel sick.

The phone rang. From the cool tone of her mother's voice Mira knew it must be Michael. But she felt worn thin, transparent as ice—she didn't want to talk to anyone. "Tell him I'm asleep," she said. She huddled down into the sheets and pulled them around her chin. When the phone rang a second time, it was Dee, calling as she'd promised. Vivian tried to pass Mira the phone, but she shrank back, keeping her hands under the blanket. Dee knew how to unlock her. Her resolve to stay calm would crack and she'd cry for sure. It was important to keep herself empty, no complications, pure and blank and white.

Mira watched "Simon and Simon" and "Hill Street Blues" while Vivian went over her script for the next day. When the eleven o'clock news came on, Mira turned out her light and put her head under the covers so Vivian's lamp wouldn't be in her eyes. She welcomed sleep—a warm white drift, a smooth blank mind.

The room is white. The room has white gauze curtains hanging like long surgical bandages. The couches are white. The chairs are white. The bed linen and the rug are white. I sit on the couch, wrapped in a winding sheet—like a mummy in its cocoon. I can't move my arms or my legs. Only my mouth is free. I argue with the tall man. He wears a white suit and a white Panama hat. I can't see his eyes, but I know why he keeps flashing those long-bladed scissors in front of my face.

I love my hair, I say, I love the way it falls across my back, I love the way it falls into my eyes. It is long and black and thick. I don't want it cut. I am begging him but now he is gone, and Vivian is standing in his place instead. The shears are in her hand. Words come from her mouth, but I can't hear them. They're flying around the room like birds who can't find the way out. She gathers my hair in one hand and begins to put the scissors through it. It hurts, it feels as though the scissors are cutting my flesh, as if she is clipping fingers, toes, tiny pieces of skin. I cry out in pain, but Vivian is relentless, keeps cutting and cutting, slicing down through me until I can't stand it anymore. With my teeth I pull on a tag of the sheet and unwind myself suddenly, I am like a yo-yo spinning down to the end of my string. I feel my head with my hands. Sunlight pours through a gap in cloud cover, anger, the room is bright white. I grab my mother's hair, a shining rope of red, a sheet of copper, and cut and cut until there is nothing left but sparse clumps and Vivian looks like a chick wet from the egg. She is ugly. She opens her mouth but now no words come out, no birds to batter at my cage. Hair grows in patches, like some strange crop, across the couches, the rug, the pillows. Now there is red on the white.

I try to open my eyes. The room is black and silent. I think I am alone. I think I am awake. I feel my hair stick in the sweat on my forehead, tears track down my cheeks.

I am coiled on the edge of the bed. I slide back toward the dream. Vivian sighs softly and rolls close to me. It makes me hot and sticky. Dreaming makes me hot and sticky. I want to stretch out from under it.

My mother's breathing deepens down into sleep. Vivian presses in on me, the dark is damp against my face, I wish I knew the time. I open my eyes. I remember my dream.

5

VIVIAN LEANED into the glass of the large mirror to retouch her mascara and saw Mira reflected, today's dress and accessories in hand, at the door of her studio dressing room. "You don't really mind, do you?" she asked.

"I guess not."

Vivian smiled, trying to ease the tension that had begun between them last night. When she'd suggested Mira come to the set today excitement was what she'd expected, not an argument. Before, her daughter had enjoyed skipping a day of classes to help out at the studio. But for the last two weeks— since the abortion—Mira'd been very subdued, silent; it seemed like she was always shut away in her room. Even in the mornings now she helped Vivian quickly and efficiently but then made some excuse to leave. Every afternoon when Vivian came home from the set, Mira's door was closed, and when she asked what Mira was doing her daughter gave schoolwork as the reason for her locked existence. Nothing seemed to draw her out—not the lure of a shopping spree or even a nice lunch midtown. Vivian was getting tired of offering treats and being refused, and when Mira'd been reluctant to come today, what had been worry about her daughter turned to irritation: how long could you sit around and mope? It was time to get on with life. Mira needed to think of somebody else besides herself. Anyway, Vivian really needed her best defender by her side today: what had started as a skirmish the night of her birthday party had escalated into a steady war with Ariella—a barrage of insinuations, nasty comments, and criticism. It all made Vivian so tense she could barely concentrate on Megan, and she wasn't sure she could take much more.

She swiveled on the stool and put out her arms, trying one last time to make a connection. Mira hesitated a minute, then set the clothes down and crossed over to give her a hug. Vivian's tension flowed outward, like ink against blotting paper, sucked up by her daughter's strength. It felt so good to be hugged again. She snuggled her head against Mira's shoulder: loneliness, fear, and anger erased themselves. She wanted just to rest there for hours—but Mira pulled away.

Having not been on the set in a few weeks, Mira was surveying the room, Vivian realized, weighing the emotional disorder. Powder, eye shadow, rouge, and Pan-Cake were strewn helter-skelter across the dressing table. A hairbrush lay in the middle of the floor and the clothing for next week's shoot was thrown across the sofa and chairs in piles—bright red silk, yellow cotton, deep blue challis. Vivian hadn't made any attempt to pick up in over a week and the chaos worked. Mira began to straighten up. Vivian smiled: her ally was back.

"What's going on?" Mira put her back to the wall and slid down on the floor cross-legged. She started to fold a snarl of scarves into a box, trying to push away her irritation. Her mother thought that it was all okay now, all the same again. But it wasn't. She was still angry. The baby was gone, the pressure was off—but she was still mad. She'd spent a lot of time in her room the last couple weeks, talking to her father in the mirror. He was mad, too, at what Vivian had made her do.

"I'm getting a lot of flack." Vivian turned back to the mirror and tried to reline her left eye with charcoal pencil, but her hand was shaking.

"Ariella," Mira said with a sigh. She pushed the box of scarves aside and pulled her foot up to her crotch to retie her Nike. "What now?"

"I can just feel her out there." Vivian drew a Winston from the soft cellophane pack and lit it abruptly, then reached for the powder and blotted the creases around her nose. "Watching me, sitting in the control booth taking notes, bending Marty's ear." She mimicked the older woman's voice. "Too old. Wrong for the part."

Mira sighed. "Every week you say the same thing but nothing ever happens. You're being paranoid." Her mouth was full of a bad sour taste—her mother was always thinking of herself. She doesn't care that I'm missing classes today, Mira thought. I'm drowning I'm so far behind, all those pages and pages still to read in my history book, and Dr. Strauss stopping me in the hall yesterday. Midterms are coming. Everyone knows I'm in trouble but my own mother. Mira looked up at Vivian and saw the silent glare coming at her from the mirror.

"Okay, okay." She put up her hand like a stop sign. She didn't feel like arguing. When they argued Vivian always won. "I just meant, is there anything specific?"

"Not yet. But there will be."

"Why're you always looking for problems?"

Mira's voice was saturated with exasperation. Vivian looked down at the dressing table and traced a line with the edge of her fingernail through the spilt powder. "Just try being in my shoes." Suddenly she was tired of the silent tug-of-war they'd been playing for the last few weeks. "You think it's so easy?" There were too many things to be done, too many lines to be read, too many people to cope with, too much emotion to be swallowed, too much trivial detail, too much living. Her eyes filled with tears and she snatched a Kleenex from the box, blotting the edge of her lower lid quickly. If her makeup ran she'd have to start all over. "Why don't you just leave!" Vivian said angrily. "When you're like this you're no help anyway!"

Mira stood up and almost went out the door, but something about the curve of her mother's back stopped her, something about the way she was trying so hard not to cry. She looked at her mother's face, half-hidden, in the mirror, and felt a tug deep inside her, a strong current in which swirled all their feelings for each other, all the emotions, all the facts of their daily life together. And she knew then she couldn't just slam through the door. Like a match, her anger went out, soggy underneath her mother's tears. She crossed the room and wove her arms around Vivian's neck. They looked at each other in the mirror and, for the first time in weeks, Mira smiled.

Vivian patted her arm and pressed her cheek against the back of Mira's hand.

"So what's up with the script?" Mira asked, straightening up to inspect herself in the glass. She turned her face from side to side while she licked her fingertip and slicked her thick eyebrows down. "Last week was the defeat of the corporate takeover. Megan got to keep her fashion house. Dee got her man. And Chris got his mil in blackmail money. What's going on now?"

Vivian opened another pack of Winstons, speaking to Mira over her head in the mirror. "Yesterday we did a run-through of the scene in my office where Dee threatens to quit." She handed the script to Mira. "Next is that boring one with Sumner"—she made a face, as if her cigarette tasted bad—"where I'm pinning the material on the model and trying to explain why I'm moving Megan's World to N.Y.C." She arched one eyebrow and shot Mira a look of amusement. "Marcus Warren and Sumner are one of a kind—dumb as horses' behinds."

"Vivian, I can hear you all the way from the set." Dee stuck her head around the doorjamb. "Mira!" She grinned and leaned down to give her a kiss. "Terrific. Now you can keep this loudmouth in line."

"What's happening?"

Dee shrugged. "Everybody's edgy."

"Vivian, ready in five," Toni called, walking past the open door. "Hello, Mira!" She waved and continued on down the line.

"I'll go over to the set and check it out," Mira said, hoisting herself off the floor and rubbing her back. She'd skipped her exercises this morning. "Then I'll hang around the control booth and take my own notes—so just relax. Did you clear my being there with Marty?"

Vivian nodded, busy now with drawing a smooth red line over the rounded contours of her lips.

Mira walked back into the studio and down the length of the darkened sets. Constructed like alcoves off a central corridor, they ran side by side in two long lines. Each room was a regular location for the soap—Megan's office, her studio, the runway, the shop, her bedroom, Dee's living room and kitchen, Sumner's office and den, Chris Light's bare bachelor studio, a local restaurant and bar. Over twenty individual rooms were set up within the barnlike space of the studio, each with three walls, no ceiling, and usually no more to their dimensions than ten by ten, but clever camera angles and a wide angle lens made them appear large and complete on the home screen.

Mira's running shoes squeaked on the wooden floor and she shifted the script on her arm, flipping through to the scene they were to rehearse. Even though she hadn't wanted to come, now that she was here it didn't feel so bad. Since the abortion she'd found it especially hard to be around people, especially people like Dee or Penny, who had a knack for taking her apart and seeing what she was feeling. But here everyone was busy—they didn't have time to stop and look at her too closely. She stuck a pencil through the hair behind her ear. She knew the routines, she knew the ins and outs of a complicated, technical craft and for a while she could distract herself—from worry, depression, grades, just about anything —with her job on the set. It felt good to be doing something again.

Today they were filming in the studio where Megan created her original designs, and the set was littered with scraps of cloth and bolts of fabric that had to be changed several times an episode. Even on the set of a soap nothing was allowed to stand still. The plants on the windowsills had to grow, the piles of paper had to heap and mound in different shapes, the sketch pads and pencils had to shrink and increase as if they were being used. It might be melodrama, but the detail was as painstaking as in Flaubert's *Madame Bovary.*

The cameramen were setting up for the run-through, and their voices drifted across the empty space as they argued over the color of the gels for the spots, while the set crew worked to make Megan's studio appear more lived-in than yesterday's shoot. Across the drafting board in the center of the room they had draped the cut cloth Vivian would use today for a prop, and Mira made her way across the tangle of cables and electrical boxes to check it. The lights hit her face and she squinted against their heat and the glare. She found the place in the script where Vivian would be working with the material and talking to Marcus Warren. It wasn't a terribly exciting scene, just a synopsis that established the move to the city for the viewer who had missed yesterday's episode.

Mira fingered the pieces of violet silk and they shimmered under the white lights, shot through with silver thread. The fabric was slippery, the sort of thing that would drape sensuously without clinging. The set crew had a way of finding just the right piece of equipment or prop, from teapots and saucers to coffee-table books and pocket watches. Making little arrows on the script to flag Vivian's close-ups so that she could be aware ahead of time, Mira wandered off the set and hoped wardrobe had remembered to color-key Vivian's outfit for today with the violet silk.

"Hey!"

She looked up, startled, to see Marty negotiating his way across the web of cables and cameras.

"Talk to me." He put his arm around her and drew her down the main aisle toward the control booth. His flowery scent surrounded them. "I'm real worried about Vivian. She's tense plus."

"You're telling me?" Mira sighed and shrugged her shoulders. "I just spent half an hour cooling her out. Can't you get Ariella off her back?"

Marty's face tightened and she wondered if she'd gone too far. Mostly it seemed as if she were a member of the cast, but other times people let her know that she was just a kid, just Vivian's daughter—in the way. There were boundaries.

He sighed and shook his head. "Easy to say, hard to do." He took her hand and swung it as they walked. "Ariella's got a pin up her butt because the damn dog has prickly heat. What a bore."

A pair of hands covered Mira's eyes from behind, interrupting her reply. She stopped, knowing who it was from the feel of his forearms as they pressed against her cheeks. "Chris?" The nearness of him made her fingers sticky with perspiration.

"None other." He took his hands away and swiveled her by the shoulders toward him.

"See you in a sec, Mira," Marty said, heading toward the control booth.

Chris stuck his hands in the pockets of his jeans and rocked back and forth. "How've you been?"

Mira just nodded. As usual her tongue seemed coated with library paste.

"Lookin' good," he said, staring at her breasts through the soft yellow tee shirt.

She folded her arms across her chest, embarrassed.

"So." He ran his finger down the length of her arm. "What've you been up to?"

He was playing her, keeping the line between them taut. Mira didn't mind. She was already hooked, she wanted to be landed. "Not much."

"School on vacation or what?"

"I'm cutting." She tried to give him a nonchalant smile.

He looked at his watch. "Makeup time. See you later?"

She nodded again, and headed toward the control booth, forcing herself not to look over her shoulder as they walked in opposite directions. Maybe he'd ask her out, although she was about ready to give up.

Settling into a folding chair in the corner, she tucked her feet up out of the way. It was important to be unobtrusive here: this was the heart of the show, pumping directions, comments, orders, and criticism to the crews on the floor. It was a small room, crowded with everyone who had to be there— Marty, Toni, Ariella, and the technical people—and it was one of Marty's favors to Vivian that Mira was sometimes allowed in. She sat facing the wall of ten TV monitors as the cameramen got their positions set up. Techies sat in front of the monitors and operated a panel of levers and knobs that looked as complicated as the inside of the Gemini capsule Mira had seen in the National Air and Space Museum in Washington on the trip her class took to the capital last year.

As she leafed through the script again, apprehension crowded her stomach. Vivian had to keep herself stitched together until today's filming was finished.

"Okay, let's go," Marty said into the mike that carried down onto the set. "We're short on time."

Looking up, Mira saw that her mother and Sumner had

taken their places. Vivian's red smock was a glaring bull's-eye against the shimmering piece of violet. Someone in wardrobe had forgotten. Mira made a note on the edge of the script. The makeup on her left eye was a little heavy. The earrings looked too dressy for the working smock. Megan's irritation with Marcus Warren was too strong, as Vivian's real feelings for Sumner came through.

"Camera three pan back so we can see what she's doing."

The angle on monitor six shifted and Vivian's efforts to drape the violet silk across the mannequin filled the screen as she talked. Mira could see she was having trouble. The material was slippery and the pins wouldn't go through it. Vivian was struggling and trying not to let it show.

"Close-up on her face with number one."

Vivian turned into the camera as she spoke, knowing that this was the place in the script where Marty would probably call for a close-up. She could see her lines on the Tele-PrompTer but she ignored them: she had this scene down cold. Besides, it was hard enough to concentrate on her acting when she had to be pinning this damned purple stuff. She jabbed a pin at the shoulder, but the material hung down lopsidedly against the plastic flesh of the mannequin. Perspiration began to bead the edge of her hairline. She thought of it shining in the lights, the cameras ready to show it all. She tried another pin, stuck herself in the thumb and resolutely did not wince. Her hands were shaking.

Mira clenched her fists tightly, willing her mother to get control.

"For Chrissakes, Marty," Ariella snorted, breaking into the tense atmosphere of the control booth. "Look at those hands. What a mess she's making." 'Nando was sprawled on her lap and she covered the wet tip of his nose with tiny smacking kisses.

Mira looked down at her script, breath tight in her windpipe. She hated Ariella, hated every wrinkle and pore on her smug and pudgy face. Toni sent Mira a glance of sympathy and a smile, but it didn't help—when Ariella criticized Vivian, she dug a hole in Mira. Mira looked down at her script and made a deep black line with the point of her pencil, rubbing the lead back and forth until the paper underneath shredded with the friction.

Marty sighed and shook his head with resignation. On screen Vivian fumbled with the piece of cloth. It came unpinned and slithered to the ground, a silent flag of purple.

Mira slid to the edge of her chair.

Ariella slapped her script closed.

Marty spoke into the mike. "Honey, we've got a little trouble up here."

Vivian raised her head and looked full into the camera's eye as if she were speaking face to face with her director. *"You're having trouble!"* She snatched up the cloth and hurled it to the floor. "I can't work with this garbage! I might as well be trying to bend a piece of iron!"

"Keep it cool—don't get yourself in an uproar."

His voice came down to her, placating, tired, and she could just see Ariella up there in the control booth, making more trouble. "It's stupid!" she cried, humiliated. "I'm not a seamstress, I'm an actress! Tell Ariella to take this purple crap and"—

Mira winced in anticipation, but Marty switched off the mike so that Vivian's mouth formed the angry words in silence. From the control booth they watched her pick up the material and rip it from one end to the other. Marty moaned and put his head down on his crossed arms.

"I want her out," Ariella gasped, hugging 'Nando against her chest so tightly that he yelped. "Out!"

Marty turned to Mira. "We're running out of time. Go. Do some magic."

Mira sprinted to Vivian's dressing room. The door was locked, but Vivian opened it right away to the sound of her voice. Tears had ruined her mother's makeup—it was running down her cheeks in multicolored rivers. Mira took her by the shoulders and sat with her on the couch. She held her, rocked her, patted her shoulder, let her cry for exactly four minutes. Then she wiped off the old foundation and rouge, put a cold washcloth over her mother's eyes, stuck her head out the door and yelled for Vivian's makeup man to come in exactly ten minutes, pulled the red smock over her mother's head, and told wardrobe they had fifteen minutes to find her a new yellow one. Her own problems had vanished—absorbed by her mother's crisis—and her body vibrated with energy. She liked to rescue things.

It was eleven-thirty and airtime was noon. She poured Vivian a glass of water. "Bottoms up."

Vivian took it and sipped. "What am I going to do?" she asked plaintively, her naked eyes looking puffy and red.

"You're going back out there, that's what."

"I can't." She pressed her fingertips against her eyelids.

"You can and you will." Mira picked up the hairbrush and began the long rhythmic strokes that Vivian always found soothing. "Otherwise Ariella gets just what she wants—you walk off the set a half hour before we go on the air and she gets us fired."

Vivian's shoulders stiffened.

"The only reason you couldn't pin that stuff is because you didn't know how slippery it was going to be and you were in a bad mood to begin with. Just make up your mind to do it right this time." Mira massaged her shoulders briskly and then went to unlock the door for makeup.

She sat quietly as the makeup man redid Vivian from scratch—sculpting, smoothing, and erasing the marks of distress. The yellow smock from wardrobe arrived. The room was quiet, and she could see Vivian begin to unwind a little. Mira helped her change smocks and then squeezed her hand. "I know you'll be okay."

They walked out the door, partners, hand in hand, back to the set. Nothing was said. Vivian acted as though it were any other day. As she and Sumner took their places, and the studio tightened with the expectancy of airtime, Mira slumped down into a folding chair just off set. She knew she ought to monitor things from the control booth, but right now she needed to be near Vivian, as if her presence could magically protect her mother.

The scene began, and Vivian picked up the new swatch of cloth in a casual way, taking her time, talking to Sumner. She draped it over the mannequin's shoulder and studied it, adjusted it, gathered it in one hand, squinted at it, did everything but pin it while they talked. And it all worked perfectly.

Mira relaxed against the canvas back of the chair, glad for a minute alone to catch her breath. On his way from the booth during a sixty-second spot for Gravy Train, Marty squeezed her shoulder with thanks. She allowed herself to put her head back and close her eyes.

Half an hour later, when Vivian came looking for Mira, she was still sitting half-collapsed in the folding chair. The filming was finished for the day; Vivian's hands were shaking. She needed Mira to help her change. Pulling off the scene had required enormous effort and she didn't want anyone to see how much it had taken out of her. Mira stood, gathered her things together, and they walked back to her dressing room together. Vivian put her arm around Mira's shoulders and leaned on her, nauseated with exhaustion.

"You did it," Mira said, closing the door behind them.

Vivian pulled the smock off her shoulders and let it fall to the ground. Her knees wouldn't lock, threatening, and she sat down on the sofa abruptly. She patted the empty space beside her with her last bit of energy. "It's a good thing you were here. I nearly fell apart." She put her head down on Mira's lap. "You look as tired as I feel."

Mira was quiet, stroking the long black hair.

"I ask too much from you." Vivian turned her green eyes upward, questioning, looking for a negative. "Don't I?"

Mira sighed. Her mother reminded her of a child begging not to be spanked. "I love you." She looked down at her mother's face, the eyes closed in relief now, the tiny lines that spread out in a fan at the corners, the long lashes that touched down on her cheeks. She was proud to help and protect, but still, she wondered, what had Vivian done when Mira was a little girl, who had she relied on then? "Come on," she said, straightening her mother up and pushing aside the unanswerables. She took Vivian's shirt and jeans off the hook on the back of the door and handed them to her. "Let's get out of here—we deserve some lunch."

That had been one good thing about being at the studio yesterday, Mira thought, as she slipped through the door of the gym a few minutes late—she'd gotten out of basketball. The locker room was crowded with girls changing into the short-sleeved gym uniform that signaled the beginning of spring at Breton. She hated basketball. Running up and down, sticking your armpits and your sweaty smell in someone's face —all for the sake of a ball through a hoop. It made her feel awkward and dumb. She liked gymnastics better, the clean circles and loops above the unevens, the vault over the horse, the precision of tumbling across stiff leather mats. In basketball the bodies were too close—and you had to depend on someone else.

The changing room was a large open area with lockers and a few wooden benches running down the middle. Mira crossed to her assigned space, trying to remember the combination she always forgot, all the while concentrating on not looking at breasts swelling out of their bras, breasts floating free, nipples aimed at the ceiling, thighs and buttocks and ankles and calves. There was no privacy here. She hated the public undressing—the embarrassment of wearing an A-cup padded bra. This place is more naked than a hospital, she thought.

She spun the lock to clear it and the numbers ran together in her head. Ordinarily Janet Singleton remembered it for her, but Janet was ignoring her today. Mira concentrated. She was tired of asking for help. Out of the corner of her eye she could see Janet laughing at something with Penny Saunders and Crystal Cielo. The four of them had been good friends for years, since elementary school. They went to parties together, went shopping together, stabled their horses at the same place, and spent every July and August together at Martingale, a summer riding camp in the Berkshires. But since she'd gotten pregnant and had the abortion it was really hard to talk to any of them. The abortion still stood between them, just as her father's death stood between them. Crystal had had three abortions and for her they were a matter of convenience—she saw herself as too wild and free to be pinned down by something as civilized as birth control. Mira could see that somehow Penny admired Crystal for having been pregnant so often —she envied her the experience. Penny had never had a boyfriend, and to her an abortion meant you were loved by somebody. Janet was too smart to get caught and she was short on sympathy for anyone who did.

None of them understood Mira's reaction and they treated her as if she were fragile and unpredictable, almost as though she were a patient with a contagious disease.

"You will join us today for a little basquetbal?" Crystal now asked, turning on the bench to face Mira as she pulled her jeans down over her long legs. Her words were lightly accented. She'd been born in Nicaragua and lived there until she was nine, when her father had been kidnapped and ransomed by left-wing terrorists. Crystal still talked about "her country" with pride, but Mira couldn't understand why. She would never have wanted to live anyplace they did such terrible things. But Crystal was brave and daring. She was dark-eyed, her long black hair pulled into a high ponytail. She stood up to reach into her locker, wearing only a lace bra that pushed her breasts upward into a mountain of cleavage and a pair of transparent bikini underpants. Her underwear was famous schoolwide.

Mira fingered the top button of her blouse. The worst part of gym was the shower afterward—without even panties or a bra—where everyone looked at everyone else, comparing each last ripple, fold, and curve. At home, she'd begun to undress in her closet because Vivian always forgot to knock. The week of the abortion her mother had written her three medical excuses for all of her gym classes—menstrual cramps, the notes had said—because Mira felt too drained to run around. Then last week she'd cut once and claimed cramps twice.

"You are recovered at last?" Crystal asked.

Mira shrugged. She didn't want to talk about it.

"Bill Phillips has been after your ass for two days now," Penny said, pulling her sweater over her head and chewing her gum at a fantastic rate. Mira always wondered how Penny managed not to bite her tongue. But she was an expert, she wound it around and through her teeth like a skier attacking the slalom slope.

"We've got something on for later," Mira said, undoing the top button of her blouse.

Janet let go of a precise smile that showed her teeth. They were white and well-shaped and even—they reminded Mira of the denture ads on TV—and once she'd actually caught Janet practicing that smile in the girls' room. "I'll bet you've got a date for the auditorium—right, Mira?" Janet had a sly expression on her face as she pulled blue tennis socks that matched her uniform on over her carefully pedicured feet. "Yesterday afternoon Rich and I spent an hour there, and when we came out we ran smack into Mr. Marsten, you know, the new French teacher. He was about to ask how come we weren't in study hall, but I told him we were using the piano to practice a duet . . ."

Crystal groaned. "Little did he know."

"The point is he believed me," Janet said, her oval face soft with satisfaction. "Give credit where credit is due, Crys." She reached up to tie her honey-colored hair back with a ribbon. "Just make sure you don't use the same excuse, Mira."

"I'm surprised he even bothered to hassle you guys," Penny said. "Honor students and class presidents are above suspicion."

Those girls who didn't know Janet well had nicknamed her Virgin Mary, when, in fact, she'd been sleeping with her boyfriend since she was twelve. It was Janet who'd gone with Mira the day she'd gotten her prescription for the pill.

"What I don't get is why no one else thinks of that place," Penny said, standing up to snap her uniform closed in front. The cotton stretched tight across her hips. Mira could smell the winter sweat of thirty pairs of socks and sneakers. "I mean, it's so big no one'd ever catch on, and dark enough to do some good stuff."

"I don't really like it in there," Mira said, feeling a little faint and sitting down. The room seemed close and hot. The heat prickled behind her eyes. Her hand went to the top button of her blouse and closed it. The nausea came in waves now. She couldn't expose herself. She couldn't get undressed.

A whistle shrilled through the room, calling the girls to the gym, and, still talking loudly, everyone began to file out. "Hurry up, Mira," Penny said. "You're real late."

"Go on," she said, "I'll catch up with you."

"Are you sure you're okay?" Penny asked, sitting beside Mira and putting her arm around her. Mira fought the urge to push her away. The smell of garlic bagel and Juicy Fruit blanketed her.

"Go," Mira said. "I'm fine. You'll get in trouble."

As soon as Penny disappeared around the corner Mira slid her head between her knees. From the gym she could hear Miss Roberts calling the roll. The sick feeling went away after a minute. She went to the sink and washed her hands, hard, with water so hot it stung. She had to get out of here, she didn't care if she got caught. She picked up her books and started for the door, safety just a few yards away, the knob a cold metal lump that wouldn't turn beneath her still wet palm.

As she pulled the heavy door open, she looked back over her shoulder. Miss Roberts was behind her, watching, her arms crossed. With her cropped hair and muscles, everyone said she was just a bull dyke, and these comments floated across Mira's mind now as she stared at the teacher, wordless. From the other room she could hear the thump of the ball and the thud of feet. The action had begun.

"Cutting again, Mira?"

"I'm not cutting," she said, leaning against the edge of the door for support. "I don't feel good, I'm going to the nurse's office."

Miss Roberts eyes pressed in on her like two black bullets. "Is it your period?"

"Yes," Mira said eagerly, "yes, I have cramps."

"Fascinating. You had your period all of last week, *and* all of the week before. You must be a menstrual machine."

Mira flinched.

"Get your uniform on. Right away."

"I can't."

"What do you mean, can't? Don't you mean *won't?*"

Mira looked at the floor.

"Report to Mrs. Markham. Maybe she can figure out what's the matter with you." The teacher turned on her heel and went to the glassed-in office, where Mira saw her pick up the phone.

Mira went out into the hall and rested for a moment on a bench near the water fountain. She had to think up an excuse before she went to the principal's office. She thought of saying, "I don't want to get undressed. I want to be left alone," but it sounded silly. She didn't want to explain her feelings, not even to herself.

"Hey!"

She looked up. Michael was crossing the lobby in his gym shorts. "What's up?" she asked, as he wiped the sweat from his face on a towel.

"Water," he said, short of wind, as he bent over the fountain to drink. "You?"

"Markham's office."

"How come?"

"I just couldn't," she said, moving her hands in agitation. "That damn game! I hate this place—there's no privacy!"

Michael just looked at her. He didn't understand what she was talking about.

"I don't know." She ran her fingers through her hair. "I just didn't want to play. So I didn't, and now Roberts is being bitchy and making a big deal out of it." She stood up, using the anger to push down her fear. Mrs. Markham was waiting for her.

"Why don't you wait for a minute and calm down." His hand tugged on her arm.

"I've got to go."

He sighed. "Well, what about after school? Maybe a movie."

She shook her head. "Already got a date."

"Bill Phillips."

Mira just nodded. "Look, I've got to go now. See you in bio

lab." She hurried down the hall, her hair swinging across her back like a metronome.

No matter how many times Mira was asked out, she never felt sure of herself. As she and Bill shared a joint in the dark auditorium she wasn't listening to what he was saying. The open space around them was so black her eyes hurt from straining to see anything at all, and the silence made her nervous. She had shifted into an adrenaline high where her thoughts were just a streak in her mind. She worried about her hair, her makeup, her breath, if she was still clean from last night's bath, the chances of getting caught here, the trouble she was in. Mrs. Markham had set up another conference with Dr. Strauss, who would definitely call her mother, who would be mad.

It hurt Mira to trouble teachers who'd known her since she was six and first came to Breton. She'd always liked being bright, a teachers' favorite—reliable, dependable, and a little shy. She liked the way the faculty greeted her in the hall and called on her in class. She'd wanted to be able to explain everything to Mrs. Markham, whose disappointed, perplexed expression made it even more important. She'd wanted to make them believe in her again. But even she didn't understand what had made her refuse to play, and so she'd given Mrs. Markham the same lie she'd given Miss Roberts—she was sick to her stomach from cramps.

She rubbed her chin with the back of her hand and wished she could concentrate on what she was supposed to be doing here. Bill Phillips didn't do a lot of talking and even though they'd seen each other off and on for the better part of the year, they didn't know very much about one another. Mira couldn't talk to him about the trouble she was in. Besides, he hadn't asked her out in quite a while and she didn't want to be a drag.

Today she just needed to get high, needed to float out over her problems, to allow her mind to move onto a separate plane above her body. She closed her eyes and saw the orange and white illustration they'd studied in geometry this morning— two parallel planes that met somewhere you couldn't see, in infinity. But the situation kept pulling her back, the chairs uncomfortable, the conversation slow. It would only be a few minutes before they shifted down onto the carpeted aisle. She knew Bill's habits, she'd been here with him before. Study hall was the last period of the day, and it was crowded, easy to cut because the proctor hardly ever took attendance.

The darkness was so total that she couldn't see even his profile, only the heightened glow of the joint as he sucked hard against it. His voice, harsh and choked, came toward her in a pinched breathless way as he tried to talk without exhaling over the dope.

"Want to try upstairs?"

She imagined him pointing at the molded soundproof ceiling and did not understand what he meant. An auditorium had no upstairs. Then she remembered that Bill worked the catwalk as a techie for the drama productions. He created exits, entrances, and solos with the lightboard, Lekos, and follow spots. She'd never been up there before, never felt the slightest desire to sit on that lip, hanging out into space. It would be like sitting on the edge of a very new moon.

"Sure," she said.

He pulled her to her feet. As she stood up, a rush moved, swelled, an ocean wave from her feet to her head, pounding, exploding, beating hot against the backs of her eyeballs. Suddenly she could see through the dark. The world was magical, full of shapes. He took her hand and moved through the blackness, up over the stage, to the narrow ladder that led upstairs.

She climbed without thinking, without fear, because she wasn't worried about her body. There was no longer any danger.

High on the narrow catwalk, Mira peered over the rail into a sea of black. It looked solid enough to hold her and she imagined walking back to the ground this way, down through the air on a staircase carved out of black oxygen, like Jesus walking across the water. Bill pulled her down beside him and she felt the steel of the walk cold under her shoulders. She hated the way it was always quick and awkward, she hated her own willingness—but mostly she hated his need. He undid her blouse and slid her jeans down around her ankles, and she heard the sharp rasp of his zipper. He angled her hand through the open fly and pressed it down onto his penis. As always, she was surprised and embarrassed by its hardness, its width—too huge to fit inside her. She was glad it was dark. The mechanics of sex were a distraction. She could not fly away until the preliminaries were taken care of.

He licked her breast and for a minute she felt a flicker of desire, faint, struggling against the dark. But then it was gone. He had moved on top, kissing her, pushing her legs apart, and she arched against him—even though it made her back pinch a little—trying to make it easier, the Vaseline she had put on herself earlier helping him to get in. An image, the doctor between her knees, floated up on the surface of her eyes, but she pushed it down. Anger, but she pushed it down. This was the first time since then.

Dimly she could hear him moaning. The only pleasure was in pleasing him, and she lifted her hips to his rhythm. The teeth of his zipper were cold against her as he ground his way down. Mira closed her eyes.

I am remembering the horses. It is summer, and I am at camp. It is hot August, dusk, and we line up, twelve girls just becoming women, drawn by the spectacle and the knowledge and the smell. We sit on the fence, gripping with our thighs. We are here to watch the Friday-night breeding. The stallion comes from the barn, his hooves clatter on the wooden floors, he waves his head, he snorts and flares and grows erect, hugely erect, some great snake winds out beneath his belly, long and black and hard. It swings from side to side as he prances, he is showing it off to us, he dances in a circle and we all stare at its impossible width and length, strong as an iron bar. He comes to the mare, he sniffs her puckered slit, the breeder pulls her tail aside. She tries to kick, but the trainer holds her head tight on the lead line. She can't move. He mounts, his hooves dig into her sides, he pulls her toward him, he arches in a wave of muscle, his round haunches thrust and tense against her hind-quarters. After he is finished, the mare is walked. We climb down from the fence, we stand on weak legs, we are embarrassed by the violence and the thrill of what we have seen. Between our thighs we are wet. I am thinking of Catharine the Great, I am thinking of a book I have read for the first time that summer, *The Painted Bird*. I am thinking of women who ride barebelly beneath horses to impale themselves on that great black stake.

It is dark now. There is noise around me, a lot of noise. It is not the horse. It is Bill. He is getting ready to finish. I am trying to bring myself back, out of that dream, I am trying to get the dream out of my head.

A flashlight beam floods down into Mira's eyes. She can't see. She is blind. She can feel Bill struggling to leave her like a fish caught on the end of a hook. She is tense, she is tight, he can't get out. For an agonized moment she thinks they will be bound this way forever, trapped under the eye of that light, exposed, her legs apart to the world. But then Bill is out, and zipping up his pants in a quick greased motion.

The light plays down on Mira, it lingers there, it turns her flesh dead white, the harsh color of the neon signs on Forty-second Street that advertize bodies. It seems forever that the light inspects her. She knows she is naked, she can see her nipples pale and sunken under that light, the smell of sex thick around her. She rolls on her side, away from the light, but it follows her. It wants to see her. With one hand she clutches her blouse closed, with the other she reaches for her jeans and pulls them up over her lap to hide herself. She can hear a man's laughter. Shame rises in her mouth, bitter, and she knows suddenly that she is going to throw up. She hunches forward on her knees and her stomach slides up into her throat, the cherry yogurt from lunch backs up into her nose and mouth, foul and acid now, and slops out onto the steel of the catwalk. And still she feels the cold heat of that light against her buttocks as she kneels there, helpless.

"You kids come with me," the security guard said, still laughing. "Markham's gonna love this."

At four-thirty Eve was packing her satchel to go home when the phone interrupted her.

"Eve? Marie. We've got a new problem over here. The security guard just caught Mira Webster and Bill Phillips going at it in the auditorium, and Markham's in a rage. Webster'd already cut gym today and yesterday her mother kept her out so she could go to the TV studio and she missed a history quiz. Anyway, I think Sylvia's ready for something drastic."

"Damn!" Eve slapped the flat of her hand against the desk. "Damn that woman!"

"I knew you'd want to know. Call me if there's anything . . ."

"Sure. Thanks." Even hung up the phone with a bang, and began to pace the room. Mira had been at the back of her mind for several weeks now—ever since the last meeting when Eve had felt Mira nearly defy her mother by reaching out to a stranger. She'd seen Mira pass in the halls, head down, eyes down, and knew these were signs to leave her alone. And so she'd done just that—except for another warning about her grades—but it hadn't stopped her wondering.

She sighed and paused in front of the window; the forsythia had turned a bright Easter-egg yellow last week. So Mrs. Webster had kept her out of school yesterday. It was no consolation that her initial instincts about Mira seemed more and more correct; she would rather have been wrong. Eve twisted a curl around her index finger: there had to be a way to get that girl into therapy before Sylvia Markham kicked her out of school.

With a start Eve checked her watch. It was already quarter to five and she had to make that call now, before she did anything else, before the office closed. Never in her life had she dreaded lifting the receiver more. She had to dial twice before she reached the correct number.

"Dr. Rosenthal's office."

"This is Eve Strauss. I had a pregnancy test done this morning."

"Right. Hold a minute please."

The nurse clicked off the line, leaving Eve in silence. Her palm sweated against the receiver. More than four months had passed since the stillbirth in December, and last month she'd won her argument with Peter: in March they'd started trying to conceive again. But it was not easy; once again it was not the way Eve had always imagined making a baby would be, once again every detail had to be orchestrated. Each morning she had to remember to reach for the thermometer on waking, to get it in under her tongue before she was allowed to move arm or leg, or say hello to Peter, or even go to the john. She dutifully recorded her day's score on the temperature chart that tracked the path of her ovulation and her psyche. On days five through ten of her cycle, ignoring migraine, hot flashes, and blurred vision, Eve swallowed the high dose of Clomid—a fertility drug whose bottle cap said in loud red letters: "THIS CONTAINER NOT CHILD-PROOFED!" Toward the middle of the month there was tension, and the inevitable bargain with God as she slid the glass tube from her sticky morning mouth, praying for the sharp rise that indicated adequate ovulation. She and Peter made love on schedule, as if they were catching a train, the same train, over and over, every forty-eight hours and not a minute sooner.

All this was an echo of the attempts that had given them the child they'd lost such a short time before. Eve was not sure she was ready to take the risk of being pregnant again, but the need to hold a baby in her arms forced her to it. It was a way of fighting back.

And, as always, she was haunted by the memory of Rosenthal's face at that last checkup. "Uncertain," he'd said. His face had been almost sad. "We're not sure why you've had two misses in the second trimester. Unusual—and it makes the future uncertain." He twiddled with his pen and looked away. "I've got to be frank with you, Eve. It's not good. One more and you'll be a habitual aborter. The odds of ever carrying successfully drop to only fifty percent."

Habitual aborter: the words rang in her mind, like drug addict, jailbird, psychopath—classifications, life sentences.

With a click the nurse was back on the phone again. "Mrs. Strauss? Right. Your test was positive."

"Positive?"

"Right—you're pregnant. As long as you're on the phone, would you like to make your first prenatal appointment?"

"I'll call back," Eve said, feeling weak. She hung up, hands shaking. It was what she had wanted to hear, but it was not what she'd wanted to hear. Never before had good news been so hard to bear; never before had she been so frightened.

The sun was lowering itself into the bank of clouds over the river's horizon as Eve walked down Riverside Drive from the Ninety-sixth Street bus stop, the April air soft against her face. She had taken this circuitous route home so that she could stop for a minute at the Soldiers' and Sailors' Monument, a favorite place to sit and think. There was a permanence to this Civil War memorial, with Bull Run, Atlanta, and Gettysburg etched into the granite of its circular walls. Those battles made her own thinking clearer somehow; they put her own battles into perspective. Below, the river ran on, comforting in its steady motion and constant change. The trees over the drive were just budding out into lace, their brand new leaves limp and pale green against the dimming sky.

She would only stay for a minute, because she and Peter were having people in to dinner. But she needed this time to pull herself together, to decide how she would handle all this. Her thoughts wandered from Peter and the baby to Mira and back again: a new life within her; how to find a new life for Mira. She caught the association and smiled. She was doing it again. Mira was not her child; she mustn't confuse the issues here and get protective over someone who didn't belong to her. Still, her professional concern was valid: first an abortion, then skipping school, now Mira had let herself get caught having sex—where would it end? And at the bottom of everything, that bizarre woman, her mother.

People passed on the street and she examined their faces, wondered what they carried in their bags, where their homes were, what their children looked like, while she continued to think about Mira. The rays of light through the trees had become low and slanted; for a few minutes it made the new leaves seem an intense green, as if they had been highlighted by a paintbrush: her mother called this hour "the long green."

She stood up, finally, ready to go home. It was almost dark, the air had cooled. She needed help with Mira Webster; it was a complicated case. Her watch said six o'clock: if she hurried to a phone, she might still catch Lucy Brower in her office at Payne Whitney. And Peter was waiting. She began to run.

6

"POSITIVE!" Eve slid through the door of the kitchen to stop a few feet from Peter. Her hair was wild, in curls around her face, and she was short of breath from running.

Peter turned slowly from the sink, a carrot still in his hand. He looked at her, his face fighting for control. "How do you feel?"

"Terrified." She put her briefcase on the table and unbuttoned her coat.

He smiled tentatively. Neither of them knew what to say.

"Are you glad?" She crossed the room and put her arms around his waist as he turned back to the cutting board.

"Of course," he said, sounding a little defensive, "but it makes me remember."

"I know."

"Will we be okay?" He turned to look into her face earnestly. "If something happens this time will you be okay?"

Eve put her arms around him again and hugged him, hard. "We'll be together. We won't fight—I promise."

Peter still had a carrot in his hand and now he started to feed them alternating bites. He was beginning to function again. "What about tonight?"

"I don't want to jinx it. Even Rosenthal said we shouldn't go spreading the news yet."

"Let's wait." He poured them each a glass of wine as Eve crossed to the phone and dialed.

"This'll only take a sec," she said, pinching the receiver between shoulder and chin so that she could raid the hors d'oeuvre tray Peter was fixing. "She's probably not even there."

"Who?"

"Lucy." After a minute Eve cradled the receiver and turned back to Peter. "Gone for the day. Service's picking up."

"Why're you calling Lucy?"

"I need some advice." Lucy Brower was the head of the psychiatric residency program at Payne Whitney, and Eve had worked under her for three years to complete her training. Eve rummaged through the silver drawer and gathered forks and knives. "Anyway," she went on, changing the subject quickly, "how was your day?" She set the cutlery down on a stack of plates and linen napkins.

He ground some dried herbs in the mortar and added them to the salad dressing he was mixing. "Wrote, shopped, cooked, went to see Mom and Dad." Peter's parents had died when he was in his early twenties, each to a different kind of cancer. Every couple of months he went to the cemetery; he didn't say kaddish, or even a prayer. He just stood there and talked to them, needing to be near for a little while. He always went alone. Afterward he'd go for a long walk on the Lower East Side, where he'd grown up. He was sadder on the days he went, a little more pensive and melancholy than usual. Sometimes Eve resented it—she wished he wouldn't subject himself to the pain of remembering—but she never tried to stop him. "Are you okay?" she asked, snuzzling her face into the nape of his neck as he stood at the stove.

He sighed. "My mind was more on your test." The oval Dutch oven was bubbling as he stirred it: a spring lamb stew, with only the newest, tiniest fresh vegetables. She loved to watch him cook; he did it without measuring, throwing things in, just by the eye. It must be some kind of release, she thought to herself. In his writing there was no refuse—not a word or an experience could be discarded. He kept everything, stuffed his worksheets into file cabinets; they were his insurance policy: he used them as most people used their attics. What a relief it must be to throw out the potato peelings, chicken fat, and melon seeds.

Peter wiped his hands on his pants. He was still in his work clothes—corduroys whose nap had fallen out at the knees, crotch, and seat, a tee shirt, and sneakers—and they carried the remnants of tonight's meal. Eve hoped he'd remember to change without being reminded; he got touchy if she tried to boss him around. She went to the refrigerator to let the asparagus she had set to marinate the night before come to room temperature, and arranged it on glass plates before going to set the table in the dining room.

The silver glowed against the rosewood; Eve always set a bare board because even placemats hid the warmth of the wood. Blue-rimmed china plates, a tweedy blue and white napkin, the perfect oval globes of crystal wine glasses; and in the center of the table an ivory bowl, hand-thrown porcelain, low and open, holding the pure and delicate blush of six peaches. Their smell filled the room. Eve stood back, satisfied; she loved setting a beautiful table, making a harmony of color, texture, and line from disparate objects. At the far end of the room she opened the French doors and let in the cool April air. It was just dark; in the back courtyard the daffodils beneath the window were up and nearly opened, the magnolia had budded out deep pink over ivory. She stood with her hand on her abdomen; it was the first time she had allowed herself to think of the baby growing inside her, just five weeks old, just beginning to form. Desire for this child flickered up through her, a desire as warm and strong as the need for sex. Then she shivered.

The air was colder than she'd realized. She closed the doors. The phone rang.

"A quick consult," Eve said to Lucy Brower as she answered. "I've got company coming in half an hour."

"With you it is always quick." Lucy was a heavyset woman with gray hair cropped along the lines of her head, and eyes whose liveliness relieved the stern lines of her face. Born in Austria, she spoke with an accent, and her voice had a rasp unusual in depth and timbre for a woman; she had a habit of humming a note or two under her breath as she was thinking. The first time Eve had met her she was reminded of Pooh Bear humming Tiddly Pom as he ate his honey and she knew right then that they would be friends as well as colleagues. Lucy specialized in treating sexually abused children, and it was while Eve had been working with her on one of these cases that they'd gotten to know each other well. Even after Eve finished at Payne, they hadn't grown apart; Eve called for advice when a case got complicated or asked the older woman out for lunch just to hear a little hospital gossip.

"The patient's fourteen years old, intelligent but vulnerable," Eve went on. "Her father died a year ago. Her mother does a TV series. No financial difficulties. Her academic standing started to slip a year ago and now there're behavioral problems too. At the first interview she was in extreme depression over an abortion her mother insisted she have."

"A major depression?"

"I don't think so. At least—I didn't pick up on any of the standard symptoms."

"Why didn't she want the abortion?"

"She seemed terribly caught up in the *idea* of a child—but was quite dissociative about it. Didn't seem to know or care who the father was. Her connection between sex and babies and birth control is vague."

"Is she promiscuous?"

"She feels sex is expected of her."

"By whom? Her peers?"

"No—more her mother."

"The mother seems to figure quite prominently."

"Yesterday Mrs. Webster kept her out of school so that Mira could help her at the TV studio and Mira missed a history quiz. She thinks of her daughter as her best friend."

"A symbiotic relationship?"

Eve hesitated. "More destructive than that, I think. When you talk to her she answers all questions in terms of her mother. She misses school to help her mother out, has sex for her mother—it's like her mother is her buffer, a pacifier." Eve spoke slowly, thinking aloud. "She uses her mother to keep herself from finding out about herself, what she really wants— just sublimates herself to the more powerful identity. And she's quite isolated except for this one relationship. And then the mother—she herself is so . . ." Eve paused, looking for the right word.

"Possessive?" Lucy supplied.

"More than that. It's more like ownership."

"So you must deal with truancy, acting out, promiscuity, pregnancy, *and* a bizarre attachment between mother and daughter." Eve could hear Lucy clicking the symptoms off on her fingers. "Disturbing. Is she engaging—or engageable? Could you work with her?"

"I think so. But her mother's opposed."

"Find a way to move around the mother."

"Also," Eve hesitated again, feeling her cheeks color this time; she was glad they were not speaking face to face. "I'm a little uncertain about my own standing."

"Meaning?"

"Meaning I wonder if I'm overinvolved. I keep thinking about the Baxter boy."

She'd been in her final year of residency at Payne Whitney

when Seth Baxter had been admitted. Diagnosis by the neurological team: glioblastoma. Brain tumor. He was only thirteen years old. Eve had been called in on psychiatric consult to help him accept what was happening to him—the dark that clouded his eyes, the expanding pressure inside his head, the hair loss, the surgeries, the vomit, the bedsores, the indignity, and, incidentally, the pain. Toward the end he had refused to let them carve anymore in a place he could not even see or touch; he refused the drugs and the machines, and Eve had not been able to accept this decision. She'd thought he was too young to know. She'd argued, cajoled, lost her professional mask and manner. She couldn't eat. She couldn't concentrate on any of her other patients. She walked the corridors at night, unable to go home to Peter. You must separate yourself, Lucy Brower had said. You are there to be a doctor. Not his sister, not his mother. That is not the reality. You are here to help him come to terms with dying. You cannot save him.

It nearly broke her. But by the end, she'd been able to help his parents come to terms with his desire to die quickly, and they'd ordered the push of the needles stopped, turned off the radiation that had burned out his tissue and bone. She'd learned then that the best thing she could do was to try and restrain herself, to keep her love and her own needs leashed back.

And now there was Mira Webster. "I thought I had conquered this weakness," she said, swallowing hard, "of getting too involved."

"You expect too much. But then you always did." Lucy paused. "How many times did I tell you that this problem would not just up and vanish? To be drawn in is normal. After all, you cannot be a robot. You must guard against your emotions interfering with the analysis, but there is no cure—this is all part of being an honest therapist, of knowing your patient intimately." She sighed. "Still, it is good to recognize the weakness. This will be a complex case and you will need to be a reliable witness, to trust yourself. A therapist's intuition is her sixth sense—it must be above suspicion—and in this case it sounds as if your intuitions are appropriate."

"A reliable witness—easy to say, hard to do." Eve sighed and spun a curl around her index finger. "Any suggestions on how to convince the mother that the girl needs therapy?"

"That is what they pay *you* for. Get to work."

The leaves pressed, new and green, against the room's glass walls. The trees were lush, spotlighted by white bulbs running the length of each branch. To have ornamental lights on maples and elms seemed a little weird to Mira—like decorating a tree for Christmas in summer. Still, it made her feel as if she was sitting in a gazebo in the middle of a tropical rain forest, like in an old Clark Gable movie. The Crystal Room at Tavern on the Green really did make you forget that the cruddy sidewalks of the city were less than fifty yards away.

Sometimes she thought she'd like to leave Manhattan, just move to the country. Up in Massachusetts at her Grandma Charlotte's. They didn't even have sidewalks in Sudbury—just field after field of hay and corn, cows and tomatoes and beans. Her horse, Singapore, had been born on Grandma Charlotte's farm, in the big barn with the families of swallows that nested under the eaves. When they'd gone to visit in the summers, she and her father sat for whole afternoons on a bale of hay, drinking orange soda and letting the heat make them lazy. The swallows moved above their heads in quick wide loops, in and out, up and down, flickering their notched tails in the shadows. Her father told her how the birds could fly, drew diagrams in the hay dust with his index finger, explaining, and at night, asleep, Mira grew sleek wings, soared, arched, escaped above the dark houses, glided on downdrafts across checkerboard fields and silver strips of road, saw the land rush under her belly in a stream of cold night air.

Vivian ordered Mira another ginger ale and asked to have her own wine glass refilled. "Please cheer up," she scolded. "You're sitting there like a monkey sucking on a lemon—let's have some fun." She lit a cigarette and picked up the big menu. Vivian mostly only smoked in public, but Mira worried about it anyway. She worried about her mother's lungs, looks, and luck; sometimes she wished she had a different mother, someone easier.

She sipped at the sweet bubbles, thinking about school again. She hadn't wanted to come out at all tonight—she needed to stay home and study for her two midterms tomorrow. She was in enough trouble at school already without failing an exam. Just because Vivian had promised that they'd be in early didn't mean they would be. Mira kept wondering what Mrs. Markham was going to do to her. She'd do anything not to get kicked out. She didn't want to lose her friends, her teachers, her school—all the things that spelled safety.

"I still don't get why they were in such an uproar," Vivian said, laying the menu aside and leaning toward Mira. When the school had called this afternoon, Vivian had hung up the phone in a spasm of laughter. Mira'd thought she'd die of shame—everyone was laughing at her, even her own mother. She remembered, suddenly, being six and having an accident on the jungle gym—the way the other kids pointed at her wet pants and giggled. She felt dirty.

"This is the nineteen-eighties and you kids aren't children anymore," Vivian was saying. "I mean, maybe it's *bizarre* to think of making it in that kind of place—but at least you're imaginative."

Mira felt undressed once again. That flashlight stared down at her. Why couldn't her mother just shut up? It made her sick to talk about it. For a minute she felt angry—it seemed somehow that Vivian was to blame.

"Sylvia Markham's just out of touch." Vivian blotted her mouth carefully on a cocktail napkin—she was the only woman Mira'd ever seen who managed to make her lipstick last through an entire meal. "They must've unearthed her sometime B.C."

"Could we drop it!"

"Look, lovey, I'm not your mother for nothing. I'll throw my weight around if they start giving you trouble." She smiled. "Would you like a little of my wine as a treat?"

Mira shrugged. She was so miserable she didn't care. She wanted to go home, to sleep and forget. The astringent taste of red wine tasted like vinegar to her and she tried not to make a face.

Little by little she began to feel that they were being watched. It was like being at camp, sitting around the fire after dark in the woods. The animals were invisible in the blackness, but you always knew they were there—you could feel them. An instinct she'd developed from living with Vivian always told her when her mother had been recognized, when she was being discussed behind menus at other tables. People stared and then looked away quickly, they liked to pretend they were above it all. They stripped away her privacy. They made her feel naked in a public place.

When she was a little girl, it had been exciting, it had put her at the center of attention. But tonight she didn't want bustle and clamor. She didn't want to stand on the sidelines and watch her mother be admired. She wanted Vivian to herself, at home, alone. She wanted to talk out what they would do about the trouble she was in. She wanted to study her math and go to bed.

Mira sighed, picked up her menu, and chose without caring. Across the room a man stared at her—he was in his early twenties, with blond hair and very blue eyes. He really seemed to be looking only at her, not at her mother, she thought, a little bit of pride creeping in. Maybe this time she was the one being admired. Her cheeks were flushing, hot and pink—embarrassed, she bent her head and smoothed the black silk dress over the three round bones of her elbow, watching the way the cloth absorbed the light. Tonight she and Vivian matched. It was a new game her mother had invented—dressing them as if they were twins. Mira thought it was fun, except that the clothes Vivian picked maybe looked better on Vivian than on her. Mira wanted to look like her mother, and dressing as mirror images sometimes pointed out how unalike they really were. But her mother wanted to seem young and so she went along with it, wearing her understanding of Vivian's insecurities like a Girl Scout merit badge.

"What are you blushing about? You look like the cat that ate the canary."

"See that guy over there?" Mira asked, with a surreptitious sideways nod.

Vivian turned as if to look out the window. "What about him?"

"I think he's staring at me," Mira giggled.

Vivian took a second look. "Don't you think he's a bit beyond you, sweetie?" She reached over and patted Mira's hand.

Mira moved her hand down into her lap. She should have known. The humiliation was hot across her face. "Can we order now?" A plaintive note slipped into her tone and she could not stop it, did not want to stop it. It reminded her of car trips when she was little, of making the mistake to whine, "Are we there yet?"

Vivian looked up at her sharply. "You're hungry already?"

"I've got two exams tomorrow and I still haven't done any studying." Mira's voice was wavering out of control now, angry and defensive. Sitting here was making her tense, the carved hole in the back of the chair dug against her skin. The people and the colors pressed in. She shut her eyes. "I'm in enough trouble already—I don't want to make it worse—and you *promised* we'd be home early!"

"Stop acting like a baby!" Vivian shook her head in exasperation. "I'm not ashamed of what you did and neither should you be."

"Well *I* am!" Mira creased the corner of the thick white menu in agitation. "And you're not helping," she added in a low voice. Her heart pounded. She never fought with Vivian and it scared her.

Vivian slumped back in her chair. Mira's words had wounded her. "I guess I'm just lousy at this." Helpless and bitter and exasperated—that was how she felt. She drained her wine glass and reached to refill it. "Here I thought I was being a good mother, treating you to dinner, getting your mind off it and all." Her eyes began to glisten and she bit her lip, hoping the pain would distract her. "I just did what I'd've wanted *my* best friend to do. When I was your age I was *alone!* My mother and I never talked—about anything."

Silence. Vivian fingered the hem of her napkin, running it underneath her nail, thinking how different she and Mira were sometimes. Mira liked to stew over her problems, and that wasn't good. It worried her. You had to be able to laugh at life, you had to bounce out of any situation. Meet divorce with a little champagne and death with pâté de foie gras—that was her motto. Vivian could think of nothing better than distracting yourself with a good dinner in a nice restaurant. That was survival.

But Mira was still young, and maybe she expected too much from her. Sometimes she didn't know what was the right thing to do. She'd thought this was the perfect place: lots of people and noise, colored glass chandeliers, balloons, butter carved in the shape of giant seashells—elegance combined with whimsy, the ultimate in distraction for a fourteen-year-old. But teenagers were unpredictable. She sipped her wine, trying to remember what she'd been like when she was fourteen. Awkward, ungainly, uncertain, probably a lot like her daughter—but it hadn't taken her long to grow out of it.

"It's not your fault," Mira said, interrupting her thoughts. "I'm sorry I'm so upset—don't be mad."

Vivian felt a surge of relief and her face brightened. She reached over to squeeze Mira's hand. "Let's get something sinful for dessert—something just *soaked* in sugar, and flaming and wild, and huge," she gestured with her hands and her bracelet caught the light. "To celebrate my changeable, wonderful daughter."

Mira smiled and Vivian smiled back. Vivian loved persuading people to change their minds or their moods without even realizing they were doing it. She considered it among her most powerful weapons and greatest talents.

She decided in the spirit of the occasion to order for them both and abandon her diet, to forget about "thin" alternatives like smoked salmon and veal paillard, and stick to simple, down-home basics; Mira would like that better. She whispered the order to the waiter behind her menu so that everything would be a surprise. As they waited for the appetizer to arrive, Vivian looked around at the young man across the room—blond and good-looking—the one Mira had thought was watching her. How silly, how sad, she thought, he's really staring at me. The next time she caught him looking, she smiled. A slow half-smile, very subtle. She poured herself more wine, enjoying the effect she was having, reveling in the power.

He took out his lighter and drew on his cigarette, holding the smoke down in his lungs for a long time before he exhaled through his nose. The mannerism reminded her suddenly of Stewart, but the resemblance stopped there. Stewart hadn't looked at her that way since they were first married. She wondered if Stewart had been able to see her at all. Vivian liked a man to reflect her beauty in his eyes; she wanted to see herself mirrored in his mind. But Stewart was a clouded glass: all he could think of were the experiments in the lab that weren't working, the time he was wasting, the pressure to achieve once again. It wasn't easy to be a star when you were twenty-five and a rerun when you were forty. Stewart had simply ceased to appreciate her. He was so constantly distracted that she'd been able to take lovers easily—young men like the one across the room, men who gave her what she needed. That kind of love was her vitamin pill, it kept her young.

After the shrimp cocktail, the waiter brought Mira's favorite, rare prime rib with crisp slivers of fried potato, and Vivian was rewarded by a smile of true delight. She tried to refocus her attention, to concentrate on what her daughter was saying. She was a little fuzzy from the wine, and the lure of being admired—the very heat of it—was drawing her away from the table. At the back of her mind she was planning what she would say if he approached her, how she would explain Mira.

The waiter brought their dessert, a fiery baked Alaska, and Mira concentrated on the melting ice cream and meringue, which was one of the best things she'd ever eaten. She kept looking over to the other side of the room at her secret admirer. He seemed always to meet her eyes. He smiled at her, it distracted her. Mira wondered what his voice would sound like, what his name was, how he would look at her up close. She tried to focus on what her mother was saying. A second half-bottle of wine made Vivian loose, and she was telling stories from the set—doors that wouldn't open, phones that didn't ring on cue, lines muffed. They kept laughing—so hard Mira's cheeks hurt after a while—and she forgot about school, just as Vivian had predicted she would. For the first time all day she felt happy.

They'd finished their dessert when Mira looked up to see

him coming over to their table. Maybe she really did look pretty tonight, she thought, the flush returning to her cheeks, maybe the black dress made her eyes greener. His eyes were aquamarines. Close up, he was even more handsome than she'd guessed, maybe even more than Chris Light. She realized she was staring and, embarrassed, started to fiddle with her spoon. She lined it up over the far edge of the plate.

"Care to join me for a drink in the bar?"

Mira looked up. He smiled at her, a very warm smile. She wanted to say yes. It was exciting to be asked by someone older, it was exciting to be asked in front of her mother—to prove her mother wrong.

"My sister and I would love to," Vivian said, standing, smiling, gathering her purse. Mira looked at her in shock. To say they were sisters made her feel like some sort of imposter. She returned her mother's apologetic expression with a stony look.

Vivian was unsteady from the wine, and she leaned on his arm as they left the Crystal Room. Mira thought that another drink was a really bad idea—her mother threw up when she was drunk. She marched a step behind them, furious, forced to stop and sign the Amex bill on her way out because Vivian didn't like to check addition or figure tips when she was high.

By the time Mira got to the bar, they were already in a banquette. Her mother touched his hand as he lit her cigarette. It was like watching a snake charmer and a cobra—he was totally mesmerized. Mira just stood there, the whole horrible scene repeating over and over again in the wall of mirror behind and across from them. He'd really been after Vivian all along, she said to herself in a monotone, feeling once again the impossible weight of her mother's presence and beauty. I am only a shadow, a thin gray shadow. Tears of humiliation stung her eyes. She'd been passed over for another, a more beautiful, woman. They were laughing now. She wondered if they were laughing at her.

She walked up to the table and put down the check for Vivian's coat with a loud click. They turned toward her with surprise. They weren't laughing at her—they'd forgotten she was even around. "I'm going now," she said, her voice sounding as distant to her as if she'd had on earmuffs. "It's after ten and I've still got work to do."

"Wait." Vivian picked up her brandy snifter and drained it with a cough. "I'll go with you." She stood, uncertain of her balance, and reached for Mira's arm. She didn't want to find her way home alone—she was depending on her daughter to navigate.

Mira got their coats at the cloakroom, and steered her mother to the front door, pinching her arm hard while pretending to hold her steady. She hoped she'd have a black and blue in the morning. She asked for a cab. Vivian leaned on her heavily, and as they bent to get in she staggered against Mira.

"Park and Seventy-fourth," Mira said to the driver.

"I'm going to be sick," Vivian announced with a moan.

"Wait till we get home," Mira hissed. It served her mother right to feel bad.

Vivian shook her head. "Can't."

Furious, Mira cranked the window down. The cab sped through the Park, racing for the green lights. Mira was glad there was a plastic partition between her and the driver—he was going to yell when he saw the mess her mother made.

The acrid smell floated back into the cab, and the noise of retching made her stomach flip over. Hating herself, hating the hypocrisy, she patted her mother's back as she heaved their hundred-and-fifty-dollar meal onto the pavement. When Vivian had finished, Mira wiped her mouth with a Kleenex and smoothed the hair off her damp face. Anger turned to depression. Once again her own problems had been upstaged—once again she was holding Vivian's head when all she wanted was to put her cheek against her mother's breast and cry.

At the entrance to their building, the doorman helped her get Vivian to the elevator, where the elevator man helped support her into the bedroom. Mira was so embarrassed she didn't even say thank you. She pulled off Vivian's dress and her earrings, peeled off her stockings and her panties. She felt nauseated. Her mother's skin was damp.

"Sleep in here," Vivian said, moaning a little as Mira pulled the blankets over her.

"I have to study." Mira turned out the light. She would not be caught like that tonight.

"Don't leave me alone—Mira?"

"No," she said, closing the door behind her. The power of her refusal surged through her, hot and strong and sweet. She went into her room, and locked the door.

7

When Mira woke at 5 A.M. the anger was waiting for her, as if it had sat in the chair beside the bed and watched her sleep. It stared back at her from the mirror as she washed her face. It bit down into her morning with small sharp teeth, like a wild animal. It was part of her, whether she wanted it or not.

She did her stretching exercises against the cold smooth tile of the bathroom, and dressed in the half-light of the early spring morning, putting on a cotton sweater over her shirt because outside it might still be cold. Tiptoeing down the hall, she turned the lock as quietly as possible. She didn't want to get caught leaving and be stopped. Outside, standing on the edge of the sidewalk with her arm raised, she hailed a cab before the doorman could get to the street to whistle one in.

In five minutes the taxi stopped at the stable near Central Park where Singapore boarded, and Mira entered the barn as silently as she'd left the apartment. Sliding open the heavy door to the main floor, she paused for a minute to listen. The animals shifted in their stalls, wood creaking, hay rustling, water slurped up and sloshed against the floor. They were awake and impatient to be grained. The pungence of manure mingled with the sweet dusk of hay and the warmth of horses. On the floor were the remnants of springtime shedding. The blacksmith had been here yesterday afternoon, and hoof parings curled like old snake skins in the corner nearest Singapore's box stall.

Mira opened the stall door, her eyes adjusting slowly to the semidark. The mare was in the corner, pulling hay from the rack with a flip of her head, and Mira came to her side with a low whistle. Singapore put her chin on Mira's shoulder, asking to be scratched in her favorite place, and Mira obliged, feeling the warm breath on her hair and the soft skin of the muzzle against her cheek. Crooning with sounds, not words, she put her shoulder against the warm flank, pushed the mare's weight to the opposite foot, and bent to lift her front hoof. The blacksmith had done a good job in taking off the borium pads and studs—a horse's snowtires for the winter months—and replacing them with a lighter shoe for spring, summer, and fall. She was glad she hadn't been here yesterday. She hated watching the blacksmith shoe Singapore. Even though the horse couldn't feel the nails being driven down into her feet, Mira felt every blow of the hammer—it reminded her of the crucifixion paintings they'd studied last year in art history.

She refilled the water bucket and went to the tack room to get a bridle, a hoof pick, and a brush. Quickly—it wouldn't be long before she was due at school—she curried the mare's back, chest, and legs in circular motions, as if polishing a car. With swift strokes she picked her hooves clean of hay and manure, and the mare's munching went on, undisturbed. Then Mira brought the bit up to Singapore's mouth and the horse accepted it as if it were a licorice drop in Mira's hand.

Outside, she led her to the paddock fence and mounted, bareback, and Singapore headed right away for the path they always took on early morning rides. Central Park spread around them, leafy, new with the morning's damp, a cocoon that denied the city even existed. Mira liked to pretend she was at summer camp, high in the Berkshires, where the trails wound into mountains and she and Singapore were all by themselves, with only the wind and trees. She closed her eyes, swaying to the mare's rhythm, and smelled nearly the same smells, felt almost the same sort of peace. For the first time in months her back didn't bother her.

The sun sifted down through the new leaves, and Mira felt the anger floating out and away, like drops of water hissing off a hot pan. She shifted her weight forward just a little bit, and, as if by telepathy, the horse lifted herself instantly into a canter. Under her thighs Mira could feel the muscles in the mare's back expanding and contracting, and the seat of her jeans began to grow warm and damp with Singapore's sweat. When she rode her horse, Mira always imagined herself as a centaur.

Her father had taught her to ride when she was nine. At first they'd only walked, on hired hacks, he leading, she sitting. But she had a natural sense of balance and good hands, and within the month they were cantering side by side down the bridle paths in the Park. He'd been brought up on the back of a horse, he always said, and the South was famous for its Derby winners. He liked pulling out his battered old boots and his favorite riding shirt—plaid and nearly in pieces. He taught her that the best style in riding was comfort, not chic. They never talked much on those rides, but that didn't matter to Mira. The motion, the peace it brought—that was all that mattered. He seemed to understand that she needed something entirely her own. And so he brought Singapore down from Grandma Charlotte's farm for Mira's tenth birthday and Christmas present combined.

The trees that arched over the bridle path opened up under the pale blue sky over the lake. There was no one paddling a rowboat this early, and she was alone. Mira pulled Singapore to a halt on the bank where the grass had been worn away by the feet of too many tourists and watched a water bug skate its way across the silver surface. She and Singapore were reflected by the water, but she didn't notice. She was looking down into a flat picture, an oil painting of a sad young girl. Behind her, piles of clouds shouldered their way across a deepening blue sky, and the heads of the trees stretched and bent against the flattened plane of glass. She turned Singapore from the water and continued down the path.

She used to spend Saturdays here sometimes with her father. He liked to teach her the history of the Park, which he loved because it reminded him of North Carolina. They bought an illustrated book once and memorized the names of the gates and arches, the fountains and bridges. It was a game. He was good at classifying things. When there were flowers he taught her the scientific names—*Narcissus pseudonarcissus, Bellis perennis, Chrysanthemum leucanthemum, Convallaria majalis, Lilium candidum, Tilia tomentosa*. When the trees budded out in spring he showed her how to identify the leaves from the edges—saw-toothed or smooth—and the way they grew—singly or in clusters. She'd loved the big words that were smooth and long across her tongue. Class. Genus. Species. She'd loved pleasing him with science in a way she'd never been able to with math.

The bells of St. Patrick's struck the half hour, six-thirty. Time to head back. But she didn't want to go home. She didn't want to face her mother, who'd probably be mad that Mira'd gone off riding without telling her the night before. Even ordinary mornings with Vivian were always complicated, while riding was pure and simple—a release. Feed, water, curry. No complex demands. She wished she could stay all day.

She walked the mare back to the stable slowly. The day was already pretty warm, and it was going to take a while to cool Singapore out. In the yard they traced lopsided circles till the mare's sweat dried across her back and chest. By the time Mira was done, it was a little after seven.

Vivian had woken to the alarm clock. She was waiting at the

dressing table in her bedroom, her face pinched in anger. "Where've you been?"

"Riding."

"It's late."

"I'm sorry." Mira looked at the floor, not sorry at all, feeling her anger come back. "It took a long time to cool her out," she lied. "It's hot out."

"What the hell do I care about that?" Vivian's eyes were like hard green agate. "What I care about is that when I woke up you were nowhere to be found! Not even a note! The last thing I need on a morning when I'm hung over is you wandering off."

"Come on," Mira said, surprised to hear her own sarcasm. "You knew where I was."

"What I *knew* is that you weren't where you were supposed to be—*here*. Where I'm depending on you."

"Y'know, it wouldn't be the world's biggest tragedy if for once Elsa got your bath and coffee."

"That's not the point." Vivian's voice rose to an edge. "Those are *your* responsibilities. *You* agreed to them and now *you'll* live up to them."

I agreed to them? Mira thought. Since when had Vivian ever asked. "Like hell," she muttered, turning quickly to go to her own room.

"What was that?" Vivian came after her and caught at Mira's elbow. She pinched it hard enough to stop her.

"Nothing."

"Don't you speak to me that way. You just remember that I'm your mother."

"Funny," Mira said, her eyes glittering at the opportunity, "last night you said you were my sister."

The breath went out of Vivian's ribcage with an audible woosh and for a minute she didn't say anything. Then she opened her cigarette case and lit up. "You're such a big girl now, Mira. Too big for horses." Her voice was cool and pleasant. "That's little girl stuff." She inhaled and snapped the case closed. "For when you've got no sex life." The smoke curled out of her nostrils.

Mira didn't move. Her breath felt frozen in her lungs. Her mother's voice came at her, magnified, distorted, like someone shouting from a passing car.

"Just the other day someone was asking me if we were interested in selling Singapore," Vivian went on, leaning over to check her mascara in the mirror and flicking a piece of white lint off her bathrobe.

Mira forced herself to breathe and pushed away rage, fear, self-respect. "I'm sorry," she said. "I apologize."

"On the other hand," her mother continued, as if Mira hadn't spoken, "I know how much you love that horse. Maybe you're not quite ready to be a *real* adult."

Mira's face colored with humiliation. She didn't say anything.

"You'll be here when I get home?" Vivian asked, crossing to her closet. It was a statement, not a question.

Mira was afraid that if she tried to talk she'd cry.

Vivian smiled at her and held out her arms. "Kiss and make up?"

Mira walked to her, her legs heavy as stone pillars, and Vivian's arms came around her tightly, bands of iron. Her cheek was hard and bony. Mira wanted to push her away, but she just stood there.

"You know how much I love you," Vivian said in her ear. "You know I want what's best for you. But," she straightened up, "you've got to be responsible and stop acting like a baby. You just can't have everything you want."

Vivian released her and started to dress. Mira went to her room and pulled on clean jeans and a shirt—in the closet in case her mother came in without knocking. She was numb.

Somehow she should figure all of this out. But she couldn't. She loved her horse. She loved her mother. Why did she have to choose? Why was she being punished? Why did she feel such a boiler-full of anger and fear? She left the apartment quickly, before Vivian could call to her. She couldn't talk anymore. She couldn't say goodbye. Her mind iced over.

By eight Vivian finished dressing. She was late, but she needed to talk to Mira before she left for the set. She headed toward her daughter's bedroom. Threatening to take away Singapore was a stupid thing to do. She was sorry now that she'd gotten so carried away. She knocked on Mira's door. No answer. She pushed it open and saw the room was empty. It came as a jolt: Mira never left without saying goodbye.

Vivian sank down on the edge of the bed. Her daughter's desk was piled high with books and notepads; the bedside table held a box of Kleenex, a water glass, and a picture of Vivian and Stewart; the bookshelf was stacked with *Winnie the Pooh, Grimm's Fairy Tales, Mary Poppins, Gone with the Wind, The Grapes of Wrath, The World According to Garp,* and *Sophie's Choice.* Mira's riding boots slumped against the radiator, molded by the shape of her calves. The white walls were looped with row after row of blue, red, and yellow ribbons, and a few white cardboard circles with large black numbers— some of the winning numbers Mira had wanted to save. Trophies filled a display case in the far corner, and on the rocking chair was the threadbare pink cat Vivian had brought Mira after she and Stewart had been away on a trip once. Mira still slept with it. These were the bits and pieces of her girl.

She stood and walked into the closet. Mira was meticulous: she arranged each garment by its length, its category, and its color. Nothing was ever out of place. Her shoes were all boxed in clear plastic, arranged on the shelves like a rainbow: pink, red, orange, yellow, purple, violet, blue; black and white bordered the edges. Vivian thought of her own closet, of the disarray. As she ran her hand along the soft fabrics hanging from the bar, she wondered what had made Mira such a neat person. Here was the red silk caftan that Mira wore at the cast party. At this end were the velveteen trousers that matched her own. The closet smelled of her daughter, a young, clean, soapy smell. Vivian put her face against the fabrics, rubbed a sleeve across her cheek. The clothes seemed more Mira than Mira herself. She gathered them to her in armfuls.

Mira, her baby, her nubkin. Mira with her special laugh. Mira who understood everything even though she was only fourteen. Vivian remembered her daughter, only eight months old, one January night when Nurse was off, a night when Mira woke for the eighth time between midnight and 3 A.M., screaming with pain from teeth newly erupting. Vivian had pushed her eyes open for the third time that hour, pulled herself from under the warm sheets, her body craving sleep, her skin tingling with the slow sweet suck of sleep. Without turning on the light, she'd lifted Mira over the rail of the crib, cuddled her fuzzy, pajamaed bulk up against her in the rocking chair. She'd wanted to stuff that screaming mouth with cotton batting until there was no more noise. She'd wanted to kill her. In desperation she'd pushed her robe aside and let Mira suck for a minute—even though her milk had dried up long ago—for the sheer pleasure of it, for the comfort, the warmth of one body against another. It was a warm, human feeling, a good feeling. Mira stopped crying and dozed in Vivian's arms, the top of her head sweaty with fever, her hair matted, as soft as goosefeathers. The scent of baby shampoo rose, pure and muted as a church choir. Innocence, trust, a hand that nested inside Vivian's like a tiny bird. Hate and then love, as tightly tied as shoelaces. Standing there in the closet, she started to cry.

She didn't understand what was happening to them now; she didn't understand why they were fighting or why Mira was always in trouble. She'd always been able to count on her daughter, but now Mira was unpredictable and irritable and, worst of all, distant.

Maybe they needed to spend more time together, she thought. Maybe this summer Mira shouldn't go off to camp, but should stay here in the city so they could work everything out. Running off to the mountains was no solution. And there was a lot they could do in New York in the summer.

She straightened up and let the clothes fall back against the wall. She shook her head to stop the tears. The idea of an entire summer with Mira made her feel better. She wouldn't be alone. She wouldn't lose Mira; Mira was all she had. She wanted to hug her right now, put her arms around that perfect body which had come from hers, which was part of hers. She wanted to bind her close and never let her go. Her body ached to stroke Mira's brown hair, to lose herself in the clear green of her eyes, to make her promise that she would love her mother always. "You belong to me," she said aloud, wiping her eyes on the sleeve of her blouse and ignoring the mascara smeared across the cotton. Mira was her daughter: if she had to fight for her, she would. She was not going to give up so easily. There was magical strength in a mother's love.

Mira wandered around looking in shop windows for a while, before heading uptown to school at seven forty-five. Suddenly she wanted to hold her father's hand, she wanted to come down this street by his side, even if they didn't say a word to each other. A great wave of remembering overpowered her— his face, his voice, his smell, the textured callus of his palm. By the time she reached Breton she was exhausted.

She climbed the stairs, sliding up against the rail and hoping no one would notice her, wishing she could be invisible. She didn't hang around her locker but hurried to shove her books

in, afraid someone would stop her and tell her to go home. She
didn't wait at the mirror for Michael or even go to homeroom
—where the teacher might be waiting to send her to Mrs.
Markham's office. Instead she went to the girls' lav and sat in
one of the stalls, her feet tucked up under her on the toilet
seat. Someone came in and sat in the next cubicle, smoking a
cigarette.

"Hey, Mira—s'that you?" A face peered up at her from
underneath the metal partition.

"Penny, what're you doing?"

"I saw you come in and I waited but you never came out."

Mira climbed off the toilet seat and went to comb her hair.

Penny flushed her butt away and came out to talk. "You
look real upset." She unwrapped a new stick of Juicy Fruit.

"My mother said she might sell Singapore!" Mira burst out,
holding onto the metal shelf under the mirror.

Penny's eyes got round and wide. "Why? What for?" Her
voice was horrified. She didn't have her own horse—she always rented—because her family didn't have the money. She
envied Janet, Crystal, and Mira their horses almost more than
she envied them their boyfriends.

"I don't know." Mira shook her head and tried not to cry.
"I guess she's mad at me."

"But it's not fair. Not even my old man would be that
mean!"

"What'm I going to do?"

"I don't know."

Mira was silent, trying once again not to cry.

"Maybe you should talk to someone older," Penny said after a while. "You know, who could give you some advice." She
hesitated. "I never told you, but I went to see that counselor,
Dr. Strauss, about my weight once."

"I didn't know that," Mira lied.

Penny nodded and flushed, looking at the floor. "She's real

nice. At least she made me *feel* better—even if I don't *look* better."

The bell for first period rang. Penny stuffed her brush and cigarettes back into her purse. "Geometry," she groaned. "I'm going to flunk this midterm, I just know it."

Mira nodded and closed her bag slowly. Math was the one subject she'd always struggled with. Before her father died, she'd managed, by working very hard, to pull a B— average, but afterward it hadn't seemed important anymore, and she'd let it slip. Math was a sea in which she panicked. With the water over her head, it tossed her up and down so that she couldn't think.

As she and Penny came into the room she could feel everyone around her staring from the corners of their eyes, just the way people had stared at her mother over their menus last night. News about yesterday had obviously gotten around. She held herself straight at her desk and thumbed through her geometry book, even though she couldn't see a word. Once again, she felt naked. She wanted to run away. She looked over at Bill Phillips but he didn't look back. He was pretending to study his math book too.

Michael walked up to her desk and crouched down beside her. "Did you go over those problem sets last night?"

Mira shook her head. He didn't say a word, but she knew what he was thinking. "Get off my case!" she whispered, her voice squeaking with irritation. "I don't need this right now."

"Sure thing," he said, backing away. She could tell from his voice that she'd hurt his feelings. He went to his own seat and didn't look over at her again.

Right away she was sorry but she felt too tired to apologize, and besides, Mr. Lynch had started passing out the blue books and exam sheets. Mira's heart thudded as she watched him make the circuit of the room. He was an old man with wiry gray hair like her father's. His face was as full of wrinkles as a cotton shirt taken straight from the dryer. He said they would have one hour for the test.

Mira's hands left sweaty stains on the clean sheet of questions. She tried to read it, but the numbers shifted in front of her eyes and wouldn't hold still. Those angles and degrees and lines and planes meant nothing to her. Her brain was as blank and white as the booklet in which she was supposed to write her answers. She picked up her pencil. She stared at the numbers. She felt so tired.

Daddy is moving the numbers around with his pencil. They're jumping from the lead onto the page, they do acrobatics, they twist and turn, upside down and rightside up, they refuse to fly into my mind. Numbers are symbols, he says, but I don't understand. Numbers aren't symbols, numbers aren't abstract. Numbers are concrete. Numbers are a way of counting the oranges in the refrigerator or knowing how old I am. Word problems come when you are eleven. Algebra comes when you are eleven. Daddy tries to help with my algebra, but he gets frustrated, he isn't patient with me. I try to see the numbers as symbols, floating in the sky, meaning something else. They mean nothing to me. They are locked up. They keep their secrets.

He's angry now. He says they are a language, but I can't speak it. I try to explain that they don't want to be read, like words or French. The numbers shine in his eyes. They remind me of a cartoon where dollar signs ring up in people's pupils like cherries on a slot machine. I'm trying to climb that slippery wall of numbers, I'm trying to see their faces or their names but they twist and turn. The room is thick with numbers, there are numbers in the design of the lampshade, in the pattern of the curtains. He is banging his fist on the page. The numbers scatter. They are running away from him. They are running away from anger.

In this dream I am running too, I am running from the

anger. Anger brings death, anger corrodes, anger eats love. The numbers remind me. The numbers are symbols. I am unclean with anger. Here is Mr. Lynch. He is bending close to me, he is turning the blank pages of my exam book, he is asking me questions. I hear him and I try to answer but there are too many tears.

"Are you ill, Mira?" he asks.

I'm shaking my head. I'm crying. My hands are birds, trying to explain, trying to make a pattern of words, trying to get out of the web of anger. In my head there are only the postulates and theorems I memorized so late last night. I'm afraid to speak, I'm afraid I'm still caught in the numbers, still trapped in my dream.

He takes my hand. He pulls me to my feet. Everyone stares. He puts his arm around me and walks me out the door. I lean against him.

"I don't think you fully understand the severity of the problem, Mrs. Webster."

Eve sighed silently. Sylvia Markham had a way of putting things that would have made a hot spring run cold. She was one of those people you hated the first time you met her because she was picture-perfect: her hair perfectly molded, her linen dress without a wrinkle—and she talked like an English textbook.

"Why do you keep calling it a problem?" Vivian Webster asked angrily. "Kids are kids, and they just need a little space is all. It's not like she murdered someone, or put a bomb under Mr. Lynch's chair."

"Failing her courses would be reason enough to expel your daughter."

"That's your solution? Kick out a kid who needs a little academic help?"

"Not at all." Mrs. Markham stood and smoothed her skirt down over her hips. "We propose quite a different answer. I have another meeting at my office now, so I'll leave Dr. Strauss to explain—but do not misunderstand the gravity of this situation. We care for your daughter a great deal here at Breton, but you must help us to help her. I hope you won't let us down."

Eve watched Sylvia Markham pivot out the door and wished they'd let her do this alone; Sylvia made too many speeches. On the other hand, she had gone along with Eve's idea. The solution had come to Eve at the dinner party last night. It often happened like that: a question, a worry, solved as she ironed or walked or picked over lemons at the vegetable stand. Despite what Sylvia said, Breton had no intention of expelling Mira, but Vivian Webster didn't know that. It was a deception—and Eve didn't feel in the least bit guilty about it.

Vivian had lit a cigarette, and now she turned in her chair to look out into the back garden. Eve remembered the last time they'd met. Vivian Webster had seemed a chameleon that day —able to change color, expression, personality in an instant, depending on what was required. Somewhere, underneath the beauty she wielded as defensively as a razor blade, there had to be a vulnerable spot.

She could see that Vivian was not going to turn back to her, and she went to stand beside her chair and look out into the garden, too, as if they were at a tea party. "The view's one good thing about this office."

Vivian did not respond. She was using the time to collect herself, Eve thought, to swing the weight of the silence, like ballast, to her side of the room. She hadn't really noticed the garden. She was putting a wall around herself. Eve sat down in the chair beside her. "Mira's having more trouble than just her grades, or being caught with Bill Phillips yesterday." She paused, waiting to see if she had engaged the other woman's attention. Vivian turned her gaze back and Eve felt the power of those green eyes: they had a peculiar, unnerving depth. The woman had a knack for dressing so that you could not concentrate on anything but her. Her beauty clouded rational thought. Eve shrugged herself free of Vivian's gaze, and went on, "Mrs. Markham wanted to expel her but I'm hoping you'll accept the much less drastic idea I've suggested."

Vivian waited, her eyes meeting Eve's in a level stare.

"If you let Mira enter therapy with me she will be allowed to remain at Breton."

Vivian's eyes widened slightly. "Therapy?" Her face set itself in firm, unalterable lines. "That's blackmail. Absolutely not."

Eve felt her cheeks flush, but kept her voice level, her gaze level. This was one war she was determined to win.

"I won't have some stranger poking into our lives."

Eve allowed a small silence to fall, using it to her advantage. "Why not?"

"Privacy is important to me."

What narcissism, Eve thought. Vivian Webster reflected every question in the discussion back onto herself. She could not bear to be out of the spotlight, not even for a second. "What about Mira?"

"It's one and the same."

"What are you so afraid of?" Eve said. She was a miner: she was digging with pickaxe and shovel, looking for the core, the lode rich with emotion.

Vivian shifted in her chair and dropped her eyes as she rummaged in her purse for another cigarette. "I'm not afraid of anything. I just try to protect myself!"

Her voice took on a slight buzz and the tendons on the backs of her hands stood out, taut as wires, as she fumbled to open the lid of her cigarette lighter. Suddenly Eve heard Lucy's voice last night: "A bizarre attachment between mother and daughter." That was clearly an understatement. For an instant then, she wondered what kind of a parent she herself would be. She was glad to be pregnant now: with the baby growing inside her, taking up more and more of her attention, her body, and her heart, it would be easier to keep from getting too attached to Mira. She shook herself back to the moment. "If you love Mira—get her the help she needs."

Vivian turned to face her, angry now. "You're questioning my *love?*" Her face had reddened slightly. "I love my daughter more than anything else in the world."

"Sometimes it's *how* you love a child that counts."

"Very nice for you to say," Vivian said, with a nasty hiss to her voice. *"I'm* forced to do this by the school, and *you'll* be making money off the deal!"

"Don't confuse the issues, Mrs. Webster." Eve's voice was sharp now. *My seeing Mira will cost you exactly one Halston a month,* she said silently. She wondered how much Vivian Webster did spend on her clothes. Probably more than Mira's tuition at Breton for an entire semester. "My interest in Mira has nothing to do with money. If you take her from Breton and don't find her some kind of help—well," she spread her hands in a gesture of defeat, "I suppose I can't stop you, but surely you don't want to put her in that kind of jeopardy?" Surely you are enough of a mother, she echoed mutely.

"I could just take her to another school, you know, just enroll her somewhere else."

"Given the trouble she's been having, transferring her to another place of equal standing would be pretty hard right now." It was good she had planned out her arguments before this meeting, she thought.

Vivian ground her cigarette stub out in the ashtray. "What will you talk about in these sessions," she asked, changing tack abruptly.

"That's up to Mira."

"Her sex life? Her dreams?" She clicked her fingernails against the arm of the chair. "Mira and I share many things and it wouldn't be right for her to talk about them with you."

"I'm sure Mira will decide what she wants to discuss and what she wants to keep to herself. We won't be using any truth serum here." Eve smiled, hoping the joke might break the tension, but Vivian Webster just stared at her. Eve looked down at her lap and sighed. "Dreams are like maps, Mrs. Webster. If Mira wants to use them to understand things better, then that's what we'll do. If Mira wants to talk about sex —her sex, your sex, sex on TV, or sex in the street—that's fine too." She watched as Vivian Webster locked her hands tightly together. "There's nothing to be frightened of."

The other woman drew herself up, rigid. "I don't like it. I don't want it."

"Mira will still be Mira," Eve said, her voice gentle.

"You'll take her away from me." Vivian's voice was low. Her eyes had a peculiar sheen.

"Only as far as she wants to go." It struck Eve that Vivian spoke as if Mira were her husband and Eve the other woman. *How could she be so selfish? How could she see Mira's life only from her own bias? Maybe,* Eve thought, *it was more than merely selfish. Maybe it was more, maybe it was sick.* Suddenly she was even more sure that she had to win this argument; Mira's health depended on it. "It's not good for mothers and daughters to be too umbilically attached."

"We're best friends and I'm proud of that! I worked to make it that way." *Mira,* she thought, *my friend, my daughter, my mother, my father, my everything. My best creation, a piece of myself, she is me—the best of me. I gave her life.*

"How do you mean, best friends?"

"I cultivated Mira. Like those flowers they grow in hothouses. I brought her up to think a certain way, with a certain kind of sophistication, so that she could be a part of my world. What young girl wouldn't want that—it's glamorous."

"A hothouse isn't necessarily a healthy place to live—a lot of hot, humid air, and growth that's forced, not natural."

"Mira loves it."

"Mira's giving off signals: she's asking for your help." Vivian reminded Eve of an angry snake coiled around its wound.

"Don't you understand," Vivian said, rising half up out of her chair. "Mira and I are best friends, we *talk,* we *relate.* Don't you think I'd know if she were in trouble?"

"Maybe that's just the reason she is in trouble."

"How can love be bad? How can there be such a thing as too much love?"

No matter how deeply Eve insulated herself inside her doctor's mask, she heard the anguish in Vivian Webster's voice, and it depressed her. "Do you know what antibiosis means?" She chose the big stiff word deliberately and forced her voice to stay clinical.

Vivian said nothing. She was looking in her purse now.

"It's when two things or two people have grown together too tightly, too much," Eve went on. "When they drain each other. When they suck each other dry."

"I need my daughter's love and she needs mine. Love has nothing to do with big words and all your psychiatric garbage. You make it sound like medicine! What the hell do you know anyway? My love for Mira is private—it's just between us." How dare you, she wanted to scream in this doctor's righteous face. I did my best for Mira, I did just what my mother never did, I never left her alone, I gave her talk and touch. Even with all ten of us in Elizabeth I was always lonely. *I* had to *make up* a best friend, an imaginary little boy who came from Iowa and lived in my room. I kept a whole drawer empty for him! I slept on the edge of my bed so he'd fit too. "I won't just hand her over," she said aloud.

"Such a big love makes it hard for Mira. It's a burden."

"There's no *burden,* and if you really believe there is, then there's something wrong with *you.*"

Eve said nothing.

"But since you give me no choice," she said, her voice tight, gathering her purse and coat together. She stood.

Eve rose and offered her hand, but Vivian walked right past her to the door. "You'll see," she said, turning at the threshold. "Weave your doctor's hocus-pocus all you want—Mira loves *me.* She won't be an easy mark."

8

MIRA HESITATED on the threshold. Two months of appointments at Dr. Strauss's West Side office had made her no more sure of what she was doing here than she had been the first time she'd come. Talking couldn't really change anything —her mother was still the same and she, Mira, was still the same. It took something bigger than an hour's appointment with a shrink to make a person's life different. She felt more depressed than she had in a long time, more alone. No one had called her in weeks, not Bill or Mark, not even Janet or Penny. School was almost over and everyone but her was getting ready to go away.

Still, when she ran to catch the bus after each session and the wind lifted her hair off her back and cooled her neck, she felt free. There was something important and special in telling someone how you really felt and knowing it was as safe as if you were only talking to yourself. Everything in these sessions was secret—unless she chose to tell. Besides, she liked Dr. Strauss a lot. Penny had been right. And she was pretty, too, even if her clothes weren't exactly up to Vivian's standards.

"How about a cold drink?" Dr. Strauss said, coming up behind her in the hall. "The air conditioner's on the fritz again."

Mira hesitated. "It wouldn't be any trouble?"

Dr. Strauss smiled. "Iced tea, apple juice, soda?"

"Whatever."

As Dr. Strauss went upstairs to the kitchen Mira crossed into the room and wandered over to the desk. She was curious, she wanted to know anything about this person who knew everything about her. It was a physical craving, an itch—she needed to see how many of her fantasies were true. Sometimes she daydreamed of what Dr. Strauss might be doing right then, how she'd look as hostess at a dinner party, or shopping for groceries, or kissing her husband. What did the upstairs of the brownstone look like? Mira wondered. What sort of sheets were on the beds? What did Mr. Strauss do? What books did Dr. Strauss keep on her nightstand? What did she wear to bed? How old was she? Did she have any children?

Each week Mira searched the room for clues. This house was so different from her own—everything here was comfortable. Mira bet you could sit on all the chairs, stick your feet up on the sofa and even put a glass down without a coaster. It looked like the kind of place that could have five messy kids running around with bicycles and balls and bats. What would it be like to have Dr. Strauss as a mother? But then Mira would force herself to stop drawing pictures in her mind. Dr. Strauss was simply paid to sit and listen, she probably didn't think of Mira a single time when she wasn't in the office.

From the kitchen something warm and sweet drifted downstairs on the hot June breeze. Cinnamon, nutmeg, raisin. Mira's mouth watered. This was a house of cooking smells and every time she came through the front door she sniffed at the air first off. But she never dared ask what each delicious odor really was. She imagined a complete catering service, run on the side, with the name Strauss printed in fancy red script on cardboard cake boxes, napkins, and swizzle sticks.

A few things she'd figured out on her own. In her diary there was a whole section headed *Dr. Strauss,* and on these pages Mira wrote down every detail she uncovered, as well as all her feelings. A check of the bathroom medicine cabinet had revealed Tampax, Maalox, and a package of Saltines. The bookshelves in the office held no fiction—only psychology, history, and, surprisingly, poetry. The wastebasket beside Dr. Strauss's desk always had chocolate wrappers in it—Brach's semisweet mints. A pair of red rainboots lying on their side on the floor under the coathooks were from Chandler's, $29.99— Mira'd seen them in the store window back in April. A big bowl full of matchbooks from different Manhattan restaurants was on the mantelpiece, and every week Mira went to check and see if there were any new ones on the top—they would tell her where Dr. Strauss had been over the weekend.

On the desk were stacks of messy legal pads covered in a running scrawl. She didn't dot her *i*'s, Mira noticed. Her *r*'s looked like *n*'s. Messy. Mira's handwriting was precise, her school notebooks filled with pages of neatly formed consonants and vowels. She liked to have her details in control. For a minute, she remembered her father's notebooks, his even lettering—all the columns lined up with a ruler, each formula printed clear and bold in hard black pencil. On Dr. Strauss's desk the pencils in the earthenware jug were soft, Dixon Ticonderoga Number One, and each was scarred with teethmarks. At the corner of the desk, buried under the green and white fronds of a spider plant, something sparkled—was it a glass or a mirror? Mira reached to push away the plant. Transfixed, she drew her finger down its near edge, then reached out slowly to take it.

What she picked up was a heavy crystal paperweight, faceted and etched to reflect the light. She sat down in the bay window seat and held it up to catch the last of the afternoon sun. A rainbow, blue green gold, sparkled against the walls of the room. Mira swallowed and felt her eyes prickle with tears.

"So." Dr. Strauss put a glass of iced tea beside Mira on the bench.

"There's not much to talk about today," Mira said, turning the paperweight in her hand.

"How about starting with what we were discussing last time?"

"What was that? I can't remember."

"You told me about the night before your math midterm, at Tavern on the Green, and the next day when your mother talked about selling Singapore. How you felt."

"Oh, yeah. I said how I was angry that night," Mira answered mildly. "But I'm not anymore. I thought to myself after I left last time that it's stupid to waste time talking about something that's over."

Eve didn't answer. She watched Mira play with the paperweight for a few minutes and then decided to be a little aggressive. "You still seemed angry last week."

"No," Mira said slowly. "And I'm not today, either." She held the paperweight up to her eye and peered through it.

"I always hated that paperweight." Eve was watching how Mira used it. "But I do like what it does to the light. Someone gave it to us when we got married."

"How old were you when you got married?" Mira perked up—another detail for her diary—but Dr. Strauss just smiled and didn't answer. Mira looked down, embarrassed that she'd broken the unspoken rule. You weren't supposed to ask personal questions like that. "My father had one sort of like it," she went on, to cover her mistake. "The same shape." She kept turning the prism in her hands, playing with the light, watching it make a pattern on the ceiling. "I mean, Daddy and I bought one for Mom once."

"A gift?" Eve tried to keep her face impassive; she didn't want to look too interested. This was the first time Mira had ever brought up her father, and the first time she'd ever called Vivian "Mom."

Mira nodded. "Her birthday's October and Daddy took a whole Saturday off work to go shopping with me for a present." She looked over at Dr. Strauss, not really sure of what she would say next. She was just rambling, and the words seemed to come out of her mouth all on their own. "That's the best time in the city, I think. The fall. You know, everything feels clean, even the air does, and the street carts have chestnuts instead of popsicles, people walk down the sidewalk a different way. The sky's blue, not hazy like in summer. Everything's sort of crisp, everything has edges again. Nothing's blurred anymore." She smiled, a little embarrassed again. "D'you know what I mean?"

Dr. Strauss smiled back.

"Anyway, we went to Tiffany's to get a present." Mira sighed. "What a neat store. I think it was the first time I was ever there, at least the first time I ever remember. Diamonds, and sapphires, and rubies, all laid out on black velvet. Daddy asked me what I'd like best and I picked a beautiful ring with emeralds the exact same color as my grandmother's cat's eyes." She paused and turned the crystal again. An army of diamond dots moved across the braided rug.

"How old were you?"

"Eight. 'Course I couldn't have the ring or anything—we were just playing make-believe—but Daddy promised to buy it for me when I turned eighteen. Now though . . ." She moved the paperweight into the shifting light to make a shower of dancing arcs against the opposite wall. "Then we went upstairs to the crystal floor. The whole room sparkled with all this stuff in different shapes and sizes, all transparent, birds and ashtrays and bowls and candlesticks and hundreds of vases and statues. And they were out, where you could touch them. I thought at first that they were carved from ice, and that there was some sort of magic that made them not melt. And the paperweight," she turned it again in her hands, "was just sitting under a spotlight on a mirror, making rainbows all around. I knew first thing that was the right present for Mom, I knew she'd just love it. And Daddy explained prisms to me, how the light sneaks into the heart of the glass and then gets bent into a spectrum of color when it escapes.

"And after they wrapped it for us he took me to lunch at the Palm Court."

"At the Plaza?"

Mira nodded. "We had a little table in the corner and there was a violinist. I remember I had strawberries and whipped cream." She was silent for a minute, looking down at her lap. When she looked up again the room was blurred, Dr. Strauss faded out of focus behind the thin wash of tears. "It was such a special day. It was perfect. I had on my taffeta party dress with the petticoat that stuck out and my Mary Janes, and the add-a-pearl necklace Grandma Charlotte started for me the day I was born. Daddy even said I looked pretty."

"Did he take you out often?"

"He was busy. He was a famous scientist, just twenty-five when he did some big thing in his research, something major. Everyone made a big fuss, I think."

Stewart Webster, Eve thought to herself, the name rolling up in her mind as a block of printed text in a book. When she was still in med school she'd read of his work, originally begun as cancer research, on tissue transplants and the immune response. But it had never occurred to her that Mira's father was the same man. She nodded, wondering why Mira had chosen to remember this day, this particular piece of her emotional history, now, when they had been talking about her anger at her mother.

"He won the Lasker Prize, but my mother never cared about any of that," Mira went on, biting her lip hard. She wanted the pain to distract her. She wanted to forget the anger. "She was just mad with him all the time. Like that day, when we brought her present home, she acted as though he was *bothering* her. We came in with the present and Daddy was so excited. He loved to give her presents. But there was someone there with her. Some man she knew." Mira stopped and looked down into the crystal. Her voice was slow, coming back through her mouth now from another time. "Daddy got so mad. It was like a bad dream—one minute we were so happy, we sang Happy Birthday all the way home in the taxi and even made up a special harmony." She wanted to close her eyes, to push away the sadness.

She spun the crystal in her hands and it filled the room with flashing, shifting light, like the overhead revolving ball at an old-fashioned dance. The light made her sleepy but she couldn't put the crystal down, couldn't turn away from it. "My Daddy loves to sing. And he loves Mommy too, he wants to surprise her, but Mommy's with that man. When the man leaves she opens the box, it's a big blue box with a white satin ribbon, and she lifts out the crystal. She turns it in her hand. She doesn't like it, I can tell. I watch Daddy's face. She's hurting his feelings. Why can't she pretend? She's letting it slide from her fingers, very slowly, it's like a pearl necklace slipping one bead at a time, down onto the parquet. It cracks, it splits right down the middle like the geode we have in science class. For a minute nobody says anything, but then there are lots of words, and Daddy keeps yelling something about exposing me and Mother's laughing loud. I don't understand. I don't want to understand. I run away. I go to my room and lock the door and I put my head under the pillows on my bed but I can hear them anyway. I hear Mother calling me. Her voice is scared. I don't want to go in their room. But I have to. I go in. She's crying, lying on the floor. Her face's red and swollen on one side. There's so much I don't understand."

"What don't you understand, Mira?"

Dr. Strauss's voice came to her, noise at the end of a very long tunnel, a tunnel filled with agitated lights, shifting colors, a psychedelic dream. For a minute she couldn't answer, but then her own voice came back, like a reflex, or a boomerang out of control. "I don't understand why she is afraid."

"Who is she afraid of?"

"I don't know." Anxiety made her heart go even faster now. She was in danger. She had to get out of here. She had to get away from these questions, relentless as darts.

"Is it your father?"

"No!" Mira shook her head. "I *love* Daddy. Why would she be afraid of Daddy?"

Dr. Strauss was silent.

"He was angry. That's *all.*"

"What was wrong with her face?"

"Her face?"

"You said it was red and puffy."

"I don't know. Why do you keep asking me these things!" She was scared now. She wasn't sure exactly what she'd said. She felt as though she'd been asleep. She'd never told anyone about that day, and had never wanted to—there was too much that was a blank, a mystery in her mind. It hurt her to remember. Her head ached. She put the paperweight back on the desk with a thump.

"Why are you so upset?"

"I'm not."

"What don't you want to remember?"

"There's nothing to remember."

"You're afraid," Dr. Strauss said gently, "and you're angry. This memory is about anger. Instead of talking about how angry you were with your mother that night a few months back, you're remembering anger from a long time ago. Your parents' anger."

"What d'you mean?"

"You remember your father's anger with your mother."

"My father was a good man!"

"Can't good people get angry too?"

"I don't like to get angry."

"Why not?"

"It's scary."

"Scary how?"

"Something bad might happen."

"Like what?"

"I don't know."

"Did it make you mad that your mother called you into their argument?"

"I had to go—she needed me."

"Yes, but did it make you mad?"

"How could I be mad? It wasn't her fault that she needed help. It wouldn't've been fair to her."

"But it put you in the middle, didn't it? That wasn't fair either."

"I guess." Mira nodded.

"And what about your father—how did you feel about him after the fight?"

"You say it like I felt something special!"

Eve didn't answer. She waited. But Mira just looked at her. "What was wrong with your mother's face?" Eve asked at last. "Why did it look bruised?"

"I said I didn't know!" Mira underlined her words with a thrust of her hand. "Anyway, my time's up. I have to go."

Eve looked at her watch. "You still have five minutes." She kept her voice low-key and practical. "Let's talk about your father a little more. Do you know this is the first time you've ever talked about him to me?"

Mira shrugged. "What's there to say?"

"How you feel about him now, how you feel about his dying, how you felt when he got so angry with your mother," Eve suggested.

"I just miss him. That's all."

"Why can't you let yourself remember him here?" *Because to remember him is to admit he's dead,* Eve said silently, answering her own question in her mind. *If you don't grieve you don't let him die. If you see only his perfect side you keep him alive.*

"Sometimes I don't like you at all," Mira said, jumping up.

"What are you afraid of?"

"I'm not afraid—I'm bored. I have to go now." She left the room quickly, finding the front door almost by touch, blind, the hall seemed so dark.

"What's wrong?" Vivian put the brush down on her dressing table and swiveled toward Mira in a quick motion. One look at her daughter's white face gave her a stab of fear.

Mira shook her head. She couldn't talk. She felt very strange. She sat down on the edge of the bed and started to cry.

Vivian crossed right over and put her arms around her. "Sweetie, what is it? Tell me." She started to rock her and pat her back.

"Don't know," Mira sobbed, clinging to her mother. "I feel sad is all."

"Sad about what?"

"Daddy."

Vivian didn't answer. She just kept holding onto Mira and stroking her back.

"I talked about him to Dr. Strauss today," Mira confessed, sobs slowing. "It made me feel sort of upset."

"It's not good to go digging around in things that can't be changed." Vivian kept her voice quiet, easy.

"I know." Mira sighed and wiped her eyes with the back of her hand. "It just sort of slipped out, that's all."

"Well," Vivian said, giving her an extra-big hug. "Let's try and forget about all that. Here's a Kleenex." She took it and blotted Mira's face dry. "How about if we spoil you a little—why don't you take a bubble bath in my tub?" She bustled into the bathroom and turned the taps on full.

She helped Mira off with her dress and panties and shoes, wanting to kiss each pink inch of vulnerable daughter. Inside she was boiling with fury at that Eve Strauss. Poking into the past wasn't good—it was just upsetting Mira. Only when Mira was submerged under a thick layer of bubbles did Vivian leave her for a second to make herself a drink. Then she returned to the bedroom, sat down at the dressing table and started to finish her makeup. She hummed a little to show Mira she was still there and rummaged in her top drawer for the eyeliner sharpener. Everything was in such a mess she couldn't find it. She pawed through the clutter, shoving aside powder puffs and brushes, dried-out lipsticks, pencils, a pair of scissors, and the paperweight Stewart had given her as a birthday present the first year they were together. She lifted it up; it was small, star-shaped—she'd loved it. Not like the huge ugly carved one he'd brought her from Tiffany's a bunch of years later. The one that had broken.

It had been her thirty-second birthday, she remembered, sipping her drink. She closed her eyes for a minute. The day she'd made the mistake of asking Jack Martin, an actor from the set, to meet her at home. Stewart had known as soon as he saw the two of them together that they'd been in bed not so very long before. His face had gotten more and more angry, more and more red. She'd wanted to laugh at his impotence then. He'd lost this round and he knew it. He was worried Mira would figure out what was going on. But of course Mira already knew something was wrong. Mira was old for her age.

When Jack left they had a terrible fight, and she told him it wasn't her fault that he was limp as a dishrag. He had slapped her, hard, and her face lit up with fire. She knew what was coming next, that he was just getting warmed up. She didn't wait for more. She ran to her bedroom but he got in before she could lock the door, out of his mind with rage. She tried calling his name as she backed away from him, but as always he'd slipped into some inner recess of his mind. He couldn't hear her. Fury buzzed too loudly in his ears; it hypnotized him. Then he took a gun from his night-table drawer—a gun she hadn't even known was there. "That's right," she'd said, "use that instead—at least it's hard." And known in the same instant that she'd gone too far: he was further over the edge than ever before, she might not be able to stop him this time. He loaded it, snapping each bullet into the chamber with deliberate precision. She stood still in the middle of the room, afraid to move, sure he was going to kill her. He made her lie down on the floor. He called her a whore. He cocked the gun and shoved the muzzle up into her mouth. Its snout burrowed down her throat like a cold animal and she gagged on it. He told her she could do what she wanted anywhere else, but not in his bed. Then he threw the gun down and started slapping her, pinning her shoulders with his knees so she couldn't move. She cried out, two syllables of high reedlike fear that reverberated through the apartment. It was Mira who came, not the maid, not the police, Mira who tugged on her father's arm and brought him back to what he was doing, Mira who told him to go and get a cold washcloth. He brought it as though nothing had happened. Mira sponged Vivian's face, made the air normal once again. Stewart didn't seem surprised when Vivian went into their daughter's bedroom and locked the door. She was so frightened that she refused to come out for dinner and she'd slept curled around Mira that night. Just being near her daughter had comforted her.

Hiding in Mira's room was like hiding under her bed when she was little, after she'd broken a lamp while whirling around the living room or torn a hole in the dress she'd borrowed from her oldest sister's closet without asking. She was always in trouble: it was her status within the family. Oscar would come for her, his belt in his hand, a long snake. He knew she was under the bed, it was no good hiding there, but she refused to just sit and wait. He pulled her out by the ankle and marched her downstairs. She had to bend over, to pull down her pants—even when she was sixteen—and then he laid the strap across her behind, counting the strokes just the way he counted the pills in the store: never more, never less, than the prescribed dose. And her mother stood there, a silent witness, peeling her vegetables at the kitchen sink, her hands brown with potato dust. When her father was finished, Edna would bring him a root beer. "Ox," she'd say, "I'm sorry about her." Then she'd sigh, and put her hand through her dun-colored hair. The anger would start up inside Vivian as if someone were holding a lighter underneath her heart. When she'd asked Edna why Daddy was allowed to hit her but she couldn't hit Bobby, her mother had said, "Because you belong to us, because it's a parent's job to teach their children right." And so Vivian took her pain and kept it quiet: she hardened it into an armor.

If Stewart had ever touched Mira she would have left him right away. Besides, she'd been too smart to stay intimidated by him. It wasn't enough to hide in Mira's room. She'd taught herself how to load the gun, how to free the safety, and practiced with it in front of a mirror until she was confident enough to use it. Then she moved it to the drawer in her dressing table.

Vivian snapped off the lamp beside her mirror and went to lie down on her bed in the dark for a minute. The light from the bathroom fell in a long yellow shaft across the floor. The darkness helped her eyes. She rubbed her forehead, willing her headache to disappear, but she was so tense it hurt just to lift her arm. The sound of the water sloshing as Mira soaped herself was somehow a comfort.

The thought of Mira, how upset she was, made up her mind as even her headache had not: she picked up the phone and canceled her date. She should stay home with her daughter tonight—after all, wasn't that what a mother was for?

The water was so hot it made her shiver. Mira slid down, her nipples hardening against the heat, and watched her body disappear under the bubbles. She didn't close her eyes. She still felt frightened—as if something was about to show itself on the screen of her eyelids—and for a minute it seemed as if someone was really under the bubbles, gurgling, gasping like a hooked fish, a white face waterlogged, a moon beneath the surface of the water. She tightened her fists by her side. She would like to extinguish the past like a cigarette in a puddle—with a hiss.

The washcloth floated across her feet and she caught it with her big toe and draped it over her face. The warm steam felt good on her eyes. Crying had made them dry and sandpapery. Sometimes Vivian surprised her by doing just what she would've wanted a mother to do. More than anything in the world she'd wanted to be held, and Vivian had held her. Vivian had drawn her a bath. These were small safety valves. If you could take a bath it meant you were okay.

Vivian put her head through the door. "Feel better?"

Mira smiled. "Thanks."

"How about dinner?"

"Just a little," she said anxiously. "Just a doll-sized dish."

Vivian nodded. "I'll tell Elsa." She closed the door again.

A doll-sized dish, Mira thought, rolling onto her belly and

propping her chin on her hands. Her hair floated out around her in the water like seaweed. When she was little she'd pretended to be a mermaid. When she was little she'd been allowed a bath in her mother's tub once a week as a special treat. When she was very little Vivian had come in with her sometimes, but Mira didn't remember that. It was too long ago. It just seemed a part of her memory because she'd been told about it so many times—just the way she was sure she must've once met Jesus because she'd painted him in her mind, on the high hill surrounded by heaps of bread and small gold fish. When she was little and sick she'd had her dinner on a tray in bed, a tiny portion. She'd called it a doll-sized dish and once, to be funny, Vivian had served her a whole meal on the porcelain china of her doll's tea set. A miniature plate of chicken cut up bite-size, a small mound of string beans, a dollop of mashed potato as big as a fifty-cent piece. And a big glass of milk, cold and pure against the scratch of her red throat. How good it had all tasted. The taste of peace and comfort. Safety. Someone else taking care.

Mira turned on her side, her cotton baby-dolls bunching comfortably around her hips. She put down *Ethan Frome* and reached for her geometry textbook. Vivian had insisted that she spend the night on homework—no matter how depressed she felt. Both her English and math finals were tomorrow. The phone rang and it was Penny, asking a question about tomorrow's math test, but Mira didn't know the answer. She asked Penny if she wanted to go riding later in the week, when all their exams were over, and was relieved to hear her say sure.

On the other twin bed, Vivian was stretched out in lounging pajamas—having finished her dinner she was now working her way through to the bottom of a half-bottle of red wine. Mira was glad she'd stayed home tonight to keep her company. It was funny, but sometimes she still felt like she really needed her mother, especially right now, when everyone else felt so far away.

"I'm awful sleepy." Mira rubbed her eyes. "I don't think I'm getting too much out of this."

"Why don't you come to my room?" Vivian suggested, getting up and snapping off the TV. "I'll read and give you a backrub, and then you can just slide in for a good snooze."

"I should probably stay here." Mira hesitated.

"Nonsense." Vivian got up and came over to pull her off the bed. "I don't want you to be alone tonight."

Mira didn't feel much like being alone and so she followed Vivian into the other room, and they peeled the bed down together. Even though talking on the phone and studying had somehow made this afternoon's fears seem silly, and even though everything'd felt okay again after dinner, the idea of sleep—where images and dreams rioted without control—was still scary. Beside her mother she'd be protected.

Mira moved into the center of the bed and snuggled against her mother's warmth. She stretched her toes down into the cool cotton of the sheets. Vivian stroked her head, a light touch that paralyzed her with pleasure. Goosebumps raised on the back of her neck and sleep took her away like a rush, a wave of high, a colored slipping-down-in. Toes. Knees. Elbows. Chin.

Something is waking her up, something irritating, a noise you don't want to hear, a shade bumping in the wind, a cat's whine. It nags at her, like worrying about whether she locked the front door before bed. She tries to bury herself in sleep again but it's no good. The bed is moving, a faint jiggle, and when she opens her eyes to the dark she wonders why she ever came in here tonight. She curls around herself tightly. She

wishes she were as small as an embryo. She is tired. She only
wants to sleep.

Her mother moves closer. Mira presses herself against the
edge of the mattress. There is nowhere else to go. The sheets
bind her like a cliff at the side of the road. Mira pretends to be
asleep. She uses the darkness. But her mother says *hold me*
and the whisper is a suction cup. It attaches to her heart. It
reminds her of all Vivian did for her today, of all the love.
Love, as sweet as a peppermint drop. She turns on her back,
hoping this time it will be different. She remembers the first
times they cuddled like this when she was little. How nice it
was then not to be alone, to be curled into her mother's arms,
to feel safe and warm and loved after her parents had argued.
It was always after they had argued.

Vivian twines her leg over Mira's thigh. She presses close.
Mira fights the urge to pull away. This wasn't how it was at
first. There was no need then. There was only love. Mira
doesn't understand need. She's read enough books to know
what it is, to recognize it the way an inexperienced doctor
diagnoses a strange new disease with textbook precision. Need
is as dangerous, as communicable, as infectious. But she never
touches herself there except to wash in the tub, never allows
herself to feel even the faintest tingle. She tells herself she does
not want to know what it would be like. She wants to stay
safely locked in her own body. Need is a loss of power, a
sickening, a weakening.

Her mother's breath is damp against her neck and the smell
of wine turns her stomach. She sets her teeth edge to edge and
waits. It'll be over soon. Vivian has learned to be fast. Mira
feels her mother's rhythm pick up, the pressure of her leg
tighten, the friction increase. A minute later and Vivian holds
tight, quivers. And then she slumps, her muscles loose, relaxed, her lips paint a small moan on the dark air, and suddenly she's gone, taking her sticky touch with her.

The cold draft of the air conditioner brushes Mira's face, the wings of a moth. She's awake now. She can't sleep, she wants to fill the bathroom with a fog of scalding steam. She wants to lose herself in another drowning tub, to wash away her mother's sweat. She wants to be a mermaid, or, better yet, a child.

2

9

EVE DECIDED to walk the rest of the way to Payne Whitney and got off the crosstown bus at Eighty-sixth and Lexington. She crossed the street, stepping around a sidewalk array of imitation Gucci purses and wallets and Louis Vuitton totes. The restlessness that had made her call Lucy Brower this morning began to ease, but her depression didn't. After yesterday afternoon's appointment with Mira, Eve couldn't get rid of the feeling that she'd missed some essential, some key in their dialogue, that would bring her the insight she needed. Today this case seemed overwhelming and complicated—once again she needed Lucy's advice.

As she wound her way further downtown the sidewalks became thick with people out on their noontime break; the smell of souvlaki and pizza crowded the air the same way Mira crowded her mind. She'd never before had a patient who was so blocked, so afraid of her own memories, that she'd had to run from a therapy session.

On the corner of Seventy-ninth and Lexington a black man in a print shirt waved his hand over his wares like a magician: gold chains, earrings, pins, silk scarves, and umbrellas. In cardboard boxes beside him purple grapes and cherries baked under the hot sun, giving up their sweet odor to the city. A Chipwich pushcart was surrounded by a swarm of small children. Waiting for the light, Eve thought of the Good Humor truck that had rung its bell through her Brookline neighborhood—how you scrambled for a nickle and two pennies and ran from the house to get an orange popsicle or Creamsicle, a Push-Up, a Fudgsicle, a Nutty-Buddy.

But Manhattan was Mira's world: bag ladies and winos, the fleshy press of crowds, the silent glide of stretch limos, the shriek of ambulances trapped in gridlock, Tiffany's, Cartier, Bottega Veneta, Cerruti's, E.A.T. The pressure of expensive excitements elbow-to-elbow with poverty. These sharp contrasts were what Mira had been raised on—not a quiet, tree-lined street whose peace was disturbed only by the ice-cream man's bell.

For a minute Eve remembered the dry and woody smell of Saturdays in October when she was a child—the smell of burning. Eve and her sisters would sneak up behind their father, who was still sweaty from raking, and leap into the piles of leaves that stood high as a blizzard's snowbanks. When they emerged, dog-doo smeared in a sticky brown patch across one knee, he'd say "Servesyouright," and until she was eight she'd thought the three words were one, a long magical incantation meaning "Iloveyou." Then he'd let one of them hold his cigarette lighter to the mounds he'd pushed into the gutter, and they squatted on the curbstone to watch fire eat up what had been spring only a few months before. But, as Mira had said yesterday, she hadn't minded when summer slowly lost its heat to fall, because fall meant a snap in the air and pumpkins and cool rain and, best of all, the start of school: a fresh Bic pen, clean white notepaper, a blue looseleaf folder, and a new plaid dress.

Her childhood had been different from Mira's; they'd learned to expect different things from life. Sometimes she couldn't even imagine what it must be like to be Mira, fourteen, with a mother who asked so much, in a place that moved so fast. As Vivian had said, Mira was a hothouse flower, spreading her roots in a garden of adult sophistications. It was important for Eve to remember all the differences between Mira at fourteen and Eve at fourteen. She had to paint this background around Mira's face—not her own. She turned in the hospital gate.

Lucy was waiting for her in the lobby of the clinic. "Our favorite restaurant, I presume?" They went back out the front door and down the drive.

"I smelled it on my way in." Eve's mouth began to water. Under the humid sunshine the Sabrett's cart waited, its yellow and blue umbrella opened against the heat.

"Frankie, look whom I've brought." Lucy propelled Eve forward by the elbow. The smell of hot dogs, knishes, and sauerkraut floated over them.

"My old friend!" Frankie's face was as wrinkled as a peanut in a shell. "But how come you never stop by anymore, Dr. Strauss?" He pushed his lower lip out in petulant reproach.

"Maybe you could wheel your cart over to the West Side?" Eve put her hand on his arm and laughed. "This is a little out of my way now."

"And your husband, how's he?"

"Fine. But he still doesn't like your goyische hot dogs."

"Would Frankie sell you trayf? My cart is all beef!" His face was a study in indignation.

"Not Hebrew National, though."

"You want Israeli, go to Israel. Here we eat official New York dogs. Pure beef." He grinned, a wide smile that showed the gaps in his teeth, yellowed by nicotine. He pushed his Yankees cap to the side of his head at a jaunty slant. "The usual?"

When Eve opened her wallet he turned his back on her and waited on another customer. She took the bills out and tried to press them into his back pocket but he only shook her off with a glare. "You want I should report you for harassment?"

"But Frankie . . ."

"Come again soon." He filled another order. "A pretty face is good for business."

They walked back into the hospital courtyard, and settled quickly on a bench under the arms of a giant maple. Lucy munched her hot dogs with precision. "So." She picked up her soda can and sucked deeply on the straw. "How are you progressing with the Webster girl?"

"She's getting worse." Eve took a bite. "I'm afraid there're signs of a major depression starting—she's losing weight, though she denies it, and she complains of insomnia a lot." Eve shook her head and Lucy waited for her to go on. "Yesterday she ran out of my office after stirring up a painful memory. I'm pretty sure she's blocked something important—some kind of family violence. Her father striking her mother maybe. But even that's not what's worrying me."

"What is?"

"The *way* she remembered." Eve hesitated. "Have you ever had a patient hypnotize herself?"

"Autohypnosis? You don't mean a fugue state?"

"She was totally lucid and coherent. It was simply as if she were back in her past, eight years old and in the middle of an argument between her parents. But she couldn't allow herself to stay there for too long, or to see the whole picture. When she returned to the present she was extremely disoriented—as if she didn't know where she was. Most of the time she has very little affect. Regressing to an angry childhood memory seemed to be the only way she could let me in on the rage she now feels toward her parents."

Lucy wiped her hands on her napkin and didn't speak for a moment. This was the rhythm of their conversations: syncopation and then a rest; a waterfall of information and then a pause to synthesize. "So it would seem that your initial instincts about her were correct," Lucy said at last. "Such trouble here. And the home environment—do you know more?"

"Yesterday's incident indicates violence. Her father and mother probably didn't keep their arguments verbal."

"Consider what you told me the last time we spoke," Lucy said, crumpling up her napkin and draining the last of her soda. "The girl is promiscuous, rebellious, truant, isolated. She has a grave lack of self-esteem. These are all characteristic of a child who comes from a violent home. Is it possible she herself is part of the violence?"

"You mean—is she being physically abused?" Eve shook her head. "I don't know. Without a doubt there's emotional abuse."

"What of the mother?"

"Still next to nothing. This is a case of dead ends."

Lucy hummed a little under her breath. "If the mother is middle-aged, or at a difficult point in the middle of her career, or isolated, or frustrated with her life—all these are warning signs."

"Think how many middle-aged adults you know who fit that description and have never laid a hand on their kids."

"Yes, but I am remembering something else." Lucy laced her hands behind her head and leaned back against the tree. "I am remembering your description of this woman the last time we talked on the phone. Her domineering attitude toward the child—you called it 'ownership.' It seems to me abuse of any kind is just one way to take possession of another person, to say, 'You're mine.' To control both body and mind."

Eve didn't say anything for a minute, just stared at the other woman. "Great." She put down her second hot dog, only halfway eaten, her appetite gone.

"So much is written these days about television violence, about the effects of capital punishment on society—" Lucy cut herself off by slashing her hand through the air. "But it's the *family* that teaches violence. People who are violent with their children generally grew up in violent homes themselves—they were the *first* victims." She underlined the words with her index finger. "We hand violence down through the generations like a cake recipe and children are the witnesses. I wonder about the guilt and self-hatred these parents must bear—to repeat themselves the act that scarred them originally."

"But Vivian Webster's history is a blank. I've got nothing at all."

"It's always difficult." Lucy shook her head, and shrugged. "In my work at the sex-abuse clinic I find it impossible to get this kind of information. I keep wishing I were clairvoyant."

"My rotation on that service was the most depressing year I've ever spent." Eve rubbed her hand across her eyes. "Why you do it voluntarily is beyond me."

Lucy shrugged. "Because it's necessary. Because it's important. Whenever I explain to a new group of med students that there are more sexually abused children now than battered children—over a million—and that the abuse isn't just one isolated sexual encounter, that these children are trapped in sexual *relationships* with adults in more than forty percent of the cases, I can see they don't want to believe me." With a sigh she leaned back against the tree again. "Most people don't want to hear that the majority of the time it's someone the child knows and trusts, not a stranger." She shook her head. "Or that about a third live in the same home. That they use the child's affection and loyalty as a lure. A seduction so intricate and subtle that a child couldn't possibly see it for what it is until it's too late." The wind lifted her hair from her forehead and they were both quiet for a minute. "I don't know. I suppose I like working with something so extreme, so terrible, that the average person can't begin to confront it. Even when I'm called in at five o'clock in the morning I can't resent it."

"I still couldn't deal with it day-to-day," Eve said, sighing. "It makes me too mad. It makes me crazy."

"You have to keep your emotions back," Lucy said with a grim smile. "When you see two thirds of these children becoming emotionally disturbed and nearly another sixth dysfunctional you stop thinking about yourself and just get involved in helping them the best you can."

"Could we get back to my problem?" Eve wiped her mouth on her napkin. "How am I going to help her when she's running out of my office? This is a bit more extreme than the average therapy resistance."

"She's learned to hide her feelings, to trust no one. Now you ask her to open up," Lucy mused. "She runs to protect herself."

"She'll need a lot of ego strength to put a stop to whatever's going on at home. I'm not sure she's ready to say no to her mother." Eve sighed. "She's so fragile. It's like waiting for a soufflé to rise—I don't dare open the oven door."

"Think how hard it is for her to expose all this. Even to herself—let alone to a stranger. She must sense it will eventually force her to leave her home, her mother—and that home, that relationship, is really the only tangible security she has right now. She's just fourteen." Lucy shook her head in despair. "This kind of conflict can be devastating for a child so young. You must move with care."

"I know, I know." Eve ran her straw back and forth between her fingers. "But don't forget that abused children have an increased tendency toward suicide. I don't know how much time I have for caution."

"She may be able to make the conscious decision to protest," Lucy said. "The opposite of self-destruction, a vote for herself, for her own life. How's her insight?"

"Right now, next to nil." Eve sighed. "I came for reassurance," she said, thinking aloud. "But I'm more worried now than I was before."

"You knew I wouldn't be able to give you definitive solutions." Lucy smiled. "The best of us need to share the worry a little. This is a difficult case, more complicated possibly than you ever dreamed."

"I feel very insecure," Eve admitted, plucking a blade of grass and shredding it between her fingers. "Very vulnerable. As if the entire thing is slipping away from me, as if I'm running on a treadmill and not keeping up. It's a continual crisis of confidence."

"And otherwise, how are things now?"

"Great." The words came easily. Then she saw the lie. "No, that's not right. I'm very tense."

Lucy lifted her left eyebrow and hummed a bit.

"There was that second miscarriage last December," she kept her voice flat and rigid, controlled, "in the sixth month."

Eve had been working with Lucy when she'd lost the first baby. Lucy had been one of the few who understood. Now she just nodded quietly, waiting for Eve to continue.

There were no words to describe that pain, Eve thought; how could she try to redefine it now? She thought of Peter, of his pads and pencils for capturing and reliving pain; Peter wrote it all down and in that way purged himself of it. He gave it away to his reader. "I'm pregnant again." Her hand slipped across her belly. "I have nightmares."

"I thought you were expecting—either that or you've been sneaking to Frankie's cart on the sly."

"You can tell?"

Lucy laughed. "Ordinarily you are thin as a reed. Now you are stuffed into your clothes. It was not hard to guess."

"I should buy something that fits."

She smiled. "At least you would be comfortable in body, if not in heart."

"I'm afraid to go into a maternity shop, I'm afraid to tell people, I'm afraid to know it myself. I'm afraid that if I acknowledge the baby something will take it away again." She put her face in her hands. "I can't face a third loss. My marriage can't stand a third loss."

"You are always stronger than you think," Lucy said gently, waving a fly off her knee. "Besides, you know that buying clothes has nothing to do with stillbirth. Allowing yourself to feel the joy will not jinx you. That's just magical thinking."

"And why not?" Eve looked at her in despair. "Cover me up with degrees, a career, a husband, a baby—and here I am, still a child underneath it all." She fiddled with the straw in her soda can. "I need magical thinking to survive. It gives me the illusion that I still have some control over the world. It explains how I lost a son and a daughter."

"But there is just as much magic in reality." Lucy stretched her back against the tree and looked upward into the leaves. "There is magic in your new baby. Feel it growing. Love *it.*"

"Love *it,*" Eve repeated, "instead of *Mira.* Is that what you mean?"

Lucy smiled. Her eyes reflected Eve's thoughts back at her.

"Loving Mira is safer? Less risk because the love is less real?" Eve paused. "Transference is less threatening?" The force of the revelation came over her, a warm shower after a walk in cold rain. "I worry about Mira because I cannot let myself worry about my own baby. I'm projecting the fear." It made so much sense. It explained so much. She put back her head and laughed.

"What are the medical odds that you will carry this baby to term?"

"I don't know. I go to the doctor this afternoon for the first time."

"To grieve for one lost child, let alone two, is normal. You fear for the next one—that too is normal. But keep the fear in proportion to reality. You cannot afford to have it mix in with your work, your marriage." Lucy collected her trash in one hand and stood. "Already you confine the problem by talking about it."

"I rely on you too much."

Lucy put her arm around Eve's shoulder. "When it bothers me I will tell you."

They stood, smiling, and Eve stooped to pick up a leaf. "I'll walk you back to the lobby, I know you've got a one o'clock." She threw her trash in the barrel as they walked by, and folded the leaf's soft fabric around her little finger.

It was *The Bath,* dated 1892, on loan from the Art Institute of Chicago, that stopped her as she wandered through the Mary Cassatt Exhibition in the Museum of Modern Art. She was stalling, trying to distract herself from sitting and staring at the clock: her first prenatal appointment with Dr. Rosenthal was for four o'clock, the ultrasound scheduled for five. Sometimes a few hours in a museum helped her clear out tangled ideas and feelings. She needed to look at something else besides her own life for a while.

The soft tones of lavender, pink, and moss green made the woman glow as she bent to bathe the little girl's feet in the crockery basin. The colors drew Eve in, the soft stripes of the dress moved her into the scene and she felt the absorption of the pair before her. She envied them their quiet connection: it seemed to her then as if bathing a child's feet were the most peaceful, dignified task a woman could undertake, for the benefit of no one, for the sole and simple purpose of ten pink clean toes.

There was plenty of time before she had to catch her bus and the museum was cool, so she sat on a bench opposite the framed oil to stare at it for a while. She ignored the painting beside it at first, wishing that *The Bath* could have had a stark white wall all its own. The other was an annoyance: it distracted her from the serenity, the harmony of the oil she had chosen to view. Her eye kept trailing over to the next canvas, to the woman with a sunflower pinned to her dress, to the child on her lap. Something about the sunflower painting nagged at her. The lines were less clear, less boldly drawn, the colors softer—yellows, greens, soft auburns, and oranges. A woman held a child on her lap before a large square mirror. She brought a small round hand mirror before the child's face and they grasped it together.

How clever, Eve thought, to use two mirrors. The pair was only profiled in the larger mirror, but the child's face was full front in the reflection of the smaller mirror because the woman held it at just the right angle. A duality between the mirrors, between the sets of reflected, echoed images, fascinated her. The small glass brought the better view. Were they really mother and daughter, she wondered, leaning forward, elbows on knees; could the viewer know for sure? She looked hard at the painting: their hands nearly joined, one atop the other, in grasping the handle of the mirror. The colors were of spring, of growing, the softness of trees, daffodils, new grass. The lines were soft, even the small mirror was a circle, not a square. This is a madonna, she thought, the stereotypic woman with the stereotypic child. Still, there is something else too, something that stops you from stopping there. Something that says, "Look beneath the glow, look at what I am saying underneath." The mother's hand controls. The mother sets the angle of the mirror. The mother shapes the child's vision. Mira's face floated up before Eve: Vivian Webster kept the mirror aimed constantly on herself; she never let Mira see anything else. And Lucy's voice came back to her, replayed: "The children are the witnesses." What had Vivian showed Mira about the world?

Eve leaned back against the pillar behind her bench and shivered. The mother, she thought, teaches her daughter what and how to see, perceive, understand. What to expect from life. A mother does that more completely, with more finality, than anyone else. Nothing in the painting binds them except that mirror, and yet it binds them solidly. The mother is a person of consummate power, more omnipotent than president, or dictator, or king. For a time, at least, she controls the world of her child, and even when dethroned she will have left her imprint. Even if Mira could say no to her mother, Vivian's mark would remain.

A woman in blue jeans came into the other end of the room, pulling behind her a small boy in purple Oshkosh corduroys. She moved from painting to painting, absorbed, the small child bobbing on the end of her arm like a buoy in a strong tide. He had had enough, Eve saw, of all this quiet, of all this watching. He wanted a hamburger, some noise, other kids. His three-year-old whine was shrill, thin, an angry buzz. He called her, "Mommy!", and proclaimed his needs. The woman turned with exasperation and told him to be patient, just one more minute, but he had no concept of time, he would have none of it. He needed what he needed, now. He did not notice the crease around his mother's mouth, he could not understand her frustration, he could not know her needs. She was simply Mother: procurer, provider.

As they left the room, child towing mother this time, Eve turned again to the painting, but it had altered for her somehow. Now she saw the little girl's sturdy hands, fixed in determination around the base of the hand mirror, demanding to be shown. The child controlled too. We know nothing of this woman except that she is a mother, Eve realized: the child on her lap tells us who and what she is; the child defines the woman; the child gives her an identity. Eve laid her hand across the swell of her belly: somewhere in the dark of her body a baby moved, kicked, turned somersaults. This baby would change her place in the world. With its birth she would be something she could not have been without it. An easy, terrifying slide down into a new life. A small face, a mirror of herself. A chain of metered words lingered in her memory, a line from some poem, somewhere, read sometime: "I made you to find me." The bodies of Cassatt's mother and child merged; the same flesh tone made them nearly one, extensions of each other.

The idea drew her, tempted her like a bowl of warm apple-sauce and cinnamon on a snowy afternoon. But there was also something wrong with it that eluded her. *How then are they to separate,* she asked herself, *where are the lines between them? If it were true, how could Mira ever leave Vivian behind?* Eve did not believe that this was what she was meant to carry away from the painting, but the scramble of ideas swirled in her mind. She could not settle them or sort them through.

And her time here was up. The painting would remain un-resolved, the questions about Mira would remain without an-swers for now, but if she hurried there would still be five min-utes to stop in the gift shop on her way out and buy a print of this oil. She did not have the key to it yet—but she would, and soon. And when she did she would understand more about Mira and Vivian. And herself.

Sweat stained the paper sheet in a circle under her crotch. A draft from the air conditioner traced the soles of her bare feet and Eve shivered, tried to draw the disposable gown tighter around her, but it tore at the armpit.

With a knock on the door, Jason Rosenthal came into the examining room, wearing Hush Puppies and a white jacket over his corduroy trousers. His dark hair fell a little long over the collar, his eyes were clear blue, his skin had an olive tone that passed for tan year round, and his full mustache made him seem foreign. Eve was attracted to him, but she fought it: thinking your gynecologist was sexy led to things like worrying about how you smelled, whether your legs were shaved close enough, or if you had too much pubic hair.

No nurse accompanied him and Eve liked that. She never felt self-conscious during a pelvic unless there was a nurse hanging around to watch the proceedings like some kind of voyeur. He reached out to shake her hand and she liked that too: it meant he was not afraid to touch her as a person.

He smiled. "How're you feeling, Eve?"

"Nauseated. Nervous."

"Well, let's see what's going on in there."

She lay back and folded her arms across her breasts for protection. She couldn't see him behind the white mountain. The examining light at the end of the table clicked on; a rubber glove snapped; a clank of metal announced the presence of a speculum. He ran his finger down the inside of her thigh and she shivered: it always struck her as a curiously intimate gesture, although she knew he was only letting her know where his hands were. Three months ago, Mira had been on her back in just this way—but not for life, for death.

"Can you relax this muscle here?" He pushed down with his fingers inside her. His nod indicated that she'd succeeded. She watched his face for a sign, and laced her arms tighter to keep from quivering. There was nothing tentative about the way he touched her, nothing embarrassed; he looked right into her eyes through it all. Nothing was worse than a gynecologist who pretended he was just squeezing fruit at the market while he examined you.

He backed away and stripped off the rubber glove. "Get dressed, come into my office and we'll figure out your due date."

"You mean I'm okay?" She sat up on one elbow, an uncertain smile beginning. Relief. Amazement. Joy.

He laughed and leaned over to pat her knee. "Will you relax?" He put his hands in his pockets. "You feel totally normal for a twelve-week pregnancy."

"Okay." She scrambled up and swung her legs over the edge of the table, suddenly feeling very, very pregnant. "I'll be right in."

Behind his desk he always seemed more removed. Eve sat on the edge of a chair while he finished making notes in her file.

"Your basal chart?" He reached into the top drawer and took out a flat cardboard wheel.

Eve took the graph with its map of their sex life from her purse and handed it over, and he scanned it quickly. "This looks like," he paused, sliding the wheel with its arrows and lines, "you're due December fifth. Almost a Christmas baby." He looked up at her with a smile. "Happy?"

"Yes." She shifted in her chair. "But worried too."

"Try not to be." He hesitated and fiddled with his pen. "Just be prepared."

"Is there anything I'm supposed to do differently?"

He shook his head.

"Extra vitamins? Extra rest? No sex? Something?"

He picked up his pen and clicked it in and out. "You want me to give you an answer for what happened in December, and I don't have an answer." He hesitated again. "We've talked about your DES exposure before. Women who were exposed to the drug in utero may possibly have more complicated pregnancies, and their abortion rate may be higher. This might be what gave you trouble the last two times. And it might not. There's been a controversy about it in the journals in the past couple years."

"Do they understand the problem any better?"

"The theory continues to link certain uterine deformities with DES exposure in utero. But I still say the studies are skewed. And inconclusive." He smiled at her. "We don't consider you a habitual aborter until you've lost your third pregnancy. So let's not worry yet."

She looked at him with despair, knowing she appeared irrational, that her fear seemed irrational, but she didn't see how she could "prepare" to lose a third baby. He was a doctor. He dealt in statistics and odds, and he'd seen far worse than hers. "Easy to say, hard to do."

"Feeling helpless is the worst part of my job, and it's even worse for my patients. The sonogram should allay some of your anxiety." He pulled the prescription pad toward him.

Her time was up. The pregnancy was their problem collectively, but the fear was hers alone. No matter how long she stayed and pestered him with questions he could not help her through that. It occurred to her then that this was probably how her patients felt when they left her at the end of their hour still in crisis: dissatisfied, scared, lonely.

There was no waiting room for sonography, just a long cement hallway with a row of hard wooden chairs. Because the test required a full bladder, Eve sat drinking her fourth paper cup of water, waiting for Peter to come, wishing he'd hurry up, eyeing the two women waiting beside her. They were too old to be pregnant; they must be here for other things. She hoped she got taken soon.

As the cup emptied she became more and more uncomfortable, and by the time Peter came down the corridor she was hunched over in her seat.

He sat down beside her and took her hand. "How long have you been full?"

"Maybe ten minutes. It's just starting to hurt."

"Did they say how long?"

She shook her head.

"Want me to ask?"

"They don't tell you anything."

They sat and waited. The hall seemed as bleak and hopeless as a bus terminal. She tried to concentrate on Mira, on the problems with her other patients; she tried to replay the conversation with Lucy in her head. She kept thinking about the painting, rolled in a tube beside her. She tried to push away her anxiety, but it was stubborn, it was rooted like a tuber. She could tell from the way Peter gripped her hand that he was as nervous as she, and that was somehow a comfort. But when the technician put his head out the door and called her name the fear pounded back: what if Rosenthal was wrong, what if the baby was dead?

An old supply closet was now a dim dressing room, and Eve arranged her skirt and bikinis across the back of a chair and wrapped the cotton sheet around her waist. Being scared made her be especially neat. Peter helped her climb up on the table. The sheet was pulled down below her abdomen and a long squirt of cold gel hit her belly like toothpaste lining the brush. The machinery hummed beside her right ear. Peter stood at her feet, his fingers patting her toes. The technician lowered the arm of the machine and began stroking the cameralike eye up and down in a pattern over her stomach. Eve looked at the screen but could see nothing except gray and grainy pie-shaped wedges. The technician frowned and pressed the probe harder. Eve's palms got wet and cold and she arched her back against the paper sheet to keep from trembling: there was something wrong. The silence, the frown, the blurred and fuzzing screen—it all meant something was wrong. She closed her eyes, and tried to think about breathing evenly. The tips of her toes were getting numb, her fingers prickled; she was hyperventilating.

"Look." Peter's voice was choked to a whisper. "Look at that."

She opened her eyes and twisted her head to see the screen. Something blurred, something moved. A large head turned, aiming down. In the air, a pair of feet pedaled an imaginary bicycle. Arms waved, fingers clutched, and then, with a sudden flip-flop, the position was reversed, head up and feet down. Then another somersault and the fetus did a headstand again.

"Is that"—Eve tried to swallow, but her throat was too dry. She turned to look at the technician—"is that my baby?"

"Active little bugger." He clicked a pedal with his foot. "Wish he'd hold still so I could get a measurement."

They watched the baby move and move again: a close-up enlargement of its hands, fingers fanned out in a perfect half-moon, like the petals on a daisy; feet pedaling too fast to be caught in slow-motion detail. They were as spellbound as children at a magic show. When she looked at Peter his eyes were red, as though he had been rubbing them. The technician clicked on, taking his films, unaware, impervious to their emotions and their awe.

"A miracle," Peter said, squeezing Eve's foot.

A miracle, she thought. To be able to see inside her body as easily as looking through a shop window, to record size and development, heartbeat and motion. A miracle. If Mira had seen this would she ever have had her abortion?

"Fourteen weeks from last menstrual date," the technician said, and the screen went dark as he clicked it off. "About 6.5 centimeters crown–rump." Eve wanted to yell at him and make him turn it back on. She wanted to stay with the baby and watch it all day long. But he just wiped the gel from her abdomen and pulled the drape up over her. He smiled and handed her a Polaroid snapshot. "A souvenir for your scrap-book."

Eve looked down at her child, caught in black and white, and in that instant made the transition from single to double, from lean to ripe, from daughter to mother. Her body spread out under the idea like a peacock fanning its tail feathers in the sun: she was lush, she was beautiful, she was going to have a baby.

Eve was sitting on the toilet, the blood shooting out of her in a geyser: the stream was strong and hot and sharp; it was cutting her. She looked down between thighs pressed wide against the white seat and saw a membrane, a balloon of trans-parent tissue, fall into the water. She tried to catch it with her fingers but it slid to the bottom, lost in the red. She called for Peter but it was Mira who came. It was Mira who reached for the toilet handle to flush it all away. "No," Eve said. She must stop Mira, before everything was gone with one pure rush and the toilet was once again clean and utilitarian. She pushed her away and knelt before the bowl, put her arm elbow-deep in the red water and felt the sac slither away from her touch like a live fish. She had to catch it. As she reached down into the pool, its surface shimmered up at her like a flat pane of glass and she saw her face reflected there. She was reaching into herself, into her body, into her blind womb. She cradled the sac between two hands, lifted it up and brought it into the light. It was a transparent globe, a crystal ball, the thinnest soap bubble. She held it close to her face and looked inside. She saw him there: a little boy with brown hair, and ears perfect as shells, sitting in the rowboat, holding tight to his balloons as he moved across the water. "Why?" she shouted at Mira, holding the bubble as carefully as if it were a snowflake or a ruby. "Why did you show me all I would miss?"

It was dark. She was moaning. Peter was shaking her. He drew her against him and cradled her with his arms. "Eating two whole batches of brownies—it's no wonder you've got nightmares." He kissed the top of her head. Eve's pregnancy cravings were for sweets, and at eleven o'clock it'd been a double batch of homemade butterscotch brownies. She'd eaten all but the three Peter had managed to grab for himself.

"My mother always said sugar helps you sleep." Eve sighed and grinned at him in the dark. "That's the last time I listen to my mother." They laughed and then were quiet again. Her hands rested on her abdomen and she wondered whether her baby were awake or asleep. What an awful nightmare, she thought, and there was Mira right in the middle of it all, Mira who dealt with all her feelings by hiding them, by trying to flush them away. Mira who had shown her—despite her desire to keep her emotions out of it—what having a daughter might be like: Mira who had shown her all she would miss if she lost this baby. She'd grown attached to Mira despite the precautions and the warnings.

Eve did not need to tell Peter what she'd dreamed. He knew. They curled together, animals bracing against a storm, and dozed until the dark began to gray into morning.

10

THE SMELL of boiling eggs in the humid kitchen was nauseating. Mira breathed through her mouth as Mrs. Saunders pulled the pot off the gas and drained it. "Penny, you start on the celery," she directed, running the eggs under cold water, "while Mira gives me a hand here."

It was one of the things she liked best about going to Penny's house, Mira decided—the way her mother made everybody pitch in. At the Saunders's Mira had discovered that she liked to cook—nothing fancy, just plain soups and sandwiches, pies and cakes, but everything tasted good and it was fun to make a mess bumping into each other in the small space. Mrs. Saunders's square hands dipped in and out of the water as she shelled the eggs deftly. From the back of the apartment a buzzer growled. "I can finish here," Mira offered, "if you need to get that."

"Thanks—I've still got a lot of washing to do." Mrs. Saunders dried her hands on the checkerboard dishtowel hanging from a roller above the sink and went to take care of her laundry.

"Will you see Dr. Strauss all summer long?" Penny asked, once they were alone again.

Mira nodded. She'd switched her afternoon appointment to

nine o'clock this morning so that she could go riding with Penny, Crystal, and Janet after lunch.

"What do you talk about for a whole hour?"

"Different things different days. Not much really."

"Does it ever get boring?"

Mira hesitated. Penny really seemed to want to know. "No, I guess mostly because I like talking to her. Like you said— she's nice." Mira stopped and thought for a minute, running her fingers over the hard smooth egg. Nice wasn't really the right word—her feelings for Dr. Strauss were more complicated and intense than that. Dr. Strauss was the keeper of all her secrets, and it was a relief to tell her things she'd felt for a long time but been afraid to say. It was like giving them to her to take care of for a while. "I feel like she's my friend most of the time and that feels, you know, safe."

Penny nodded. "You can really say anything you want."

Mira frowned. "But then sometimes she kind of pushes— did she ever do that with you?"

Penny shook her head and stopped chopping for a minute. "Not really."

"Well, sometimes she asks questions that I don't know the answers to."

"What kind of questions? About your classes or something?"

"No—about me, or my family."

"Like what?"

Mira shrugged. "I can't remember them mostly." But she did remember them, she thought, as Penny put the celery into a big yellow mixing bowl. Like today's questions. They were almost all about Vivian. Dr. Strauss had been very curious, almost like a scavenger picking over emotional trash. She'd wanted to talk a lot about their last session, and the way Mira'd run out. Her questions made Mira's brain go into slow motion and she didn't like that. Some things she didn't talk

about or even think about. Some things she packed away and
forgot as soon as they happened. The small blank spaces in her
mind didn't bother her anymore—unless someone or something pushed at them. They were just like the empty gap the
dentist left after he'd pulled out one of her molars when she
was ten.

The doorbell rang and the girls could hear Mrs. Saunders's
sneakers squeak over the floor as she went to answer it. Crystal
and Janet clumped into the kitchen in their riding boots.

"Sorry we're late, guys," Janet said, "but last night knocked
me out. Talk about sleep of the dead, I didn't even hear the
alarm."

"A fan-tas-tic party," Crystal agreed. Fantastic was her favorite word—she liked to draw it out, long and smooth, ac-
centing the second syllable and making the *s* hiss. "I snuck in
after four, but luckily my father was asleep."

Mira wondered whose party they'd all been to and turned so
they couldn't see her face. She worked very hard at blotting
the eggs with a paper towel and blinked against the prickly
feeling in her eyes. Janet and Crystal went on discussing the
boys and the food and the music. Bill hadn't asked her out
since that time in the auditorium, and he'd been there last
night with Marta Geiss. Mira straightened her shoulders. She
wouldn't let them know how much it hurt to be left out or to
hear about her replacement. What had happened to the time
when they did everything together?

Penny gave her gum an extra loud pop, and the knife clat-
tered against the formica as she began to slice the eggs Mira
brought her. The faster she chopped, the faster she chewed her
gum. Even when she rode, she chewed in rhythm to the
horse's gait. "Are you guys hungry yet?" She took the mayonnaise from the fridge and gave Janet a look that stopped their
gossip about the party.

"When are you driving up to Martingale?" Janet flipped the

pop-top on her Coke and leaned against the refrigerator door so she could talk to Mira while she worked.

"I'm not." Mira took the bowl of yolks and started to mash them with a fork.

"You're not?"

"Mira's not going," Penny said, getting a loaf of pumpernickel from the breadbox.

"My mother wanted me to hang around the city this summer." Mira handed Penny the bowl and squeezed herself into a chair between the wall and the table.

"How come?" Janet asked, following her over and sitting down on the other side.

"She was lonely last year when I was at camp." Mira looked over at Penny. "She sort of relies on me."

"You should've said no." Crystal opened the refrigerator and got a 7-Up off the door. "Staying at home'll be a bore."

"She thinks I'm getting too old for camp, and there'll be a lot to do here." Mira shrugged, trying to sound casual, bringing her chin up and hooking her feet over the chair rung. There wasn't much room for her legs. "This afternoon I'm going to Montauk with Michael's family for a week. When I get back I'll be on the set with Vivian every day. As her assistant—cue her, rehearse her, check wardrobe, and stuff like that."

"Really?" Crystal sounded interested now. "That might be as good as the summer circuit."

Mira smiled and nodded. She didn't say what she really felt —that nothing could be better than the circuit of summer showing, with its trophies and trailers, the rolling wave of anxiety and excitement. She couldn't say that she wasn't looking forward to being alone in the city at all. But she wanted them to think she wanted to stay, almost as if it were her idea. She realized, for the first time, that she hadn't even argued when her mother said she wouldn't be going to camp this summer, much less dared to say no. She'd felt mad—an anger that was scary it was so big—but that feeling had gone away, and then she'd just been depressed again. Suddenly she felt resentful. Why hadn't she put up more of a fight?

What would Vivian do if she came home today and just announced that she was going to camp? The idea was like a fantasy—she played out the scene in her mind step by step. She would be reasonable, logical, sure of herself, in the right. Her mother would laugh at first, then try to talk her out of it, then get ticked off. And then finally she'd be furious—like that morning a couple months ago when Mira was late after riding. Sometimes it seemed that Vivian was jealous of Singapore, as if the mare were a person who could take Mira away.

"Are you getting paid?" Janet cut into her daydream.

"Get serious." Mira flipped her hair back off her shoulder. "What do I need with money?" Usually she didn't talk about her large allowance, or the things her mother was always buying her—especially in front of Penny—but now she was on the defensive and it felt good to have a weapon.

"And you'll get to see Chris Light every day." Crystal sat down across from Mira and took a handful of potato chips out of the bag in the middle of the table. She was always impressed by Mira's proximity to good-looking actors.

"Really, really," Janet said, nodding approval. "A definite improvement over Michael Ross."

"Wouldn't take much." Crystal laughed.

"What have you guys got against Michael?"

"He's boring," Crystal said.

"Juvenile," Janet corrected. "He hangs all over you."

"He does not! He's a good friend."

"How're you girls doing out here?" Mrs. Saunders asked, walking in and interrupting the conversation. She crossed to where Penny was mixing the egg salad, put her finger in the bowl, and licked it. "Salt and pepper, and a little more mayonnaise."

"All right already, Mom," Penny said, annoyed. "I think I'm up to making a few sandwiches."

"You watch your mouth," Mrs. Saunders said mildly, handing her the mayonnaise jar.

"Not too much mayo," Crystal interrupted, "we're on diets."

Mira looked down, embarrassed at Crystal's insensitivity. Like her daughter, Mrs. Saunders needed to lose about twenty pounds, and a denim wrap skirt and madras shirt didn't help any.

But Mrs. Saunders was smiling. "If that's so," she said, teasing, "you'd better move those chips."

Mira and Janet laughed as Crystal's hand froze inside the bag. "Here," Mrs. Saunders said, handing Janet a bunch of napkins and some paper plates, "why don't you put these out and then I'll let you girls alone."

"Aren't you going to stay and eat with us?" Mira asked politely, knowing that her own mother would've been too interested to eat her lunch someplace else.

Mrs. Saunders shook her head. "I'm going to put my feet up in the other room." She set the plate of sandwiches in the middle of the table, took two for herself, and headed out the door. "Don't play that radio too loud—Timmy's taking a nap."

"Seriously, though," Crystal said around a mouthful of egg salad, returning to the subject like a bloodhound now that Mrs. Saunders was out of the way. "I still don't get it—*why* won't she let you go?"

Mira picked at a piece of lettuce. She wished Crystal would just drop the subject. Talking about camp hurt. She thought of the showing, the jump-offs, the before-breakfast rides she would miss this summer. She thought of how she would feel without her friends.

"It's weird," Crystal insisted. "You aren't her slave. You have a life of your own." She reached over and turned the volume up so they could hear The Police's "Synchronicity" better.

Janet tapped the rim of her Coke can against her teeth in time to the beat. "Your mother depends on you an awful lot. Doesn't it bug you?"

"Why should it?" Mira said defensively. The music was irritating. It was giving her a headache.

"All that responsibility." She shrugged and made a face. "Like when my grandmother started losing it upstairs and came to live with us—my Mom had to give up practically everything to take care of her. But *you* really get into the whole thing."

"Why are you so down on my mother?" Their words swarmed around her. She wanted to swat them away. "It's just since my father died—she's lonely, that's all."

"*Your* mother lonely?" Crystal hooted with laughter. "Your mother has more guys on a string than she could take care of in a year—no wonder your father had a heart attack."

"What's that supposed to mean?" Mira's skin prickled up in a wave of heat. The table was too close to the wall and too crowded. She tried to move her chair to make more room but she was wedged in. It was too hot to breathe.

"Mira, everybody knows how your mother carried on right in front of your father. My mother says it was probably your mother that gave him his coronary."

"I don't care what your dumb old mother says," Mira shouted, pushing her chair back and jumping up.

"In my country women do not chase after men."

"In *your* country they kidnap people!"

"Take a hint, Crys!" Penny's voice was sharp. "C'mon, Mira, sit down." She reached and tugged on her arm.

"Don't touch me!" Her flesh stung from the contact. Nauseated and sweaty and hot—she had to get out. "I've got to go." Her voice came back at her and echoed in her ears.

"She was just kidding around," Penny said. "Don't get so bummed."

"I have to go!"

"I thought we were going riding!"

"You're not my friends."

"You're getting weirder and weirder," Crystal said. "What's wrong with you these days anyhow?"

Their faces were flattened, like paintings or puzzles. They drew back. They didn't understand. They acted as if she were contagious.

What was she doing here and what did these people matter? They talked about her when she wasn't around. They didn't really like her. She never wanted to see them again. She was running from the hot kitchen down a dark hall, going down into the earth in a small cage that lurched, running out onto bright wet cement. Her eyes hurt, her head was zinging with meteors, strange lights. She had to call. There was a phone booth, there were the buttons. She wanted to shut the door to the closet. She must have privacy. She was pushing the numbers. They made music. There was ringing now. She thought of it ringing in the room with plants and a crystal and a scrawl of papers. The rain was wetting her face, wetting the glass, she was speaking into the phone, Will you come for me, can I stay at your house, can I sit on your floor, curl up in your lap, will you hold me for this one afternoon? But there was no answer. The ringing kept on. The light was very bright. Her eyes hurt. She hung up the phone. There was silence. Meteors. Numbers. The sky was dark. She was alone.

Concentrate, Mira said to herself as the small wooden squares rattled against the open lid of the box. Mrs. Ross mixed them up and then began to turn their printed faces downward. Don't think about this afternoon, about Crystal or Janet, about Vivian or camp. Concentrate on having fun.

Mrs. Ross opened the gray-green Scrabble board with its gridiron of pink, blue, and red, and set it across the scarred oak table. "I hope I remember how to play," Mira said, studying the rules printed inside the box top.

Mrs. Ross smiled and leaned back in the old rocker with the frayed yellow cushion. "It'll come to you—like riding a bike."

Mira looked back into the kitchen alcove where Michael and Steven were washing up the spaghetti dishes from supper. She had been so upset this afternoon she almost hadn't come with the Rosses to Montauk. She hadn't wanted to be near people who knew her so well, who could read her mood like meteorologists read weather maps. But Michael had insisted, and come to pick her up.

"How long've you been summering in Montauk?" Mira asked, although she already knew. She was making conversation so Mrs. Ross wouldn't look at her too closely.

"Since the boys were," she paused, counting back in her head, "probably two and eight. We rented at first." She tucked her bare feet up tailor-fashion and blew across the surface of her steaming mug of coffee. Her fingers were long and slender, like her toes, and they made you aware of all the other bones in her body. "The house didn't come till they were older." The net of gray in her dark hair caught the fading light. Mira had always liked Michael's mother, and she knew Mrs. Ross liked her just as much. Everything about Michael's mother was so wonderfully normal—from her weathered dungarees and man-tailored shirt to her freckles.

Mira'd been up to the house on the Old Montauk Highway
a couple of weekends last year. Before she came the first time
she'd always imagined the Rosses' Long Island summer home
on a road whizzing with cars, a tacky place full of plastic
furniture, and beaches that were covered by scum from the
Sound. But the "highway" turned out to be a meandering road
banked by shrubbery, trees, and hedges on the left and the
ocean on the right. The house was a small frame Cape Cod set
against the side of a hill that sloped down to the sea, with a
screened porch that overlooked a patch of green lawn and a
drift of clean white beach. Mrs. Ross was a shell collector, and
a large glass case stood in the living room, filled with her sea-
bleached finds.

Today, after fighting weekend traffic for three hours on the
Long Island Expressway and trying to keep her face silent,
even unloading the car felt good and Mira's mood had lifted a
little. It was good to be out of the city and away from Vivian.

The sun had started to go down now, turning the water a
rolling liquid gold and the sky magenta. Darkness moved up
from under the bushes to cover the lawn and the hammock
under the scrub oaks. Mira could feel the shadows against her
face. The smell of salt came in on the breeze, and the distant
rhythm of the waves pounded in her ears like a heartbeat.

"Let's go," Steve said, throwing himself down in the lounge
and crossing his long legs. He had big feet, Mira noticed, with
clean, well-shaped nails. The thick wooly hair on his calves
reminded her of her father.

Michael sat down beside Mira on the wicker glider and they
began picking their letters.

"You guys have the life." Steve eyed Mira and sent Michael
a half-smile. "Mom would never let me have a girl up here for
a week while she was at work in the city."

Mira blushed, glad for the dim light, and wondered why
everyone was always making cracks about Michael and her.

Michael frowned at his older brother. "Dartmouth's polluted your mind. Don't you have any women *friends?*"

"Times change," Mrs. Ross said, bending forward to pick out her seven pieces. She winked at Mira and clicked them down onto the little wooden stand, squinting at them in the half-light.

Michael held a match to the thick red candle at the edge of the table. The wick caught and the details of their faces mushroomed up in the yellow flicker. Mira and Michael chose their pieces and concentrated in silence for a minute.

"Check this out—I bet Michael's got all the good consonants again." Steve moaned and tugged at a piece of hair hanging down over his forehead. "Age before beauty, Mom—you start."

"With a son like you!" She snorted and laid down the first word to the left of the star in the center of the board. "F-A-N-T-A-S-Y. For twenty-eight plus the fifty-point bonus."

"All your letters?" Steve shook his head. "You're too much. Why didn't you just hit the triple word score—then we could pack it in right now."

With a pencil, Michael divided a sheet of paper into four columns and put his mother's score down while she drew seven new letters. "Mira's turn."

"Can I have a minute?" She stared down at the line of letters but her mind refused to work. There weren't any possibilities. Her letters were just a random scramble, gibberish. I E G M. She looked up at Michael and he smiled. When she looked back at the board she had an idea. "How about I-M-A-G-E?" she spelled, working off FANTASY's second A. "What's that worth?"

"Triple on the I makes three, plus three for six, seven, eight, nine, and the triple on E makes twelve." Michael wrote it on the pad. "Not bad, Mira."

Steve moaned again. "This eats it." He laid down an O and a D off the N in FANTASY. "NOD for four."

Michael wrote it down and then moved his pieces in. "N-O-D-U-L-A-R." He frowned. "For sixteen."

"Punk!" Steve said, noogying him in the shoulder. "How'd you think of that?"

Michael smiled and tapped the side of his head. "Kidneys."

The dog whined at the screen door and Michael got up to let him in. He bounded over to Mira, his tail pumping like a whip, a blur of black and white spots, which nearly swept the pieces off the board.

"Caesar!" Steve reached for his tail as it arced from side to side, but it was as useless as trying to hold on to a slippery fish. The dog shoved his nose in Mira's lap and began to inhale. She squirmed away so no one would notice but he burrowed right back in, and when she put her hand under his muzzle to unglue him he pushed back, hard.

"Come here, you old crotch hound." Mrs. Ross snapped her fingers and pointed at a spot on the floor beside her chair. "Mira, just smack his snoot."

The dalmation sprang back at the slap and wagged his way over to Mrs. Ross. Scrooching down beside her, his muscular tail beat a loud drum on the wooden planking. "Too damned friendly for his own good." She squinted at the board again, and shuffled the letters on her stand with a sigh. As they waited for her to decide, Mira studied the board with its small solid blocks of words and language and connection, the open spaces and the possibilities. It seemed to her like a network, a chain, linking the three absorbed faces around her, a backbone fusing the joints of their time together. Mrs. Ross, Steve, and Michael interlocked just like the letters on the board. Their lives seamed together along the edges, crisscrossed along certain lines, but each one still kept its own clean and separate meaning.

"V-A-R-N-I-S-H," Mrs. Ross cried triumphantly, using NODULAR's A. "That's worth thirty-six!"

Steve turned to Mira with disgust. "We're definitely outclassed."

They played until all the tiles were gone and no one could think of another syllable. Then Steve made hot fudge sundaes and they sat in the dark slurping up the thick sauce and whipped cream, listening to the crickets rasp in the shrubbery. The creaking rhythm lulled Mira near to sleep.

As she flipped out the light in the small bedroom next to Mrs. Ross's she didn't bother with a nightie or her toothbrush, but just peeled off her shorts and shirt. A pocket of fudge sauce was caught in the crack of a molar and her tongue sucked at the sweet. The sheets were cool, tucked rough and tight against her body as the pillow nested up around her head. The smell of starch and chocolate and salt comforted her. Sleep slipped in easily, a warmth that started at her toes and crept up until her eyelids ached to slide shut. Her breath whistled down against her cheek, her fingers curled upward into loose fists. A cool breeze came from the window, the sound of the sea, and the colors moved in, blooming blues and reds and yellows.

It was a ringing that wouldn't stop, a shrill noise that drilled into her sleep. Mira tossed against it, fought it, without waking. It was the voice, arguing, that prodded her up out of her dream.

"It's after midnight and she's asleep. Won't it keep till morning?"

A shifting in the blackness of the hallway.

"But she was so tired."

A sigh.

"You're sure you want me to wake her?"

A creak of old pine floorboards, a fumbling in the dark. The door to Mira's room opened and she sat up.

"What's wrong?"

"Nothing's wrong, don't worry." Mrs. Ross pulled the covers back and took the quilt from the bottom of the bed to wrap around Mira's shoulders. "It's just your mother." She sighed. "I tried to tell her you'd been asleep."

"I'm sorry she woke you," Mira whispered, stepping on her sneaker and stumbling in the dark. "I'll be quiet—please go back to bed."

Mrs. Ross peered at her and yawned. "If you need anything, just knock."

"What took so long?" Vivian's voice came over the wire with a whine.

"I was asleep. What's going on?"

"I got home a while ago." There was a rustle as Vivian adjusted her position and Mira could just see her, lying in bed with the lamp on the table beside her adjusted low, hair loose over her shoulders. "I miss you."

"I've only been gone a few *hours.*" There was exasperation in her tone now.

"Well, I'm here alone."

"It's just for a week." Mira rubbed the sleep out of her eyes. She wasn't going to feel guilty about one week at the beach—not after Vivian had made her stay in the city all summer. "What's going on?" she asked, changing the subject deliberately.

"Ariella and Toni came up with a big new scene for me. For Tuesday. One of the best things they've ever given me and they do it on short notice." Vivian sighed. "I just *have* to have some time with you to go over it."

"But the scripts are always done weeks in advance," Mira said, confused.

"This was a last-minute thing. Anyway, I don't want to blow it. I need you here."

Mira didn't say anything. Her heart started to pound and she stalled by poking her fingers one by one into the dial holes of the old black phone.

"Come on, you know how much I rely on you—you're my best coach."

"Look, I've only got a week here—is that so much to ask?"

"I thought you'd want to come back." Vivian sounded hurt.

"This's the only vacation I get all summer long!"

"What's happening with you, Mira?" Vivian's voice was sharp with anger now, louder. "I used to be able to depend on you."

"You used to be able to *use* me." Mira didn't even have to shout. The truth was loud enough. Don't be guilty, be angry—that was what Dr. Strauss had said at their last session.

Vivian was so silent that, for a minute, Mira thought she'd hung up. "I know who's been giving you these ideas, and I'm not going to take much more of it," Vivian said after a minute, her voice thin and sharp as an icicle. "Just think about that next time you feel like getting fresh. I'm still your mother." She took a deep breath. "And don't be so selfish. Sometimes you can't just do what you feel like—you've got to learn to be more responsible."

"Are you saying I *have* to come home?" Mira's hands were sweating now as she held the receiver. Vivian's subtle threat about Dr. Strauss had had an effect. After all, Vivian paid the bills.

"I'm sorry, sweetie, I really am," Vivian said in a low, husky wheedle. "But you still have the whole weekend there."

Mira's voice curled up out of her throat like a wisp of smoke. "See you Monday morning."

"Love you," Vivian said, making a goodnight kiss across the wire and clicking off.

Mira put the receiver down. She pulled the quilt around her
and went back to her room. The sheets felt cold and damp now
and she huddled face down, fetal, on top of the blankets. She
wanted to cry but held back, pushing her fists into her
eyesockets until burning white lights rose and burst behind her
lids. She despised herself for giving in and pinched herself,
hard. "I hate you," she said aloud and banged her forehead
against the headboard, again and then again. After a while she
stopped. It hurt a lot. There was no way to get back to sleep
now. She lay still and waited for morning.

At six o'clock she pulled on her robe and went to sit on the
porch in the early light. The floorboards were cool under her
bare feet. She had an ache at the bottom of her stomach, like
when she was about to get her period, and not getting any
sleep had made her numb. Her forehead hurt, too. In the
glider she hugged her legs to her chest for comfort. The sun
was just coming up over the waves.

Mrs. Ross set a pitcher of orange juice down on the table
and poured them each a big glass. "Sleep well?" She sank into
an armchair and propped her feet up on the table.

"I have to go back."

Mrs. Ross didn't answer, just sipped her juice and stared at
the water.

"I don't want to, but I have to." Mira's voice quavered and
she bit her lip. She didn't want to cry in front of Mrs. Ross.

"Why?"

"My mother wants help with a scene."

"You told her you wanted to stay?"

Mira nodded.

"And she still says you have to?"

She nodded again.

Mrs. Ross was silent once more. Mira knew that Michael's

mother wouldn't say anything nasty about Vivian in front of
her—even though she was definitely thinking something not
very nice. She had to say something, anything, to fill in the
silence. "If Daddy was here he'd help."

"Help?"

"She wasn't needing me so much when Daddy was alive,"
Mira explained. "She wasn't like this before the accident."

Mrs. Ross gave her a startled, puzzled look. "I thought your
father died of a heart attack." She set her glass down. "But
you said an accident?"

Mira stared at her, confused. "Did I say accident?" she
asked quickly, faking. "I don't know why I said that." The
words had slipped out of her mouth and away from her, slippery, hard to catch or stop.

"Are you all right?" Mrs. Ross got up and came to sit beside
her on the glider. She put her hand on Mira's forehead.
"You're warm."

Her touch was too much. A mother's hand, dry and capable
and smooth—she demanded nothing, she simply gave. I love
you, Mira wanted to say, it wasn't an accident, she wanted to
say, but the words jumbled in her head like towels going round
in a dryer and she just looked at Mrs. Ross.

She felt the tears gathering. Rushing, unstoppable, they
poured out, flood water, full of mud and silt and debris, and
she was crying, her body shook, the anger burned and choked,
she couldn't talk, only the tears came, like words they fell, one
great long sentence. Mrs. Ross put her arms around Mira,
patted her on the back. "Let me call your doctor, Mira." She
spoke right through the sobbing. "You need to talk to her."

The wails came from deep in Mira's chest, ripping their way
out. There was the sensation of weight shifting, a crack, a fault
line. Things held back were escaping, like gas, along the edges.

"Where is the number? Do you carry it in your purse?"
Mrs. Ross put her arms around Mira tightly and helped her to

stand, as gently as if she had broken all the bones in her body.
"Let's go," she said, her voice a soft croon, a lullaby. "Let's go
call."

Mira slumped against her, shaking, still sobbing. "I'm
alone," she cried. "No way out."

"Nonsense," said Mrs. Ross. "I'm here."

Kettledrums. Or thunder. A sound so big it filled up her
ears. The water tugged at her ankles, cold and slate blue, and
suctioned the sand from under her feet in a strong undertow.
It wanted to take her, it wanted to roll her around like a stone
or a buoy. The sea had jaws and they sucked wide and fast
against the shore. Her first beach, at six, had been the forty-
foot dunes of Truro. Near the fingertip of Cape Cod, the cliffs
were pressed—like that special German cake Grandma Charlotte made, sacher torte—into alternating stripes of ocher,
brown, and beige, and they made the narrow strip of sand
below look very small. Mira had been afraid of the ocean that
first time, had stopped short and looked down from the height
of the path over the dunes, down to the beach, down to the
thunder and crash, thinking that Columbus was wrong—this
was the edge of the earth.

"Mom wants you to come back next weekend and spend the
rest of the summer with us," Michael said, as they walked
across the sand toward their blanket. "She's worried about
you."

"Don't be silly. I'm all right." There was no conviction in
her voice. "Talking to Dr. Strauss helped." She lay down
heavily and turned onto her stomach. "If I could just get some
sleep."

"Didn't you go back to bed after your mother called last
night?" Michael unscrewed the cap of the Coppertone and
poured a puddle into his palm.

"Yeah, but I only slept for a few minutes. And I wished I hadn't." Mira dug her big toe down into the sand until she could feel the cold wet layer grit up under the nail.

"I can't believe you said you'd go back." Michael's voice was flat. His hand, greasy with lotion, rubbed the same part of his leg over and over again.

"If your mother had told *you* to come home would *you've* said no?" Mira rolled off her stomach onto her back and squinted up at him, shading her eyes from the harsh noontime sun. "I didn't have a choice. You make it sound like I did."

"My mother wouldn't have made me." Michael screwed the yellow cap back on the bottle. "I guess that's the difference. You say you're such best friends with your mother—but here she is making you do something real unfair. I think having a mom is better than having a best friend." He lay back on his towel, hands behind his head. His armpits were the only part of his body with any hair yet—long brown tufts that reminded Mira of a goat's beard. "Why did you wish you hadn't gone back to sleep?" he asked after a minute.

"It's a dream I have a lot." She propped herself on one elbow and looked out at the ocean. "I'm in this forest, like some African jungle, with huge tangled plants and vines and creepers. I'm hunting, I think. Or maybe it's that someone's chasing me. I don't know what it is, but there's just this feeling of . . ." she paused, looking for the word, "well, pressure, I guess. To get away from whatever it is. The leaves are really wet and humid and they keep catching at me and slapping me. They're slowing me down, holding me back so I can't run. Then all of a sudden I'm in this little clearing. There are birds there. They're very noisy and talking in some language I can't understand—because the language is all numbers. The numbers keep coming out of their mouths, 'five six, minus ten, triplicate the sum.' They keep flitting from tree to tree, all blue and green and gold, and these small black numbers keep falling from their beaks onto the ground. They're like shiny pieces of glass. I pick them up. I can see myself in them—an eye, a nose, a mouth—all broken apart, cracked. I want to be a bird, to get away, just fly out of the jungle. They're trying to tell me how, but they keep talking in numbers, the numbers are falling on the ground like shooting stars, or messages from heaven, and I keep picking them up but it doesn't help. I still don't understand. There isn't much time left. I keep looking at my face in the pieces of glass. Then I wake up." Mira turned to look at Michael. He was on his side, watching her with a serious expression on his face.

"Did you tell Dr. Strauss about your dream?"

Mira shook her head. "It's too complicated to talk about on the phone." She hesitated. "Besides, I'd feel dumb."

"D'you understand it?"

"No. I wish I did." Mira sat up and scratched her leg where the sand made it itch. "Dr. Strauss says dreams can sometimes tell you things."

Michael didn't say anything. He just stared at her.

Mira laughed uncomfortably. "Look, I know the dream's a little weird—but don't stare at me like I'm mental."

"What d'you want me to do, Mira?" He sat up straight and suddenly. "Applaud or something?"

"Why're you getting so mad?"

"Because I'm scared, that's why. All this bizarre stuff, your mother getting queerer by the minute—and all you can do is sit around." He stood up and threw a stick down the beach. Caesar took off after it, barking. "You should be telling this junk to your doctor."

A chill raised goose pimples on her forearms. He didn't want to hear it—just like the others. She scared him. "I don't want to talk about this stuff to anyone but you."

"Well, that's bad. I can't fix it. It's too much."

Mira lay down again and hugged her arms against her tummy. Soon Michael would be gone too.

Caesar bounded up with the stick, throwing a spray of sand across Mira's back, and Michael sighed. He knelt down and brushed it off. "Dumb dog."

She turned her head to look at him.

"Forget what I said. Let's swim."

"To where?"

He pointed. "About two miles down there's a small private beach that I go to a lot."

"I'm not sure I can do two miles and back again."

"Bet you can." He smiled, a tease. "If you drown I'll buy you a two-pound lobster at Gosman's tonight."

Mira smiled but still looked uncertain.

"C'mon." He pulled her to her feet. "If you get real tired we can always get out and walk."

"What about Caesar?"

"He's a surf bum."

They waded into the water hand in hand, but Mira pulled back as the waves moved up her calves to her thighs. "Too cold," she protested. "Freezing!"

"You'll get used to it." Michael dove through the surface of a breaking wave and rolled up on his back like a porpoise. "Come on! I'll swim right beside you."

Caesar splashed in and began to paddle after Michael, his nose like the long prow of a ship as his head parted the waves.

Mira took a deep breath, held it, and dove down into the froth of frigid green. Salt burned her eyes. Her arms were stiff, unable to move through the cold. Ahead of her she could see Michael's feet flutter-kicking, and Caesar's legs in a four-beat dog paddle. They swam out just far enough so they wouldn't be caught in the breakers and then headed north, moving parallel to the shore, fast—before long Mira's joints unlocked and she kicked through the water easily. Below her the bottom was invisible. She wondered whether it was sandy or stony or just rows of seaweed, and pushed away thoughts of Portuguese men-of-war and crabs and sharks. Ahead, Michael's head bobbed, a reassuring marker. The surf pushed her body from side to side in a rhythmic sway—it was like trying to walk up the aisle of a train, she thought as she bubbled the air out through her nose. She concentrated on regulating her breathing, on matching the stroke and pull of her arms to the kick of her legs. She wanted to swim the whole way. It was keeping her from thinking of other things. It was keeping the dream away. It was keeping the anger away. In the water tears weren't tears, just part of the ocean. She got lightheaded after a while, and stopped thinking at all. Her body moved on its own—jointless, boneless, greased, cutting through the water like a well-designed canoe. Across the tops of the swell she was an arrow aimed at the soft interior of some sandy shore. She would swim until she hit China.

Michael stopped to tread water and caught her by the shoulder. He pointed the way in and she followed. Caesar was waiting for them, shaking his coat dry.

The rocks and pebbles cut her feet and when the water was only knee-high she stumbled in the undertow, out of her element on land. Michael put his arm around her and they burrowed into the warm sand behind a large stone outcropping. Mira lay on her back and watched the sky shift under clouds. For a long time they didn't speak. To breathe was painful. Her ribs and lungs ached—she was unaccustomed to air, a mermaid. The sun faded under passing cumulus and she shivered.

"Cold?" Michael drew her against him. His skin was cold, slippery, and wet, but warm too. She'd never been so close to him before. He turned her on her side facing outward and wrapped himself around her, a blanket. Being so close reminded her of Bill, of other boys, of other times. But this was different. This was gentle. He made her warm, the way he held her now made her tingle. She pushed away the feeling. Michael wasn't the right person for that. With Michael she felt safe and she wanted it to stay that way. Safe was enough.

Mira let herself drowse, the rocking of the ocean replaced by the rhythm of his chest as it rose and fell. His body cupped hers, his breath heated the nape of her neck, his arms were a tight close circle, his knees reflected back the warmth of her own pulse point. She dipped into sleep.

11

"NICE TAN." Chris looked Mira over. "Been to the beach?"

Mira nodded, her resentment at being forced to come home dimming a little. There were some good things about being on the set. Although it had been a long morning, she now forgot how tired she was and smiled as if she'd just had a nap. "Montauk," she said. "Caught some rays over the weekend."

"You around all summer?"

She pointed at herself with a grin. "Vivian's *un*official manager."

"I hear you handle her real well."

She shrugged.

"I still say you're too young for this line of work." He gave her a half-smile.

She straightened up. "Not so young."

"Oh yeah?" His voice was a challenge. "How old?"

"Old enough."

"Sure," he grinned back. "How about dinner tonight?"

"Sure." She flushed, a deep dark red, trying to look nonchalant and keep her elation from showing.

She couldn't imagine what she would say to him for so many hours, or what she would wear. Her mother wouldn't like it, but she didn't care. She was going, that much was definite. "Fantastic." She threw her hair over her shoulder the way Crystal did, hoping her afterbath spray hadn't worn off.

"Uzie's at eight?"

"Eight," she echoed, already nervous. "Well, I really should be up there. See you." She turned and walked to the control booth, script under her arm. She watched her feet carefully—she didn't want to trip in case he was still looking at her—and hoped her jeans looked good from the back. She opened the door to the booth and walked in, wondering how she would explain it to her mother.

An hour later, Mira handed Vivian her skirt and blouse and watched as she took off her makeup at the mirror in her dressing room. They were going out to lunch and a lot of stage makeup just made her mother more recognizable. "Summerhouse?" Vivian asked, polishing her forehead with tissue and Abolene. "Then we can spend this afternoon going over the new scene."

"Okay." Mira took her brush from her purse and straightened out the tangles in her own hair. "Then tonight I've got a date with Chris," she said, trying just to slip it in.

Vivian swiveled away from the mirror, hair pulled back from her face so tightly the bones jutted against the skin, cold cream in a lather across her cheeks. "You what?"

Mira zipped her bag shut and got ready for the arguments.

"But he's too old for you—he's nearly my age!"

"He's only nineteen. That's closer to me than you."

Vivian closed her mouth with a snap and began scrubbing the white cream from her face with a tissue. "I just can't see it."

"I think he likes me."

Vivian gave her a look in the mirror.

"Isn't it *possible* he could like me?" Mira used sarcasm as a defense against her mother's doubt. "You know, some people actually think I'm cute—and interesting too."

"I suppose this's your way of paying me back," Vivian said after a minute.

"Paying you back?" Mira was confused.

"For asking you to come home. You knew I'd think he was too old." She twisted her mouth into a smile. "You're just doing it to upset me."

"Does everything I do have to have something to do with you?" Mira asked, angry now. "Can't I do something just because I feel like it?"

Vivian didn't answer, she just kept scrubbing at her face. She applied a light layer of daytime base and rouge with quick circular strokes—as if they'd never even begun to argue.

"If you don't have time to help me rehearse," Vivian drew a careful line of deep green charcoal around each eye and smudged it in with the tip of her little finger, "that's okay." Her voice was heavy with fortitude. "If you're too busy, I mean."

Mira stared as Vivian colored the bows of her lips with a thick red lipstick. "We have a good seven hours before I have to go." She was furious—why should she feel guilty? "That's plenty of time."

Vivian shrugged. "If you say so."

"Don't make *me* the heavy." Mira could see her anger in the mirror. "I'm giving you my whole afternoon."

"Only if you want to."

"Why d'you have to be so manipulative?" Mira asked. "You know I didn't *want* to come back—but I did!"

"Another big word from your shrink?" Vivian's eyebrows went up, mocking her. "That woman's getting to be a real pain in the derriere."

"I'll see you outside when you're ready," Mira said with disgust. She closed the door behind her, hard, and went to get a drink at the water cooler. She wasn't going to react to Vivian's comments about Dr. Strauss anymore. She was just going to ignore them.

Dee was sitting there, opening a brown paper bag from the coffee shop. "Are you two fighting about Chris again?"

"Among other things," Mira said angrily.

"You guys aren't getting along at all." Dee pried the plastic lid off her coffee. "What's the matter?"

"I'm ticked off." Mira tore the edge off her longest fingernail. "She's just not fair, not about anything."

"Life's never fair." Dee shrugged. "And Chris has always been too old for you."

"He's more my age than he is hers." Mira leaned against the cold metal of the water fountain.

"So what?" Dee took a big bite of her tuna on rye and wiped mayonnaise from the corner of her mouth with her pinky. "He lives in a different world than you do," she said around a mouthful. "It's not good for you to be with someone like Chris."

"Why do you keep saying that!" She didn't want to hear any of this. She was tired of being patronized.

"If you want to choose the fast and racy life when you're older—well, that's okay. But you're only fourteen!" Dee stopped and looked up at the ceiling in exasperation. "He's a user. I *told* you."

Mira didn't say anything. What Dee said embarrassed her, made her feel silly and young—just like her mother had.

"Sorry." Dee put her sandwich down and reached over to give Mira's hand a gentle tug. "I didn't mean it to sound like that. But don't you see? You've got plenty of time to be a grown-up. Can't you enjoy being a kid for a while?"

"Are you saying this is my fault?" Mira looked at her directly. "*I* wanted to go to camp this summer! *I* wanted to stay with my friend Michael out at Montauk this week—she's the one dragged me back here!"

"Your mother was wrong to keep you in the city this summer." Dee's voice was quiet. "It was selfish of her."

Mira didn't answer, surprised—at last someone was taking her side. She'd never heard Dee speak against Vivian.

"When you're fourteen you're not supposed to carry the world on your shoulders, you're not supposed to be responsible for everything and everybody."

"So what *am* I supposed to do?"

"Try saying no for a change. Stick up for yourself." Dee began to peel a tangerine, and the bitter smell of citrus floated over the dusty air of the set. "People hardly ever move in straight lines. Stop expecting your mother to live her life around yours—she's always going to put her needs first. That's just the way she is."

"She wouldn't listen if I said no."

"So leave for a while. Go to Montauk for the rest of the summer." She handed Mira a few pieces of her fruit.

Mira stopped short, anger giving way to shock—she couldn't even imagine leaving for the entire rest of the summer. "How would she get along without me?"

"How did she get along before you?"

Mira didn't answer, she played with a piece of tangerine. The idea of leaving Vivian, of breaking away like that, scared her. As much as she was angry, as much as she hated her mother right now and as much as she wanted to get away, she also wanted to stay—where she knew what to do, where things were safe and sure and predictable. Being needed at least gave you a direction. She didn't want to think about leaving for good, or being on her own.

"Sometimes you have to go just so you can come back again." Dee finished her sandwich and shoved the wrappings down into the maw of the trash can. "I'm going to the john before I run through tomorrow's scene with Marty in ten minutes—but call me tonight and let me know how you're doing. Maybe we could hit the beach on Saturday?"

Mira nodded and smiled. "Thanks." She watched Dee walk away and dropped the piece of tangerine into the trash. She bent over the water fountain, although she wasn't really thirsty. The water was cool against her lips and teeth and she wiped her mouth with the back of her hand. What Dee'd said made up her mind in one way at least. She wanted to go with Chris to Uzie's and she would—she didn't care what anyone said. It was bad enough she'd had to come back from Montauk. She'd be damned if she wasn't going to have a great time tonight. She straightened up and tried to picture her insides as a core of steel, a tempered band that didn't bend, that was at its heart a razor-thin edge.

Uzie's was a chic, noisy place that served good Northern Italian food, but that wasn't how it'd made its name. You went to Uzie's to be seen, to be noticed on a small scale, with the added bonus of being able to pick up someone without looking as though you'd come in just for that reason. You had to yell to be heard over the music, and Mira's throat was raw, despite a glass of wine. They'd both broken their diets and ordered tortellini alla panna, scooping up the rich cream sauce with oversized spoons. They'd shared a salad, and a fruit tart for dessert, and now Mira was so full she was afraid she was going to burp. That the maître d' had recognized Chris and given them a table at the center of the hubbub didn't get to her as it would have if she'd been with her mother—this time it was a mark of status, a light in which she shared because she was his date.

Everything about him seemed like magic. The scent of his cologne was subtle, but it was there. His blue sports shirt was open at the neck, but only a few buttons down, just enough to show the curl of black hair on his chest. He stroked the stem of his wine glass between two long fingers, and Mira was hypnotized by the movement, lulled away from her earlier anxiety. He made her laugh, he made her forget she was someone's daughter, he made her feel glad to be Mira. He didn't mention her mother—not even once.

He talked about his ambitions, how hard he'd worked for his spot on "Megan's World," how long it had taken and how desperate he'd been, how he'd keep it no matter what—even if it meant brown-nosing Marty and Ariella. He wouldn't let them write him out until he was ready to move on. He filled the table with himself and let Mira relax. She stopped worrying about what to say.

She scraped her fork over the sticky glaze the tart had left on her dessert plate. She didn't want it to end, and she certainly didn't want to go home. "It's nearly eleven," she said, reluctantly. "Vivian'll be waiting."

"Your mother always wants what she doesn't have." His eyes had a peculiar glitter.

"What d'you mean?" Mira said, uncertain.

"Just that one more hour won't hurt." He paid the check with five new twenties and stood to pull back her chair. "My place?"

She hesitated and then gave in, feeling relaxed and loose from all the wine. "Where?"

"Right around the corner—Seventy-first and Third."

They sauntered out into the humid summer air, into the heart of the singles district. The sidewalks were alive even though it was Monday night, the neon from stores and restaurants lit the pavement in front of them in colored splotches. They steered around the window-shoppers, the lovers hand in hand. Chris's apartment building was a limestone high rise with a fountain in front, a doorman who called him by name, a lobby with pillars and aggressively green plants. The elevator climbed slowly to thirty-nine.

He smiled at her and for the first time she wondered whether or not this was a good idea. She felt nervous again. A diffuse orange light was already on as they came in, as if they'd been expected. The couches in the living room were low, soft, like long barges you could nestle into. A bar glittered with crystal. An Oriental rug crunched under her feet when she stepped out of her shoes. As she sat down she saw herself reflected in the mirror opposite the couch and thought that she should go and comb her hair, but she was too tired. She sank back and shut her eyes.

Something landed in her lap and she jumped. It was a cat, a silky reddish-brown cat with enormous green eyes. It inspected her with a glare. After a minute it lifted its chin and left her lap for a cushion. For the first time she realized she was cold, and she rubbed her bare arms.

"What's its name?" she asked Chris as he stood crushing ice at the bar.

"It's a he. Marlowe."

It took her a minute to catch the allusion—she'd only seen the Elizabeth Taylor TV adaptation of *Dr. Faustus*. "That face'll never launch a thousand ships."

He laughed. "Well, I almost sold my soul to get him—Abyssinians are mucho dinero. How about a Black Russian?"

For a minute she thought he was talking about another type of cat, but then she saw he meant some sort of drink. She was too embarrassed to admit she didn't know what it was, so she just nodded, wishing it were a cup of hot chocolate instead. "Why d'you have a cat in the city?"

"I like cats—the way they preen. I like that they're a hundred percent, unashamedly self-centered."

The sofa shifted as he dropped down beside her and handed her a brandy snifter filled with crushed ice and a creamy con-

coction. He reached into a box on the table. Sipping her drink
—sweet and smooth as a coffee milkshake—she wondered how
she could say no to the grass. She'd been avoiding it since that
time in the auditorium with Bill. It stretched her perception,
blurred her borders and limits, when she needed to stay in
control. But Chris had already lit up, handing it to her carefully pinched between forefinger and thumb, and she didn't
want him to think her young or immature, so she took it and
inhaled against the harshness, praying she wouldn't cough.
Coughing tagged you as a straight.

The high came right away, making her warm. Chris said the
grass had been sprayed with opium, and Mira let herself float,
up and out, on the cushion. When he kissed her, desire covered her up like a thick blanket. She put her head back and let
him take her mouth. His tongue was soft and warm, it probed
deep inside her, it made her lips tingle. His face scratched
against her cheek. He sucked on her earlobe. He licked her
neck. Her body arched outward. Marlowe growled from the
other side of the couch.

Chris pulled her up and she rose like a swan from water.
Never before had she been so graceful, so long of limb. In the
bedroom he turned her toward the wall, a row of full-length
mirrors, and, putting her back to his chest, he unbuttoned her
blouse, he let her skirt drop, he pulled down her panties. She
was standing naked so that they both could see her in the
glass. She wasn't embarrassed. The cat had followed them and
was twining himself around and through Chris's ankles. Mira
could hear his angry purr as Chris piled her long hair on top of
her head in a knot and kissed the exposed flesh at the base of
her neck. He pulled off his own clothes and then drew a line
across her throat, a line where the color of her makeup ended
and her smooth skin tone began. "Shower," he said. "I want
you clean."

The water beat down on them, a waterfall of heat after the

refrigerated air of the apartment. He scrubbed her face, her shoulder blades, the backs of her knees. He put his tongue in her mouth again, he rubbed himself between her legs. She rubbed her face on the straightened black hair of his chest, she drank the small pool of water that collected in the hollow of his collarbone.

Marlowe was waiting for them on the bath mat. They didn't dry off—they shook like dogs. Chris went back to the bedroom and she followed, and Marlowe followed them both. Chris pushed her down on the bed and positioned her so that she could see each detail of what they were doing. Without makeup her face looked so young, her body a new bud, with none of the heavy sex, the full bloom, she'd always imagined men must want. His long tongue circled her nipples like a snake, he drew them outward into hard points. She was hypnotized by the red flick, the wet streaks it left behind as he worked his way downward, a slick trail across her navel and down into the dark curves she'd never seen before. But he held her open in front of the mirror, and she saw herself for the first time, a peony, pink against the pearl of her body. Watching made her more excited. The cat was rubbing his face against Chris's back, trying to distract him. Mira stifled the urge to push Marlowe away. Chris bent his head and nestled his tongue into her. He was buried between her legs in the mirror and she closed her eyes and let the heat wash her down, let everything become part of an urgency she'd never felt before, a hot wave, a final push upward into pleasure sweet as ice cream. And then he flipped her on her stomach, he moved over her, and lowered himself in. She moaned a little at the opening of what had been so tight before.

After a while he rolled off, lay back on the bed, separate. He hadn't made a noise, or shuddered, or anything. She watched him. He was still hard, glistening with the slick from her body. She wasn't sure she'd satisfied him. When he turned to her his eyes were the same cool electric blue they'd been at dinner. She wanted to ask him but she was afraid. Marlowe jumped on his chest, and Chris stroked his fur, scratched behind his ears and at the side of his face. Then he got up and went into the bathroom, Marlowe padding after him. The water ran for a while. He came back with a towel for her, carrying the cat. She sat up, dried herself off, and he helped button her back into her clothes. She was still high.

Downstairs the doorman hailed a cab. Chris tucked her in and kissed her on the cheek while she touched his arm again one last time, pretending to be casual. She wanted to say "I love you," she wanted to hear "I love you." She leaned back into the dark anonymity of the vinyl seat and remembered how he'd made her feel. She couldn't believe they'd done those things, or how good it had felt. She turned and looked through the back window of the taxi, watching the lights and the pavement blur. She'd never tell Vivian about any of this, no matter what. He was her secret.

12

JULY WAS a dangerous month. Breathing was unhealthy, living was unhealthy. Every morning on the "Today" show, Willard Scott announced that yesterday's air inversion over New York City continued. A record was set for the most hot, humid, and hazy days back-to-back since 1902. Vivian went to get a facial once a week instead of just every other—she felt dirty, she complained, her pores were clogged with the bad air —but Mira rode Singapore each afternoon, abandoning the comfort of air conditioning to sweat, flesh to fur, along with her horse. She liked the heat.

The thirteenth day of the heat wave came on the last day of the month. When Marty cut the afternoon run-through short because cast and crew were ready to pass out from the glare of the lights, Mira went to the stable, even though it was one hundred and three in the shade. She came home as wet as if she'd been swimming, as tired as if she'd run a marathon. Exhaustion was the weapon she used now against loneliness, against the depression fueled by weekly postcards from Penny and Mrs. Ross's invitations to return to Montauk. She was mired in the work on the set, in her mother's various obsessions, in the inert heat of the city. And in waiting for Chris.

Today she went straight to her room to check for a message from him. He'd been preoccupied on the set today and hadn't mentioned getting together tonight. She was sure he would've called by now to tell her where to meet him, but her bulletin board was empty.

She spun the shower dial hard right, ice cold, and just stood there until she could breathe again, telling herself that it didn't matter. Still, it was the first Friday in weeks they hadn't been together and she wondered if something was wrong. She peeled off her tee shirt and jeans, wrung them out, and slung them over the towel rack, where they dripped a spreading puddle of water on the tile. Then she soaped herself and hung her head against the spray.

After a long time she shut the water off. In one of her father's old tee shirts, she padded around the room barefoot, putting away her hard hat and straightening up. Red, pink, yellow, green. Her closet was now in rainbow order. She stuffed the wooden trees into her riding boots and pushed away the questions that kept popping up in her mind like a jack-in-the-box—where was he, why didn't he call, who was he with? Knowing she would see him on the set each day had made it easier to get up in the mornings, Friday nights in his apartment had made her less resentful about staying in the city this summer. And the sex—this was the very first time she'd ever really wanted it, the first time she'd felt she just couldn't wait. She depended on it, and now that scared her.

Chris was a bulwark between Vivian and Mira. She used him as a shield, waved him like a banner or a hunting trophy, while insisting to her mother that they were just friends. She refused to discuss him with Vivian, or how she felt, or where they went, or what they did. It was a way of staying separate. It was a way of paying Vivian back. Everything she would have ordinarily confided to her mother she recorded instead in graphic detail in the diary she hid under her mattress, page after page of intimacies she wouldn't let Vivian share. And it felt good. Even Dr. Strauss said it was a good thing. Progress, she'd called it.

Mira flipped the light switch down and went to Vivian's room, angry that she felt so vulnerable. "Any messages for me?" She hated to ask, hated to admit she was still waiting to hear from him. She perched on the edge of the bed.

Vivian was at her dressing table, fastening a jade choker around her neck. She shook her head. "Been riding?" She looked up at Mira in the mirror before bending her head again to try and catch the clasp.

Mira nodded as she crossed over to help her. "Here." She pushed Vivian's hands away and clicked the loop and circle closed. "You going somewhere?"

Vivian smiled as she loaded up her lipstick brush. "A date." The color went on in a slick red smear.

Mira picked up a comb and began to untangle her wet hair. "Who with?"

"Chris."

Mira's arm stopped in midstroke, as though she'd rusted in place while looking at her reflection in the mirror.

Vivian smiled. A crafty, mean smile, Mira thought.

"Don't be like that." Vivian blotted her lipstick on a tissue. "We're just *friends.*"

Mira caught her mother's sarcasm—her own words used against her. She was so mad, shocked, that she was silent. Her anger was like a braid—thick enough to run through her fingers, to be used. She wanted to put it around Vivian's neck, like the hangman game her class had played in the second grade when they were learning to spell.

Mira didn't move or speak. She watched her mother's face in the glass. It was a tableau, she thought, her mother smoothing her hair, talking to her through the mirror as if she were a ghost, as if she didn't really exist.

"He asked me to Grenouille," Vivian went on, "just to talk

about work. It's good politics." Pleasure and shame twined together when she saw the pain on Mira's face. All summer long Mira had kept anything to do with Chris from Vivian; all summer long Mira had kept her heart a secret. Vivian had to resort to the diary under the mattress to know what was going on—stealing back what had once been hers—and each time she read a new entry she grew angrier and angrier: Mira now belonged to Chris. Vivian bent her head over her compact to hide the shine of tears in her eyes.

"It's hot in here," Mira said, breaking away from their reflection. "The air conditioner must be broken."

"You're just overheated is all." Vivian stood up and went to the bureau to pack her evening bag. She swiveled in front of the mirror. The white silk dress was cut in a V from her shoulders to her waist, and her black hair was loose, waving down to the small of her back. She complimented herself silently: perfecto.

"And you're overdressed."

Vivian turned to look at her daughter. "What do you mean?"

"For a business dinner. You're overdressed." Mira heard her own sarcasm and didn't try to stop it.

"Stop being childish." Vivian's voice was cold now. "You don't own him."

Mira didn't answer, she just kept picturing Chris, how he would look as Vivian walked toward him. There was no way he could help responding to her mother. She was simply too beautiful.

Mira looked at every detail of that beauty—her eyes made more green by the jade at her ears and throat, the tiny circle of waist, the full high breasts—and, for the first time in her life, she really hated her. Not irritation. Not anger. Hate.

"I won't be late." Vivian checked her hair in the mirror one last time. "Wait up, and I'll give you a rundown." She picked up her evening cape and went to call a cab. Mira stood in the middle of the room.

She thought about calling Dr. Strauss, but then pulled back from the idea. She didn't want to bother her. Don't think about them together, she said to herself, just forget you know where he is, pretend she was already gone when you came home. And so she bricked up knowledge like a corpse, like that Edgar Allan Poe story they'd read in Mr. Samuel's class last year, and after a while went into the kitchen to ask for dinner. Elsa set it up in front of the television in the library but Mira wasn't hungry. She pushed the peas and potatoes around on her plate, she let her ice cream melt in a puddle and then stirred it up like soup, let it drip in strands from the spoon back onto the plate.

"You should eat something," Elsa said when she came to clear it away. "You're getting thinner and thinner."

There was nothing to watch on television except repeats of "Dallas" and "Falcon Crest," episodes she'd already seen. Mira opened the cassette drawer in the stereo cabinet and chose a movie for the VCR. When Vivian had bought *The Deerhunter* a few years ago she'd refused to let Mira watch it —too violent, she'd said, too explicit. Too much death.

The tape clicked into place and the titles crossed the screen. Vietnam, a place so full of hate and fear it made Mira's stomach go around. Helicopters, flamethrowers, the bodies on fire, the heat and sweat, the palm trees and jungle grass, the underwater cages where men swam with rats, and water, endless water. War. Russian roulette. That they died seemed unimportant to Mira. The torture of waiting to die was what counted. Brotherhood and brutality, she thought—what one person can mean to another, what one person can do to another. The kind of place where one friend helps another to pull the trigger, where the center of everything is charred. I know how that feels, Mira said to herself, you don't have to go far away to find that. The need to die was strong, like an addiction, in this movie. Putting a gun to your head every night for money was better than race car driving or blackjack. What a rush to dare to die so many times and beat it. There were people who were angry about this movie, she remembered, like Jane Fonda— they said it was prowar. That's not right, she decided. It's just about gambling. War or Russian roulette. Blood odds.

She didn't cry at the end when Nick stapled a bullet in his head and his friend tried to catch the jet of blood by putting his finger in the hole. She was too numb, she felt battered, bruised. She only wondered if it was realistic. Could a bullet make such a perfect circle?

The credits came up on the screen. In a while there was a click as the machine stopped and then whirred to rewind. Mira looked at the green digitals on the front of the tape deck. After eleven. Time to sleep. But she wasn't sleepy. "Wait up," her mother had said. She wandered down the hall toward the bedrooms.

The apartment went dark. After a minute she could hear Elsa's voice coming from the kitchen and then a pool of light wavered down the hall toward her.

"A blackout," Elsa said, satisfaction ringing in her tone, "all those air conditioners and you see what happens."

"Yes," Mira said, taking the candle offered to her. She went into her room and stared at the flame. She pinched it out between two fingers without feeling the sting. Undressed, she lay on top of the sheet with her eyes open. It was too dark to see. Sweat started in the small of her back. The room had gotten hot quickly. The apartment was silent without the hum of the air conditioners. She pictured herself in a strange country, floating down a muddy river on a big branch.

The ticking of Vivian's grandmother clock seemed very loud. Even with her ears covered it still came in. She lit the candle, went into the master bedroom, and stopped the pendulum. She sat down on the bed. Her mother's smell was still in the room. A particular perfume. In the mirror she saw a thin girl in a cotton nightgown on a green bedspread. She thought about the movie, about how even the river was angry. She watched herself put her finger to her forehead. She wondered how it would feel.

The candle had gotten short. She left it burning on her mother's dresser and went back to her own room in the dark. She lay down on her bed to wait.

From the bottom of sleep she hears voices. They're moving down the hall toward her, whispers so she won't hear them, but the laughter's there. She struggles to wake up, to look at her watch. The luminous dial is blurry. She rubs her eyes hard. Two o'clock.

The voices move past her door, left open to catch any cool air in the blackout. The power must be back on, she realizes, she can see two heads silhouetted against the light in the hall. She leans forward on her elbow and starts to call out, then stops. Two silhouettes. Not one. She lies back. The light goes out. The door to Vivian's bedroom closes. She holds her eyes open against the blackness. It's just like a nightmare, she says, and nightmares are always gone by morning. I'll wait, she says. I'll wait for the light.

13

AUGUST AND PREGNANCY weren't going to be good partners, Eve decided, feeling nauseated as she took the eggs from the refrigerator. Peter set out marmalade, pumpernickel, and Nova Scotia. The eggshells were cold and hard against Eve's palm as she cracked them and emptied them into the mixing bowl. She started thinking about Mira. Their regular Monday appointment was this afternoon and Eve wondered what shape Mira would be in: from session to session she was never sure whether her patient would be honest and show her depression or be cheerful and withdraw. She took the pitcher of orange juice and poured two glasses. Already the air that came through the window was muggy and hot. She sighed. She hated heat. It always seemed to precipitate trouble. Peter ground the coffee and put it into the Melitta.

Mira's therapy had intensified—she'd learned to trust Eve more, to depend on her, but only in a tentative way. She was still evasive and continued to steer around certain subjects as though she were navigating a coral reef. And her doctor's pregnancy was a threat: last week was probably the tenth time Mira had seen Eve in a maternity smock; she'd asked, finally, shyly, if Eve were pregnant. And at the end of the hour she'd wanted to know if Eve could still be her doctor after the baby came.

As each week passed Mira had grown more and more depressed, and once again Eve's instincts were humming like electrical wires with a full load: the therapy was at a break point. There was a ripeness to the girl now—a hesitation before she shut herself off, where previously the reaction had been automatic—and although there had been no repeat performances of the autohypnosis Eve had observed in June, she felt certain this was only because Mira was trying to keep all painful subjects submerged. Like waiting for an earthquake, it was only a question of time: neither scientists nor witches could predict the exact moment of slippage.

Eve turned from the window where she'd been peering out, trying to catch a glimpse of sun through the pollution that squashed the sky, and started to beat the eggs. Peter crossed the room as the kettle whistled and placed a restraining hand on her arm. "Slow down."

She looked from his face to the bowl. She was beating the eggs at a furious rate, her fork whipping a tornado into their sticky yellow hearts. She stopped, wiped her hands on the back of her shorts, and commanded herself to relax. A tickle came from deep inside her then, as gentle as the brush of an eyelash on a cheek, like the butterfly kisses she used to give her mother when she was little. Eve held her breath and prayed for it to come back. It did. The baby was moving inside her. She turned to Peter slowly. "It's moving," she said, whispering so she wouldn't disturb the sensation. "I can feel it."

He pulled her to him in a strong hug, pressed the small of her back into him so that the hard mound of her belly pushed against the flat of his. "I love you."

"It's going to be all right this time," she said. "It really is."

"Damned straight." He grinned. "Hey, I'm starved—let's feed that kid!" He slid the eggs into the frying pan, and they hissed as they hit the hot butter.

"He was just using me." Mira's voice was bitter. "He practically admitted it this afternoon."

"You went to see him?" Eve sat back and took a swallow of her iced tea to cover up her own horror, indignation, anger. Right now she hated Vivian Webster.

Mira nodded. "I just had to know *why.*" Her voice quavered on the last word. "He said Vivian could be helpful to him—an *ally* was the way he put it." She rubbed her eyes with the back of her hand. "Then he called me naive."

"Why?" The pain of this must be so terrible for her, Eve thought, surely she will cry.

"To think of love or anything like that. 'I never promised you anything' was what he said." She started to cry with a dry retching sound. "It's so awful."

"Losing him is awful?"

"Yes, yes."

The sound grew louder, like vomiting when there is nothing left to vomit, Eve thought.

"And just being an easy way to get to *her.* That's the worst."

"What did you say to your mother the next morning?"

"Nothing." Mira grabbed a Kleenex from the box on the desk.

"Nothing?" Eve could hear her own incredulity and struggled to bring her tone back into line.

"I haven't seen her. I took off for Michael's early Saturday morning." She used the facts to get control again—she hated crying in front of Dr. Strauss. She'd left a note on Vivian's dressing table. 'Gone to Montauk. Back Sunday night—M.' It seemed treasonous to go without asking for permission. That's why she'd signed her name with just the initial—as if it weren't really she who'd written it. The note was shorthand, staccato, a telegram of her feelings.

She'd been sure Vivian would call Mrs. Ross and make a scene, and all weekend long she'd flinched when the phone rang. But nothing had happened, and after a while she began to worry. And she'd started dreaming the new nightmare. She came home to find Vivian in the hospital, tied to the bed as if it were a crucifix. The stigmata were perfect circles in her mother's palms and feet and forehead. She dreamt of her father, too —on the beach one July when she was a child, leaping to catch the ball she had thrown, and later, standing together at the water's edge where a mermaid lay beached and struggling for air under the shimmering heat, its breasts bright red with sunburn. When she woke in the morning she knew she should stop to piece the dreams together, butt their edges corner to corner and crack to crack. But she didn't. Thinking about dreams seemed dangerous. She'd gotten up right away and scrubbed her face because she didn't want to remember them. She wanted them to fade like smoke from her memory, but even under direct sunlight they were still somehow there, edging into her awake world. It made her feel strange, disoriented, out of place. She didn't mention the dreams to Michael or his mother.

When she'd come home on Sunday night she'd expected a confrontation, an explosion. Instead there'd been only silence. An empty apartment. Sunday was Elsa's night off and Vivian was out too. There hadn't even been a note on Mira's bulletin board, and for the first time she felt a little bit scared. Maybe she'd gone too far. Maybe Vivian was as mad as she was. Or madder. Or maybe something had happened to her. Or maybe she was with Chris. Mira went to bed early but left her door open. She couldn't sleep. By midnight the questions came in alternating currents—worry and rage. Vivian returned at one o'clock, passed by the open door without speaking, and closed her own. Mira's room seemed stuffy even with the air conditioner. The sheets stuck to her back. At four she put her head under the pillow in desperation and then this morning didn't wake till nine, after Vivian had gone to the set.

"How did you feel when your mother said she was going out with him in the first place?" Dr. Strauss asked.

"I don't know." Mira looked down at the floor, wishing she could close her eyes. She felt so washed out.

Eve waited.

Mira looked up at her. She knew what the silence meant. Dr. Strauss thought she wasn't being honest. "I was mad," she said angrily. "Is that what you want me to say? He was mine, he was the only thing I had that she couldn't touch—is that what you want to hear?"

"I don't *want* you to say anything." Eve tried to keep her expression impassive. Mira had never been so angry before. Even if the emotion was transferred onto her, at least it was a response.

"You're always pushing at me! You're as bad as she is!" Mira stood up and paced the length of the room, hurling the words at Dr. Strauss as if she were Vivian, as if yelling would clean out her heart. "All right—she *stole* him!" Mira turned on her heel. "She *stole* him to get at me, to get me back, to get back at me for keeping him a secret. And I was so stupid I didn't even say anything." She started to cry again, the anger running down her face in streaks. "I should have paid her back that night!"

"Paid her back how?" Eve kept her voice low, unobtrusive.

"I wish I'd showed her."

"Showed her what?"

"That she can't run me. That she can't grab hold of me again. That it'll *never* be like before." She underlined her words in desperation. She wanted Dr. Strauss to understand what she meant. "I wanted to show her that it's *my* life."

"What was 'before' like? Why are you so angry?"

Mira dropped her gaze. "I just am. That's all." She wiped the tears off her face with the back of her hand.

"Is it just Chris? Or are you mad about more than that?"

Mira shifted on the window seat and picked at the weave of her cotton shorts. "Isn't that enough?" She was silent again. A few minutes went by. "Everything's messed up since Daddy's accident."

"Accident?"

"Heart attack."

"You said accident." Eve didn't move or fidget in her chair. She wanted nothing to disturb the room's tension. The pulse was here: in another moment she would have it between her fingers.

"I didn't mean to," Mira said, reluctantly.

"How is a heart attack an accident?"

"It isn't. In an accident it's no one's fault."

"But when your father died it was someone's fault?"

"I don't know!" Mira looked at her lap, twisting her fingers together. "You're confusing me," she said, her voice shaking with agitation.

"Tell me how your father died."

Mira sighed. "He had a bad heart—his doctors warned us after the second attack. 'You have to be careful,' they said. He wasn't allowed to exercise or anything. They wouldn't even let him go hunting. It was like walking on ice. And I was scared to make him mad." She sighed again. "But Vivian—well, you know, they were always fighting about something, the stupidest fights. Sometimes about what kind of soap was the best, sometimes about whose party to go to." Mira stopped short and looked out the window into the leaves of the magnolia tree. She felt lethargic, exhausted, almost sleepy. The droning in her ears made her eyelids feel gritty and she wanted to put her head down right there. Her chest was tight, as if her blouse were too small, and it made it hard to breathe. It must be the heat, and the late afternoon light, she thought. "It's late, it's nearly five o'clock. When I get home from riding Singapore I go right to Mother's room to tell her I'm back because it's sleeting hard and she may be worrying, but the door is closed. It seems so strange, I mean, her door is never closed in the afternoon. I try the handle and it opens and there she is with some guy from the set, in the middle of the bed. It makes me sick—I run to my bathroom and I lock the door and keep flushing the toilet. I don't want to hear them. They're in *Daddy's* bed. It's gross." Mira put her face in her hands and started to cry. "And I know he's coming home soon, she's doing it so he'll catch her. She *wants* him to know. I phone the lab, but my hands are shaking and I keep having to do it over. I want to make him stay there but he's already left for home so I get down by the edge of my bed and I pray for God to keep Daddy safe. And when the front door opens I go into my closet and I pretend I'm fixing my clothes. Daddy comes down the hall and goes into their bedroom, he's shouting, mother's screaming at him, footsteps run past my door and the front door bangs shut, and I can hear them yelling through the wall. I just want to die, go anywhere but here. I have to get out but my mother is screaming Mira! Mira! and I don't want to go in there but she keeps screaming and I have to, I go in, and he's banging her head against the wall, he's slamming her over and over and then they slide to the ground, he's kneeling on her, he's pinned her shoulders with his knees, he's punching her face, he doesn't know what he's doing, her nose is bloody and she's trying to get out from under him, and I'm pulling at him, I'm trying to help but he's strong, he's heavy. He slumps over her now, he doesn't move anymore, he's red in the face, his mouth is open. He weighs so much. He's not breathing."

Mira was sobbing, curled into a ball on the window seat, knees hugged to chest. Eve had to strain to catch the words.

"I try to breathe into his mouth, but I've only seen it in the movies, I don't really know how, I keep begging her to help but she's frozen, she doesn't move. I keep blowing down his throat, it's like a wide empty hallway, his lips are all loose, he tastes bad, and there's no breath. I want to help him but he's dead. I can't save him."

Eve baited the hook. "So it was your fault that he died?"

Mira hears a voice from far away, it is asking her questions, it is pounding at her, it is relentless. Her voice answers yes, yes, it's my fault, but at those words a metallic taste singes her mouth, a taste of smoke and burning, and the big bubble in her chest heaves upward, she thinks she is going to be sick, it's all going to come out now, she can't keep it down any longer. "No! It's *her* fault! She says it was an accident that he caught them, but she's a liar, it's no *accident*—she wanted it, she made it happen!"

"Are you blaming her?"

"Yes!"

"She took your father away—just like she took Chris away?"

"I hate her!" The words are bursting from her mouth, they are blooming, red and ugly, into the white air of the room, it's like throwing up poison. The tightness in her chest is gone. She is confused, she is not sure where she is.

"Mira, do you know where you are?"

"I was in my room," she says, starting to cry again.

"Yes, but where are you now?"

"I don't know!" She puts her arms over her face.

"You're safe." Eve crossed over to sit beside Mira on the window seat. "Do you remember coming here today?"

Mira looked around her, dazed. "Now I remember. This is your office."

"Is this the first time you've talked about the day your father died?"

"It hurts. It hurts to remember. I never let it hurt before."

"I know. But it's better to remember." Eve put her arm around Mira.

"Don't do that." Mira pulled away.

"Why not?"

"Touching hurts."

"How does it hurt?"

"It reminds me."

"Of what?"

"I have to leave now." She stood up. "My hour's done. Vivian's waiting."

"Don't run away, Mira. You can't use your mother as an excuse."

"I'll tell you next time," she said. "When I come back on Friday."

"I want you to come again sooner than that. Friday's too far away."

Mira shook her head. "I can't."

Eve just looked at her. "You have to." She forced her voice to be firm, unsure of how far she could push but knowing she had no choice.

Mira gave her a queer, clear look—like a child startled from deep sleep. "I want to hurt her," she said, "just like she hurt me. I want her to be sorry." The words came out of her mouth like hard smooth stones. She thrust them at Eve as if this offering would force the doctor to release her.

"Maybe we could talk a bit longer today," Eve said, breaking all the rules in the urgency of the situation.

Mira started to cry again. "I have to go."

Reluctantly Eve opened the door. "Promise you'll call if you need me."

Mira nodded, and then walked quickly through the hall, out into the heat. She didn't close the front door behind her.

"Something's going to happen," Eve said to Peter, whom she had dragged away from his fourth-floor cubbyhole after Mira left. "And I've got to do something before it does." She paced in a circle around the kitchen, trying to rub out the image of Stewart Webster's death: another violent scene, recalled once again in an hypnotic state. She wondered why Mira remembered only in this way and why she did not like to be touched.

"Evie, be realistic." Peter swiveled in his chair to track her as she paced. "What *can* you do?"

"Nothing." She slumped down in a chair across from him.

"Why don't you call Brower? At least it would make you feel better."

She sighed and shook her head. "It's *my* patient, *my* problem." She picked up the sugar spoon and tilted it so that the granules slid in a shower back down into the bowl. "I don't need her to tell me the danger. Mira's self-destructive urges are obvious. I know the percentages, the risks, the patterns. What I don't know is how to stop it. Why doesn't her mother call back?" Eve stood up and paced again, her maternity blouse billowing around her as she moved. She stopped beside the phone, sweat sticking the cotton to the small of her back. "It's too damned hot!"

"Instead of just sitting here and waiting for it to ring, let's *do* something."

"Like what?"

He smiled. "It's nearly suppertime. How about making some dessert?"

Eve's mouth started to water. "Brownies?" she asked, sounding hopeful.

He laughed, and his dark eyes crinkled at the corners. Shrinkles, Eve and her family always called them—the wrinkles acquired through long years of laughter. Another reason she'd married Peter.

"I'll get fat," she warned.

"So this time you'll only eat half a pan." He went to the refrigerator and started setting things onto the table: butter, eggs, milk; from the cabinet: brown sugar, chocolate bars, coconut. It was one of the few recipes he had from his mother. He lit the oven and the room vibrated with heat.

"Ouch," Eve stood very still and her heart began to pound. "That hurts."

"What does?" Peter was reaching for a measuring cup, talking to her over his shoulder.

Another sharp pain flickered through her, quick and to the point—like lightning. For a minute she couldn't talk. She gritted her teeth. It couldn't be. She wouldn't let it be. "Just gas," she said, trying to put authority in her tone, as if to convince her body. The pain diminished. She held her breath, waited. A minute passed. She smiled at Peter. His face let go of some of the fear.

And then, suddenly, there was another pain, harder than the last, grinding from one hip bone to the other. And a wet tickle. She felt it run down the inside of her thigh and looked to see a line of red on the instep of her sandal. "I'm bleeding." Her voice was calm and mechanical, simply stating facts.

"No," Peter said. "No."

In the emergency room they made her wait, upright on a hard plastic chair, while the TV set overhead ran one diaper ad after another. Peter kept going to the desk and pleading with them to hurry. She willed the contractions to stop, setting her body against them, feeling the baby's blood seep out with every rhythmic cramp. Peter held her hand.

Half an hour later they put her in a treatment room and Rosenthal appeared. "How far apart are the contractions?" he asked, as he shoved his hand into a sterile glove.

Peter held up two fingers. They'd started timing them in the cab on the way to the hospital.

Rosenthal guided Eve's feet into the metal stirrups and she felt his hand inside her. Another contraction started and she set her teeth against it but a low moan escaped. It felt as if someone had set baling hooks in her hipbones and was jerking them simultaneously in opposite directions—like being slowly drawn and quartered. She watched Rosenthal's face. It didn't change. She'd been through this enough times to know that was a bad sign. Whenever a doctor or technician didn't say anything, it was bad.

He stood beside her and took a fetoscope from the pocket of his white jacket. Cold jelly squirted onto her round abdomen and the head of the instrument pressed in. Eve held her breath, praying. And then there it was: quick, two beats to her one— the baby's heartbeat. Hope, relief: her child was alive. Maybe there was a chance.

Rosenthal pulled a stool up beside the head of the stretcher. "Eve," he took her hand, "this baby's coming. You're five fingers dilated. There's nothing I can do to stop it."

"But it's alive!"

"Yes." He nodded. "But it can't survive now. Too small at eighteen weeks—probably a half pound at most."

"What about an antilabor drug?"

He shook his head and patted her hand. "You're too far gone for that."

She opened her mouth to protest, but another contraction pressed in. She couldn't talk.

"We're moving you to a labor room. We'll give you some medication to help the pains."

Walls flashing by, faces looking down, and the pain. She wanted more than anything in the world to close her legs and hold the baby inside her, but she couldn't. There was an urgent need to push down and out, to be relieved of the pressure, to bring the baby forth. She was in the labor unit now, she could hear other women scream in pain, in ecstasy, as they shoved their sons and daughters onward to life. She refused medication. She did not want to lose these last moments with her baby, did not want to forget what was happening. She did not want to be drugged and dopey, as she had been with Evan, did not want to wake in Recovery and have to relearn the death of her child. Peter held her hand. Through the large plate glass window the Hudson was gold under a sun that had just set. Eve focused on that river, focused on the strength of its currents, and prayed that the baby might live despite the odds, might be as strong as the river, might be a fighter like the river, might be as determined to survive.

The monitors stood silent in the corner. No preparations were made, no incubators heated, no sterile gloves snapped open, no neonatologists summoned, no forceps or scalpels laid out, no sutures threaded for the episiotomy. There was only the panting heave of her body and the sweat of her failure.

The baby slid out between her legs in a warm wet rush of amniotic fluid.

"He's breathing," Rosenthal said, cutting the cord.

Eve stretched out her arms.

"Are you sure you want to see him?"

The need to hold him was as strong as the urge to deliver him had been. "Give me my baby."

He was bloody but perfectly formed. His chest pumped, ferocious with exertion, using every bit of muscle to grab for oxygen. Ten fingers and toes were where they should be. His legs were soft and flexible because his bones were not hardened yet, and his skin was thin and red for lack of subcutaneous fat, protected by a layer of vernix. He had a light fringe of auburn hair. His mouth was an elongated curve, a perfect replica of his father's. He looked about twelve inches long.

Rosenthal and the nurses moved silently from the room.

Peter sat on the edge of the bed and began to cry. "His name is Max," he said. He reached to touch the baby's hand, and the tiny thin fingers clung to his in a reflex motion.

Eve sheltered her son against her breast, gave him her warmth as his breathing slowed. She looked down into his face, the tiny mouth that tried to suck despite it all, the eyes that were still sealed shut, the fingers that already knew enough to curl around life.

She knew Max for only a minute before he died.

14

IT IS NIGHT and I am climbing the long hill from the beach to the house. It is Michael's house in Montauk, with its green shutters and wooden porch, the moon makes long blue shadows as I walk past the glider through the kitchen to my bedroom. The hall is very black, the bathroom door is ajar, there is no one home, the light coming from my room flickers, as if someone is showing a home movie. I push open the door. There is a perfect circle in the center of her forehead, like someone stamped her with a cookie cutter, I can see her blue brain pulse against the bone. She is tied to the bed with tubing, it runs in and out of her body like red telephone wires, it is siphoning off her blood like water from a fish tank. The blue light flickers through the window, as if the moon outside is switching itself on and off. She is mute, her mouth is open, a perfect circle, she looks at me with eyes of glass, she is not dead yet. The walls of the room are mirrors, they reflect me back at me, they reflect her over and over, we repeat through time. I will stand here for days, months, years, I am rooted here, this is my punishment, yes, this is one of Dante's circles. Her tongue flickers out like a lizard's. It pulls me down close to the eyes of glass, her breath whistles in her open mouth, an empty cavity. She uses no words, but I know what she wants. I struggle to get away but her tongue is wrapped around me like strong arms. I am being pulled down into the perfect circle. I can hear the waves batter the beach outside. I am fighting, I am screaming but no sound comes out, I am being suctioned up, I am being born in reverse. Soon I will be her.

Her mouth open, Mira sat upright in bed and gasped for air, drowning in the heavy, liquid dark. Quickly she reached for the light and then got up, anything to draw a line between asleep and awake. A glass of lukewarm water from the faucet. An adjustment of the air conditioner. A quick straightening of the sheets. She sat on the edge of the bed and tried to laugh at the silliness of the nightmare, but she couldn't. This was the seventh night in a row she'd dreamed it.

At dinner for the last five nights she and Vivian had barely spoken. She hadn't looked at her mother's face. Her anger made her afraid. Last night Dee had tried to fill in the silence, and tonight Vivian had gone out. Mira hadn't asked where.

She looked over at the clock. One A.M. She'd been asleep for two hours. Her mother was probably back and in bed by now, but she wanted to wake her up and have it all out, get it over with. It was lonely being mad—and the idea of going back to sleep was scary. She wished she were still little so she could sneak into her mother's bed and be comforted. She wished she could just forget their fight and be rocked in a pair of gentle arms. Today's therapy session had been canceled and that had made everything worse. She was ready to tell Dr. Strauss about this dream. When the phone call had come early this morning she'd felt deserted.

She turned out the light, but the dark still scared her. Maybe if she just sat on the edge of her mother's bed and saw Vivian was there and whole, she would feel better. She went into the hall, feeling her way with her arms in front of her. She opened the door to her mother's bedroom, slowly, so it wouldn't squeak. The rug absorbed the noise of her feet. The edge of the bed pressed against her knees and she just stood there, listening to Vivian's breathing—heavy, even, asleep.

She was still scared. She wanted to see her mother, to be reassured by her face, to see that there was no hole in her forehead. She went back to the hall and turned on the table lamp. A path of yellow light fell across the carpet, guided her. She lowered herself onto the edge of the bed, feeling the hump of her mother's hips through the lightweight summer blanket, ready to climb in and be warmed. She jiggled the bed a little— accidentally on purpose—hoping Vivian would wake up.

But as she reached to pull back the blanket and climb in she stopped. Someone else was already there. The light caught a long fall of blond hair, another woman twined in her mother's bed.

Mira ran back to her room and locked the door, sat on the edge of the bed and tore a Kleenex into thin even strips. I can use them as bookmarks, she said to herself, admiring how her hands didn't shake, how in control they were. But what about me, she wondered suddenly, where do I belong now? My mother's sick, she thought, and she wanted to be sick, to vomit up the knowledge of women loving women, and be clean again. "She doesn't need me anymore," she said aloud as tears started to fall down onto her nightie. She made no sound. The anger idled inside her—an engine bound for satisfaction—as she rummaged in the drawer of her bedside table with one hand and her fingers touched cold metal. She couldn't remember putting it there. Had she put it there? she wondered. Or was it only a brush, a box, a piggy bank?

It feels like a dream. She is sleepy again—as in a dream. She goes over to stand in front of the mirror. She watches herself put her finger to her forehead. She wonders how it would feel. Bullets. Heavy and smooth against her fingers. She'd line them up on the dresser, six little Indians. The metal is cool. Her palm is dry. One chance in six. Blood odds. I will make the perfect circle, she says to the mirror, I will break the eyes of glass. I will bind her with guilt. She spins the cylinder, snaps it shut, sets the steel against her temple. She presses it in. The metal marks her skin in a circle. It will leave a print there, she thinks. Dr. Strauss's voice, a calm voice, as cool as the metal— turn the anger outward, where it belongs, out, not in. And another voice, as far away—wait up, I won't be late. She pictures Vivian, walking into the bedroom to a tangle of bone and blood, a cracked mirror, a stained rug. The idea makes her smile. What would her mother do? Would she sit on the edge of the bed till daylight? Would she cradle that broken china doll's head in her arms? Would she be sorry? Mira stands there, watching herself, the trigger slippery under the pad of her fingertip. It dares her. It calls to her—*pull me and see, try me and see. I am illegal, I am forbidden, I am sweet pleasure.*

Her heart is pounding so hard her body shakes. But her hand is drawn from stone. Her fingers tingle, her grip tightens. In or out, in or out, the anger is a pumping rhythm, the anger is a gathering train. Just once, she promises, just once. She pulls back against the trigger. Red light to the heart. There is a loud snap like the breaking of a bone. An empty chamber. And the anger, dark and rich and deep, eats her up.

Vivian put her hand on the knob to her daughter's bedroom door and then hesitated. What if she's not ready, she asked herself, what if Dee is wrong? After Mira went to bed Thursday night, she and Dee stayed up late, rehashing Vivian's problem. It was the first time she'd ever needed someone else's advice about Mira. A lot of what Dee'd said sounded like something she'd heard before, from a less reliable, more bitchy source.

She'd always been able to reason with Mira, to make her think the same way—but this time her daughter had simply backed off, put distance between them. It hurt Vivian to act as if she didn't care. It hurt to give Mira the freeze. And so tonight she'd escaped—gone out with a friend because she couldn't stand the tension anymore. When she'd walked into her bedroom a week ago and found that note on her dressing table she'd sat on her bed and cried for an hour; there was nothing worse than being deserted by your only child. Both days she'd woken depressed, lonely, despairing. Dee had urged her to go to Mira and make up, and she was desperate enough now to try it, even if it was the middle of the night.

But the handle wouldn't turn; Vivian tried it again quickly. It was locked. She knocked gently. No answer. "Mira," she called, and for a minute was afraid: she had always been afraid of locked doors. Her father had reversed all the locks on the house in Elizabeth so that any bedroom or bath could be turned, at his whim, into a cell. They were the old-fashioned kind of locks, with keyholes you could spy through and long-handled ornate keys. She shook the knob, her voice was louder now. "Mira!"

There was no sound from the other side of the door, not even a squeak of the bed frame or the flush of the toilet. She used her fist to bang on the heavy oak panel. The blow sent a shock through the bone of her arm. It hurt. She banged again.

With a click, Mira unlocked the door. Her eyes were dark and ringed. "What?"

"Are you okay? Your door was locked."

Mira went back to sit on her bed and just stared at Vivian. She said nothing.

Vivian felt her fear change into a mild sort of anger. "How come you locked it?"

"I need permission for that too?"

"What if there was a fire!" Vivian shut her eyes for a minute, reminding herself to stay cool. "Maybe we should talk."

"About what?"

"Chris."

"What about him?"

Vivian sighed. Mira was going to make her do all the work; teenagers were impossible. "It didn't *mean* anything. And it should show you what he's really like."

"And what is he really like?"

"A user."

"How dare you call *him* a user!"

"What the hell does that mean?" Vivian's eyes had a sudden, dangerous glint and her mouth pulled into a narrow line. The anger started to vibrate, timpani struck softly for tuning.

"*You* used him to show me! *You* used me to pacify Marty, or Ariella, or whoever you wanted! And tonight—what d'you call that?" Mira could feel the hate exploding inside her as she pointed toward her mother's bedroom.

Vivian looked confused.

"I came in a while ago to talk," Mira shouted. "But you were already busy."

"I'm sorry," Vivian said quietly, "but she's gone now."

"What do you know about being sorry!" Mira stood up. She didn't care anymore. "You're just sorry for yourself—because now I know how cheap you come."

"Don't you *ever* speak to me like that!" Vivian crossed the room in two strides and raised her hand before she realized what she was doing. "If you were younger—"

"I've never been young!" The words burst out—startling her with their truth. "You never *let* me be young!"

"You're a lot younger than I ever knew." Vivian turned away, trying to calm down. She had never, ever, struck Mira, and her own rage appalled her. "Why are you acting this way?" she cried in exasperation, feeling close to tears.

"Because you're *disgusting!*"

The words were carved in the air between them like initials on a tree, and nausea cramped Vivian's stomach. She couldn't stand the hate that was flying out of her daughter's mouth. She stared at the twisted expression on Mira's face, at the hurt, at the eyes dark and cloudy from no sleep. "You're jealous, aren't you?" she said, with sudden insight. "It threatens you when I show my love for other people too."

"That's a lie!" Mira got up abruptly and went to the closet. She walked in, closed the door, pulled her nightie off and her jeans and tee shirt on. "You and all your sex makes me sick!" She shouted the words through the door, her heart pounding. She would never have dared to say it to her mother's face. She thought she was going to throw up—the anger and the guilt were whirling around and around in her stomach.

"Since when are you such a puritan!" Vivian yelled back. "You act like some turn-of-the-century virgin!"

Ignoring her mother, Mira opened the closet door and crossed to her desk. She jerked open the drawer and stuffed a twenty-dollar bill into her jeans.

"Just where do you think you're going?"

"Wherever."

"Don't get fresh!" Vivian said, beginning to feel desperate. It was all out of control. "This is a discussion—you will *not* walk out of here." She wanted to memorize Mira's face. She'd missed her so much that her whole body ached, remembering how it felt to be without her.

"Discussion?" Mira laughed derisively. "More like you pushing me around till you get what you want!"

"That's not fair and you know it. I don't even know you when you're like this." Vivian sank down on the edge of the bed and started to cry. "How can you hurt me this way?"

"Me hurt you?" Mira gave her a queer look and started toward the door.

"No," Vivian said, pushing down the fear that came as her daughter moved. Her heart beat, hard, trying to cope with the pain that radiated around that single word. "Mira, don't go—I love you."

Mira stopped and stood there for a minute, pushing down the fear that came as her mother spoke. She didn't answer. Her heart beat, hard, as she tried to find the courage she needed to say no.

"I need you now," Vivian said softly. Need was eating her up. This was what it was like to die of cancer, every bone, every cell giving way to the invader. It made her voice wheedle —like an old woman's, like her mother's from the nursing home. *"Please* don't go."

"I have to," Mira said in a whisper. The anger was eating her up, it made her thin as a ghost. This was what it was like to die of love.

"You don't." Vivian caught Mira's hand and held it hard against her face. "You don't *have* to do anything." She could see Mira's mouth moving, could hear the words, but they were far off; the pain was muted, like that of a kidney stone felt through Demerol. Her body was cracking, splintering, fracturing, ice under too great a weight.

"I do too." Her mother's tears burned her fingers. "I just can't stay here like this anymore." Mira pulled away before she could change her mind.

We are a pair, we skate a duet, Vivian wanted to shout. Now we are spiraling apart. Bone from bone, socket from joint, love is unstitching itself. The natural order is reversed. She reached for her daughter one last time.

Mira sidestepped and went through the door.

Tears rolled down Vivian's cheeks like stage glycerine. She was sobbing. She could hear the terrible noises she was making. She was hurting so much she couldn't even worry about Mira's being out, alone, so late. She went to the library and cracked the cap off a bottle of Scotch, then went back to her bedroom. She poured herself a tall glass with no ice or water.

As she drank it the agony adjusted itself in her chest. A pilot light, she thought, as she blew her nose. A slow flame that doesn't go out. She'd wait, she'd just wait till Mira came home. And then she'd make her understand, then she'd make her love her again.

As soon as Mira got onto the sidewalk she started to cry. She ran until she saw a cab with its light on, but once inside she couldn't think of where to go. In desperation she gave the driver the address of the stable. As she swung open the barn's side door she decided not to turn on the main floor lights and felt her way down to Singapore's stall through the blackness. She switched on the bare bulb over the mare's manger.

Mira paced up and down for a while, all the things she should have said, all the things she shouldn't have said, tumbling around in her mind. The mare crunched her grain in a comforting rhythm. Her tail was a metronome and gradually Mira's pace slowed to match the horse's rhythm. After a while she went to the tack room and got Singapore's saddle and bridle, a black rubber water bucket, and her brush box. Back in the stall she spread everything out. The box was in the same meticulous order she'd left it on the Friday before Montauk— only a week ago, but it seemed as far off as if it were someone else's life. To look at her box made her feel better, calmer. Soft and hard bristle brushes laid end-to-end, a curry comb, a sweat scraper. A bar of glycerine saddlesoap, a sponge, and neat's-foot oil. Two pulling combs. Rags to clean Singapore's nose and eyes. Needle and thread for hunter braiding. A spare lead line and halter.

Mira started to clean the tack, determined to forget about her mother. It took hours to undo each buckle and strap, to soap the leather down with the bar of glycerine and a deep-sea sponge, hours to rub the lather in, to feel the leather grow supple and clean beneath her sticky fingers, hours to dig into every fold and cranny of the saddle, up under the knee flaps, down deep into the stitched seams of the pommel, along the long leather stirrup straps, hours to clean all the metal, the bit and the buckles, the stirrups and chains, to buff and polish till they shone bright as mirrors, to put the bridle back together again, the throat catch, the browband and noseband, the reins, all those interlocking pieces, all those intricate connections. It took all night, and by the time she was done, her fingers were sore and she had rubbed anger into exhaustion, diluted guilt with soapy water. It was nearly four-thirty and there was nowhere left to go but home. To bed. She hoped she was too tired to dream.

There is a perfect circle in the center of my forehead, like someone stamped me with a cookie cutter, she can see my blue brain pulse against the bone. I am tied to the bed with tubing, it runs in and out of my body like red telephone wires, it is siphoning off my blood like water from a fish tank. The blue light flickers through the window, as if the moon outside is switching itself on and off. She stands mute, her mouth is open, a perfect circle, she looks at me with eyes of glass, I am not dead yet. The walls of the room are mirrors, they reflect me back at me, they reflect her over and over, we repeat through time. I will lie here for days, months, years, she is rooted here, this is our punishment, yes, this is one of Dante's circles. Her tongue flickers out like a lizard's. It pulls me up close to her eyes of glass, her breath whistles in her open mouth, an empty cavity. She uses no words, but I know what she wants. I struggle to get away but her tongue is wrapped around me like strong arms. I am being pulled up into the perfect circle. I can hear the waves batter the beach outside. I am fighting, I am screaming but no sound comes out, I am being suctioned up, I am being born in reverse. Soon I will be her.

I am struggling against her, I am pushing her away, I hear my hands, thud thud, her flesh is thick and warm, she is holding me so tight I can't breathe, I hear her voice now, it has come back, Mira, Mira she is saying, she is shaking me now, I think I am waking up, I think this is only a dream. Her face is all right again, she has no hole in her forehead, I can just see her in the light that comes through the door from the hall. I can feel her arms around me now, they are not the arms of before, they are the comforting arms, I am safe now, oh mother, hold me I say, I need you I say, and you do. I am little and there is a thunderstorm in the dark and you let me into your bed, you say it's all right, I won't let anything hurt you, and Daddy wants me to go back to my bed, but you let me stay. Do you forgive me, you say, I'm sorry about Chris, about everything, and I hardly remember what you mean, I say yes of course yes and I hold you even tighter and this one time, just this once, I am the little girl and you are the mommy, someone else is taking care. You are soft, you are a pillow, we are cuddled so close I can smell the lemon soap of your hair and the Scotch of your breath, I need you I say and you say yes, I need you too Mira, and you rub your cheek against mine, you kiss my mouth and I can smell the Scotch, it's strong, I turn my head but you are following me, it reminds me of that dream, that open mouth, that circle that has no words, just a tongue, and your weight shifts, you are heavy, I can feel you press against me, Mommy I say, Mommy please not now, but the dream is here now, you are over me, heavy, heavy, I think of Daddy, how heavy he is as I try to pull him off, his loose mouth, his empty breath, I kissed him to try and bring him back, and you kiss me, you are trying to bring me back but your lips are rubbery, there is only a tongue, your arms are too tight, your body too close, too heavy, no I say, not again you won't use me again, and I push you back, I am up now, I am awake now, I am a tower of rock, I am at the drawer, I did put it here, it wasn't a dream, I will make the perfect circle, I will break the eyes of glass, and the metal is cool and powerful, I can see myself in the mirror, and there is Daddy too, this is his gun, this is his short thick gun, this is how he will make you mind, this is how he will make you feel good, this is how he will punish you. He stands over you, he watches me, he is here to help. My arm swings up, I am the hunter, I see your mouth now, it is open but no sound comes out, it is the perfect circle. I will make more perfect circles, I will not say yes any longer, I will say no, I will not give you what you want, I see your eyes, they are soft with fear, you are pinned under my headlight, no I say, I will I say.

I watch the thrust of the bullet into your head, I watch your face in the mirror and see ecstasy push your eyes skyward, I see the glass explode and the blood pulse up in a jet that I do not try to stop with my finger, I do not want to plug this dike, I want the red anger to flood out across the room and wet my feet, I want to lap it up, it makes me sticky, it feels good. The lava from the volcano I have made will petrify you for all time, you will be a bronze statue where everything else is charred, no one else will touch you, you will be mine to stroke, I can remember you just the way I want. I am tired now, I turn from the mirror, I let the gun drop by my side, I have to go but I don't know where, I am still looking. I kneel over you, I look down into your eyes, they are broken now, they cannot reach me now, I bend down to kiss your empty mouth one last time and I lay my forehead against your forehead, my breast against your breast, my life against your life. Oh mother I say, we are born in reverse.

It is getting gray out. I am in a tunnel or maybe it is a street. I am walking, I am walking to someone who I cannot see and who I do not know. The leaves speak to me, they say go Mira go, the leaves are my friends, the leaves guide me down the path, across the bridges, past the statues where I stop to look for my mother's face, along the edge of the water where my mother will never row, past the bushes where no one hides tonight, I am on the other side, the leaves whisper goodbye, the neon blinks hello as I cross, this street is gray too, it must still be late, there is only a knocker in the shape of the moon, no bell here, the sky is soft as I wait, my hands are colored with your red, out, out, she said, the anger is out I say, as they glow invisible like the Lady's. I hear her coming, I hear the lock, here is her face. I do not know what to say, I was canceled today, there are no words to tell what is happening to me, she does not seem to mind. Mother I say, I love you I say, and she puts her arms around me and at last I am held.

3

15

"ANY MESSAGES?" Eve rested her elbows on the high counter at the nurses' station and put all her weight on one foot; her new shoes were giving her a blister on her heel.

Without looking up, the ward secretary shook her head and went on with her coffee and paperwork.

Eve's tone sharpened. "I'd like Mira Webster's chart." She only needed to use her admitting privileges at Payne Whitney once in a while, but she expected respect when she did—she wasn't a resident anymore. The clerk handed it over with a shrug, and, still annoyed, Eve flipped the metal cover back: temperature, blood pressure, mood, attitude. She squinted, trying to read the resident's notes from last night: "Patient withdrawn and depressed." Eve sighed. She wished she could make everything easier for Mira.

As she walked down the hall she nodded at two patients playing Ping-Pong, and scanned the clusters of stiff conversation on the living room couches. Sunday was a big day for visiting: families sat for a few hours to try and talk with the one who had been stolen from their homes for no comprehensible reason—not for a tumor or a broken bone, not for a heart attack or even pneumonia—usually to discover there was too much to say and no way to say it. They had lost wives, daughters, mothers, or husbands, sons, and fathers to the fortress of mental illness.

A young woman in a bathrobe sat on the floor of her room playing with a small boy in overalls. They smiled at Eve as she passed, but she looked away. It hurt too much. Even coming to the hospital, as she had each day this week and the week before, hurt too much. It reminded her, and she really did not want to be reminded.

This baby they had buried. Not quite three weeks ago, in the cemetery out on Long Island, beside Peter's parents. In another month there would be a small carved headstone: Max Seidel, August 7, 1984—something that declared he had been real, drawn breath, been loved. It was all a way of limiting the grief and keeping it confined to one place and time. They were making sure it did not take over what remained of their lives.

This time there had been a feeling of acceptance, or maybe it was simply resignation, running through the sorrow. The disaster they'd tensed against for five months had finally happened—like turning over your watch and cash to a mugger who's been shadowing you for twelve blocks. It was a relief to give up.

Lucy Brower had come to visit Eve on her second and last day at the hospital. "How are you?"

Eve wasn't sure she wanted to answer the question. Lucy would expect honesty and Eve didn't want to be honest with anyone, not even herself. She'd spent ten years training to teach people how to be analytical and honest in assessing their problems, and now she couldn't even do it for herself. She was bored, angry, and exhausted with the psychiatric formula of examination, illumination, and a brave fight for acceptance. Right now it would be easier just to numb death out and live as though it hadn't happened. She pretended they had taken out her appendix—not her child. But hospital life battered at this defense; from her bed on the maternity floor she could hear the fleet of newborns trundled out at feeding time, whose piercing, primal cries of need brought her milk in although there was no mouth to suck; the nursery photographer who rushed into the room past Peter to ask if they wanted this special, irreplaceable event captured for all time. The parade of mistakes and tactless questions made the room seem small and barred, and italicized her empty arms. But still she refused to cry or believe he was gone. She refused to let it be real. She wanted to write LEAVE ME ALONE in capital letters on the door to her room. Max was just at the end of the hall in the nursery, she told herself.

"I'm rotten," she said.

Lucy reached out and took her hand. They had never touched before. Her palm was warm. "This is terrible," she said after a while.

Eve was glad Lucy hadn't tried to say anything comforting —she was tired of Hallmark faces; she needed someone to say something true and brutal.

"Would you like me to come to the cemetery tomorrow?"

And that was how it happened that she, Peter, Lucy, and a few of their closest friends stood together on the hot and windy Wednesday that they buried Max—the only people, Eve thought, who acknowledged him as a person. They'd brought the cardboard box of ashes with them in the car and set it beside the small hole. Her parents didn't come down from Boston. "You've got to think of this as a blessing in disguise," her mother had urged over the phone. "It might have been retarded or deformed. This is nature's way of sparing you. Besides, it wasn't really human yet." She sighed. "Evie, put it behind you—don't let Peter build memorials." Her father, listening on the extension, had been silent.

After the call Eve had sat for a long time with Max's box in her lap, wanting to open the lid and rake her fingers through the soft gray ash, save a chip of kneebone to hide away at the back of a drawer, to prove to them he had been real, to keep him with her. But she didn't. She wondered why for the first time she wanted a gravestone, a place to go and mourn. Her parents concealed their own disappointment behind brave words and silence. Their attitude hurt her, she realized, increased her pain by denying it existed. She remembered the first time she'd seen her mother cry: she'd been eight years old and had surprised her in the bathroom. Rachel had thought the door was locked. When Eve asked why she was sad she said she wasn't—she was just getting a "piffle of a sniffle." Rachel took pain and bounced it back at you, usually as a joke. She was afraid to let it in.

Her mother couldn't cry; she couldn't cry. But she was determined Max would have a funeral. Peter had found her sitting there in the dark and made her come upstairs to bed. He'd wanted to hold her but she couldn't stand to be touched. She'd stayed on her edge of the bed and hadn't slept.

They stood at the cemetery awkwardly. There was no service, no carefully prepared eulogy, no rabbi. No one knew what to say. *I don't want my little boy to be lonely here,* Eve said to herself, *please God let him feel his grandparents beside him.* After a while she turned to Peter and they picked Max up together and set him down in the hole; *we laid him away,* she thought, *as simply as sliding bread into the oven. We said kaddish with our hands.*

Afterward no one made any polite conversation. The Long Island Expressway went by gray and painful with potholes. Back at home no one ate, they just sat and looked at each other, ennervated by emotion. Eve could feel herself pretending it all wasn't happening. When Lucy had left, she'd said only, "Get back to work." But Eve had canceled all her appointments for that week and the next. She was ready to give up her practice, she was ready to feel depressed. She sat all day long in the kitchen rocker and stared out the window. Two nights later, Mira appeared.

It had been a shock, stumbling downstairs through the early half-dark, not knowing why she had gotten up instead of Peter —except that she never seemed to sleep anymore and for him it was the only relief left—looking through the peephole to see Mira on the stoop. Mira, so disoriented she didn't know where she was or who Eve was; Mira, a waterfall of words, all strung together, all garbled. She kept calling Eve Mother. Eve made her sit in the kitchen while she got her black bag, and gave her an injection to calm her down, to stop the endless babbling, the hysterical laughing and crying that echoed off the floor and the walls. Anything to bring her back to reality. She was afraid that Mira was too far gone, too far down into her head to resurface, and had called Payne Whitney, arranged for an ambulance and a room. Then she got Peter to sit with Mira for a minute while she dressed. "You can't go," he'd said, "you're not well enough." "I've got to, it'll keep me alive," she'd answered, understanding at last what Lucy had meant.

In the ambulance she'd held Mira's hand. The tranquilizer was working and Mira's voice was drowsy but coherent; she kept talking about Vivian as if she couldn't stop; she was just a record player switched from 78 to 33, and for the first time Eve could really hear what she was saying. I shot my mother, she said. I shot her dead on the floor. I couldn't stand it anymore. I couldn't stand her hands. The sticky heat. And Eve understood at last: "Touching hurts, we share many things"— fragments of the therapy sliding into a final alignment.

She held Mira's head when she vomited and stroked her forehead as they admitted her. She tried to speed them up, the endless forms and insurance numbers—it's an emergency, she insisted—and used her influence to make sure Mira got a good quiet room away from elevators, stairs, and the nurses' station. She sat by the bed and held Mira's hand until she fell asleep at last, pushed into oblivion by the Thorazine flowing through the IV. Eve stayed there all night long, wanting her face to be the first Mira saw in the morning, knowing she was getting too involved but squashing down the thought. She needed to care. It was good to feel something again, to be helping somebody again. *I couldn't help Max,* she thought, as she watched the sky outside the window turn from gray to mauve to pink.

Every morning since Mira's admission two weeks ago she'd been there promptly at eleven. It was like trying to patch together an old rag doll, worn seams exploding with stuffing even as she strengthened and restitched them. Now she pushed the door to Mira's room open with a feeling of gratitude.

Mira was folding her nightgown. On the bed beside her, her suitcase lay open, half-filled. She smiled at Eve.

Eve smiled back, assessing with a quick glance. Mira was drawn beneath a yellowed tan. Her hands still shook as she stroked the fabric of the nightgown and folded it into a precise square package. She was trying to be brave.

"Today's the big day," Eve said, closing the door behind her. "How do you feel?"

Mira started to shrug and then stopped herself. She looked around the room, with its bare walls. A jade tree stood on the windowsill, a gift from Michael and his mother. It was the only thing in the room with any color. "It hasn't been so bad here."

I like it here, she really wanted to say, please don't make me leave. At first she'd been scared, of the locked doors, of the loud laughter, of the pills and injections, of the way the nurses and orderlies spoke to her as if she were deaf or retarded. And the other patients scared her too—but over the last few days she'd gotten used to everything. Even Dan, whose eyes flipped up and down like headlights when he tried to talk to you, or Edie, whose arms and neck were still bandaged. Mira had even gotten confident enough to leave her room and go to the ward refrigerator for a glass of juice or to the lounge for a magazine.

Eve sat down in the single straight chair by the side of the bed. She smiled at Mira again, waiting.

"I mean," Mira went on, looking down at her hands as they smoothed the nightgown over her forearm, "I know what's going to happen here."

"You feel safe here?"

"I guess." Mira paused. "This's a safe place."

"Safe from?"

"I don't know." She drew her eyebrows together in a puzzled expression. "It just feels safe."

"And what feels dangerous?"

"Everywhere else."

"Even Montauk?" Eve asked, with a touch of surprise. Cassie Ross had volunteered to have Mira stay with them the last two weeks in August when Eve called her last Monday on the phone.

"I'm not sure. I'm not sure of anything anymore." Mira picked up the shopping bag Dr. Strauss had set on the bed for her and dumped it. Bathing suits, nightgowns, shorts, underwear and bras, sandals, a few favorite books, and at the bottom, her old stuffed pink cat. Her heart pounded, and she licked her lips to wet them. "Who packed this?"

"Your mother," Eve said, watching her closely. At every other session any mention of Vivian had sent Mira into a rage. "I thought she'd know best what you need." It had been a risk to ask Vivian to pack Mira's things, but she needed Mira to remember the other feelings that went hand in hand with her new-found anger: love, loss, guilt, ambivalence—they would all have to be worked out.

Mira didn't say anything and Eve sat in the silence, remembering the relief she'd felt the night of Mira's hospitalization when, in phoning the Webster home, she'd heard Vivian's voice. She might hate the woman but she'd certainly been glad to find her still alive. Throughout the ambulance ride and the admissions procedure she'd kept hoping that Mira's description of the shooting was just some kind of fantasy, a hallucination—that Mira hadn't been so far gone as to act out the emotional explosion of hatred. And her intuition had been right. Vivian was more than alive; nearly hysterical with anxiety, she was wondering where her fourteen-year-old daughter had run to at five in the morning.

"She's in the hospital." Eve had kept her voice flat and cool. She wanted her tone to be a wall that Vivian would run into, that would smack her and make her listen.

"Is she hurt? Did she get mugged?"

"No. It's nothing physical."

"Then what's she doing there?" Fear turned to anger and Vivian sounded indignant.

"She came to my house and told me she killed you."

"You've got to be joking!" Vivian laughed. "You're just making this up, right?"

"You had a fight, didn't you? She threatened you with your husband's gun?"

"So what?" Vivian's voice was defiant. "She certainly didn't do anything with it—as you can see." She cleared her throat and Eve heard the chink of a glass against the receiver. "Tell me where I go to pick her up."

She's thinking it'd be inconvenient to get dressed, Eve thought to herself. "Mira's heavily sedated. Seeing you now would be the worst possible thing." She struggled to keep anger out of her voice. She needed to be cool-headed. She had to stop reacting so strongly. "She's got to stay here."

"You can't do that!" Vivian shouted, seesawing back into righteous anger. "You can't keep me from my daughter! It's against the law."

"And so is child abuse, Mrs. Webster."

"What the hell is that supposed to mean?" Her question was a stunned whisper. "I've never hit Mira in my life."

"That means that if you try to get your daughter released I'll have you brought up on charges." Eve paused. "For *sexual* abuse of a juvenile."

"I don't know what you're talking about." Vivian tried to clear her throat again and failed.

"Incest is what I'm talking about."

"If Mira told you anything like that she's lying." Her voice sounded sick.

"Have you ever known Mira to lie?"

"This is ridiculous. What proof could you possibly have?"

"I have Mira's word. That's all the proof I need." Eve knew how thin the bluff really was: it was hard to prove cases of incest in court—often the child's word was not enough. Physical evidence was important: bruises, flesh beneath fingernails, a sperm count. Or a parent who admitted the act. Here there was nothing—just the look on Mira's face in the ambulance. Those were the kinds of marks incest left: shame, contempt, a child who hated herself.

"I tell you it's not true," Vivian Webster said, the tremor in her voice breaking to a sob. "Not a *word* of it. Why would she say such a *disgusting* thing?"

"Come to my office at eleven and we'll talk."

"But you haven't told me what's wrong with her."

"She may have had a psychotic break."

"I don't know what that means."

"It doesn't matter—if we're lucky I'm wrong and she'll respond to the drugs and come around. I'll know more later."

By 11 A.M. Eve had spent two hours trying to reorient Mira and hadn't had a chance to shower or change her clothes. Vivian Webster didn't look much better. She'd been drinking and continued to deny that she and Mira had ever had anything other than a "normal" relationship. Her horror seemed so genuine that after a while Eve began to suspect that Vivian had simply blocked out what she did not want to remember, erased a memory that was shameful and incriminating. She would never admit it.

Eve's grim description of Mira's condition had frightened Vivian—"marginal" was the word she'd used—and she'd stopped threatening Eve with legal action if her daughter was not released. "She needs intensive therapy—and away from home, away from you." Vivian had flinched as Eve said the words.

That first day Mira had woken calm and rational. The Thorazine was helping but the flat look in her eyes frightened Eve. Mira did not understand what she was doing in the hospital. "Why am I here?" she'd asked.

"What do you remember?"

Mira shook her head.

"Do you know what day it is?"

Mira's face was blank.

"What year?"

Nothing.

"Can you tell me who is President of the United States?"

Mira frowned, straining. "Reagan?"

Eve smiled.

"So maybe it's 1984—but why am I here?" she repeated.

"Don't worry about that now. All you need to know is that this is a safe place, a good place for you to rest for a while. We'll figure everything else out later."

It wasn't until four days later—days in which Mira never asked about Vivian, or why she hadn't come to visit—that Mira began to resurface into reality. It was as if she needed the time and distance to feel safe enough to remember. On the Friday night one week after Mira's admission, the resident on call had summoned Eve from her bed at 2 A.M. and she'd arrived to find them putting Mira into restraints and sticking her with an IV of Thorazine. She was thrashing around, having woken incoherent and uncontrollable from a nightmare.

"No." Eve intervened to stop the sedation. "It's time for this. Let her be."

Mira was in some kind of a trance state, Eve saw, like the other times in the office when she'd revealed painful memories. Now she was reliving last Friday night; she was remembering at last. She was answering her own question about why she was there.

By 5 A.M. Mira had stopped crying and just lay there limp on the bed. The sky was beginning to turn. "Why aren't I in prison?" Mira asked.

"Would that be punishment enough for what you've done?"

"When you kill someone they send you to prison."

"How do you know your mother is dead?"

"I saw her dead. On the floor. I saw the bullets go in her."

"She could have lived," Eve suggested sensibly. "Sometimes people survive being shot. Why are you assuming she's dead?"

"Are you saying she's alive?"

"Let's say she is, hypothetically—how would you feel?"

"Scared."

"Why scared?"

"I don't know." She looked angry now. "You're playing games again!"

"Your mother's alive," Eve said in a low voice.

Mira inhaled slowly, her eyes wide. "Is she in the hospital?"

Eve shook her head. "At home. Asleep probably."

"I don't understand!"

"You didn't shoot your mother."

"I did! I saw it!"

"You saw it in your imagination. You needed to see it, so you made it up—it's a metaphor for the separation you couldn't manage in real life. You needed her to be dead, you needed to be free—so you just fantasized her away."

"I don't believe you." Mira jerked her head from side to side.

And she didn't. The next day Eve had gone to the library and brought Mira back issues of the *Times* for the past week. Mira read every article, scanned each line of type for corroboration of the guilt she knew was hers. Eve bought copies of *Newsweek, Time, Life,* and even *Soap Opera Digest.* Nothing helped. Mira continued to wait for the police to show up at the door and handcuff her.

"They won't come," Eve'd said on Monday, "and you don't need them. You're doing a fine job of punishing yourself." She'd just about decided that Mira wouldn't be able to accept the truth, that she would be stuck between her fantasy world and reality for a long time when something changed. Tuesday morning's chart read: "Came out of room for first time at 8 P.M., went to refrigerator for juice, talked with other patients." Mira'd met Eve at the door to her room that morning. "I believe you," she said.

"Why does it hurt so much to believe me?"

"Because it means I must be sick," Mira said quietly. "To have made all this up means I'm sick."

The same strength Mira had used to stay emotionally intact under Vivian's pressure was finally being applied toward healing. But it was frustrating—for each new revelation there was a new disguise—and Eve knew time was short. Mira had been at Payne over a week, and each day that passed she'd refused to see her mother. She'd made Eve promise not to let her in.

"Why d'you have to ask *her* to pack my stuff?" Mira said now, dropping the pink cat as if it were contaminated. "I told you—I don't want to see her!"

"And I gave you my word," Eve said, squinting against the sudden burst of sunlight that lit up the room. "Mrs. Ross'll be waiting for you downstairs in forty-five minutes. When you come back after Labor Day you'll go directly to Penn Station for the train to Boston. Your grandmother'll pick you up at the Route 128 station."

Boston had been Vivian's suggestion—one made in desperation after her daughter had refused to see her five days in a row. It was clear even to her that Mira would have to live apart for a while. Mira was to spend the next year with her grandmother and attend Concord Academy as a day student while entering therapy with an analyst on Marlborough Street.

"You're *sure* Vivian won't be downstairs?" Mira said suspiciously. Her worst fear was to face her mother. She wished she could just stay here, with Dr. Strauss.

Eve nodded. "How're you feeling about going to Boston?"

"Glad to get away." She looked down and began to throw the rest of the contents from the bag Dr. Strauss had brought helter-skelter into the suitcase. The pink cat stayed at the head of the bed where she'd shoved it. "I hope she falls apart on the set or something."

"You'd be glad?"

"It'd serve her right!"

Dr. Strauss didn't answer.

Mira threw another sweater on top of the pile in the suitcase. "She took so much! She stole things from me." The words burst out.

"What do you mean?"

"Chris. My father. My baby. My *privacy*. After a while—even my own body!" Mira banged her fist against the top edge of the suitcase. "I wanted to be good, I wanted to make her happy, I wanted her to love me, and she just *used* me! I hate her." Mira stood still for a minute. She looked up at Dr. Strauss. "She took my self-respect, and *I* let her. I'll hate myself for that for forever."

"You were very young when it started. You didn't know what it meant."

"But when I was older—then I knew. Then I should've said no!"

"You're punishing yourself for something that's not your fault."

"Don't you see—I *let* her do it. By keeping quiet I said *yes.* I pretended to be asleep, I just lay there, but I was still a silent partner."

"Is that an indictable offense?"

Mira cocked her head. "What d'you mean?"

"I mean that you don't need a judge or jury to sentence you to prison—you've already given yourself a life term. Maybe that's why you had to fantasize you'd killed her—to make sure you got punished well enough, to make sure you paid for your crime of silence."

Mira didn't say anything. She was working on the idea, digesting it. "Maybe," she admitted after a minute. "But it doesn't really matter, does it? It'll never be right now," she said, looking at Dr. Strauss with a clear and calm gaze.

The words sent a queasy feeling through Eve's stomach.

Mira smoothed the pile of clothes with her hand. She was quiet a long time. She looked up at the cat. "I'm still tied to her. I still worry about her, at the same time I'm mad."

"Tell me about worrying and being mad all at once."

Mira lifted her hands and let them fall again in a gesture of despair. "At first the anger feels good—it's like a knife, it lifts all the feelings away and keeps me clean—but then I start to think of how she's all alone, and the anger blurs out. When it's gone, then I feel guilty. I hate myself for loving her but the feeling won't go away." She started to cry, ashamed. It hurt to say these things. "And I'm lonely too. It's hard to be by myself. I got used to it the other way and sometimes, even with all she did, I miss her. She was my *mother.*"

"You talk about her as if she really were dead."

"In some ways she *is*—like, I can't be with her as my

mother anymore, never again." The crying was hurting her chest.

"What if being a daughter didn't mean the things it used to?"

"I still couldn't! Things would never change that much." She forced herself to stop crying and wipe her eyes.

"What do you mean?" Dr. Strauss said finally.

"It scares me!"

"What does?"

"Being close to her again now she's back."

"Back from where?"

Mira looked confused again. "From where I put her, I guess."

"And where is that?"

"I made her dead and now she's back!"

"And you're afraid that to be safe you'll have to kill her again, a second time, isn't that it?"

Mira nodded and burst into tears. Since she'd come to the hospital hearing the truth always made her cry.

"You want her back because you miss her, but you're afraid it will all be the same."

"Even if it was a bad kind of love between us, it was still *love*. Isn't a little love better than no love at all?" The tears ran down her cheeks, a sob came up from deep inside.

Eve got up and crossed over to her. She knew what Lucy would say, but she didn't care. Some things were just too hard: you had to find your own way with each patient. They sat side by side on the edge of the bed without touching. It sagged toward the floor. "Don't you think that's part of the sickness —to love the person who abuses you?"

"I'm afraid no one will ever love me again," Mira whispered, the words breaking apart into sobs.

"Mira, you need your own time and space, to grow apart, to heal."

"But it hurts—when will it stop hurting?" Her shoulders were trembling.

Eve looked down at the floor. "If you don't go now, you never will, never in all your life. And to make it stop hurting you've got to go. Do you understand?"

"Sort of. Sometimes." Mira wiped her face. "But it's not so easy."

"You're right." Dr. Strauss smiled at her gently. "Let's talk about the fantasy—can you remember what it means?"

"No." Mira got up and crossed to the window, rubbing her eyes. "After you were here yesterday I tried, I really did, to keep it in my mind, to remember what we said, but it kept sliding away. I *want* to remember. Why can't I?"

"Sometimes you think you want to remember but another part of you says no, that'll hurt too much, and it shuts off the memory, or the idea."

"You mean, like the way I couldn't talk about Daddy dying?"

Dr. Strauss nodded.

"But then I did, then I said it all out loud to you, so you could see it, so you could be there too and know what I know."

"That's what the fantasies, the trances, are for—when you can't express something in real life you put it into your dreams," Eve went on, taking the risk of saying too much. There was so little time left: she wanted Mira to go to Montauk with a lot to think out. "Tell me about the fantasy, about how you felt while you were watching yourself in the mirror."

"I was angry then, hateful." Mira bit her fingernail. "It was dangerous."

"The fantasy is a symbol for your rage," Eve said, crossing to stand beside her at the window, once again taking the chance of too much interpretation. "It's a way of acting out what you don't dare to say or do in reality. You were telling your mother to stop. Symbols are safe because they're not real."

"I was paying her back," Mira said.

"Paying her back?"

"I was killing her, killing me, stealing back what she'd stolen." Mira fingered the fat leaves on the jade tree. They stood and watched the traffic on the hospital drive for a while. Mira's hands, resting on the sill, looked white and bloodless.

"If you get out of the environment that's making you express the anger this way," Eve said, "if you go somewhere safe enough—far enough away from her—to confront how you really feel without the buffer of dreams or fantasies, why then, you'll get well."

"How do you know? Maybe I'll never get well?" Mira asked after a while. "Everything you say sounds so . . . made up. All this *interpretation!* How can you be sure I'm not just faking—how can you be sure of anything I've told you?"

"Mira, you are a maker of symbols." Eve sighed and wished she could take her hand, chafe it to bring the warmth back to the surface. "And it's my job to read your symbols."

"They say Teiresias used birds." Mira's voice was subdued now and she turned her shoulders away from Dr. Strauss, so that her face was hidden. "And what good does it do, this reading of yours?" she cried after a minute, swiveling back in anger. "It's all happened anyway. You can't control things. Life's unstoppable!"

"Is that how it feels now? Uncontrollable?"

"How sick do you think I am? What is it you write on that chart every day?"

Eve could hear the hostility in Mira's voice. It was common for patients to want to have the name of a disease assigned to them—it gave them the illusion of control—but Mira was using it here to underline her dependence. She decided to sidestep, wanting to get to the real issue: Boston. "I think you need to continue analysis. In Boston."

"Why? What difference could it make now?" Her apathy was a weapon. She was tired of being betrayed. She was angry. "I'll spend the rest of my life killing her, the rest of my life being guilty. This is who I am, forever. I can't get away from it by talking! We're sick, both of us, and our sickness won't die until we do, until we're both stamped out!"

Eve refused to look impressed. She kept to the facts. "When you don't need to use symbols anymore, when you can just say no plain and simple, when you can separate from your mother without being afraid you'll have to kill her or you—then you'll be healthy enough to have your own life. You won't need hers anymore and the pain will stop. Those are important things."

Mira looked at Dr. Strauss, distracted from her feelings for a minute by a new idea. "That's what the dream is about, the one where first she's tied to the bed and then we switch. It's about how we're the same, like twins."

Eve nodded, inwardly pleased that Mira had made the connection.

Mira pressed her nose against the glass. "I don't even know who's torturing who anymore," she said sadly. "When I thought about Russian roulette I wanted to kill myself, but I really wanted her to find me even more. It's all the same in the end, isn't it? If I'd killed her I'd have killed me and vice versa. *We are born in reverse*—I understand what that means now. We're twined together like roots, like tight dark roots. I don't think I can cut us free."

"I *know* you can."

"Have you ever seen it happen?" Mira asked with despair. "Will it take my whole life?"

"Complicated things take a long time."

"I don't want to go!" The anger was back. "Why are you

sending me away when I can talk to you, when I trust you—how do I know I'll be able to talk to this other doctor?"

For the last five sessions Mira had refused to acknowledge Dr. Hannah Baughman by name—one way, Eve thought, of keeping the intruder from being real. Mira's dependence on Eve was strong now and, as usual, Eve found herself fighting back her own emotions. She reminded herself that she was not being loved for herself, but for whom she had replaced in Mira's mind. Transference. It would only hurt Mira in the long run, she warned herself, if she allowed herself the luxury of loving back—countertransference, she thought, stifling the flash of pain and the memory of Max's face. "When you first came to see me you couldn't talk to me either, but now you can. When you get to know her, you'll be able to talk to Dr. Baughman too."

Mira went over and sat hunched up on the edge of the bed. Right now she hated Dr. Strauss for doing this to her.

Eve decided a small personal revelation might help. "Maybe you'll feel better if I tell you that I *know* Dr. Baughman. I trained under her for a while when she was on staff down here in New York a few years ago. I wouldn't send you to her if I didn't think you'd like her. If I didn't think she was the right person for you."

"I want to stay here with you." Mira raised her head to look at Eve with an imploring look. It sent shock waves through Eve's bones. From an infant that look would have meant pick me up; from a toddler cuddle me; from an adolescent love me.

She turned away to shake off the power of Mira's appeal. "Mira, you're just starting your therapy, you're just beginning to work. I can't help you anymore from here. You've got to go to Boston, it's more important than anything you've ever done before."

"I don't want to go," Mira said stubbornly.

"What's the worst that can happen?"

"I could get lost. I've never taken a train alone before."

What's that all about, Eve wondered. Mira was one of the most capable teenagers she knew. "Why are you worried about the train?"

"I don't like getting places, I don't like being in between. It scares me . . . I don't know where I really am if I'm not here or there yet."

The metaphor for her life, Eve thought, not here, but not there—yet. "Would you rather take the plane? It's quicker."

"I hate planes. Up in the air it's even worse."

"What other things scare you the same way?"

"Will you come with me?" Mira asked, avoiding the question and blurting out what she'd been thinking about before Dr. Strauss came for their appointment. "I've been thinking about it all morning—it wouldn't be nearly so hard if you'd just come with me. Just for the train ride?"

Mira was deflecting the question by dealing only with the surface issue. Eve looked at her. Her mother's heart said *yes, yes I will* but her analyst's instinct counseled caution. She considered. It was a bad idea. "This you have to do by yourself," she said quickly, reluctant to even entertain the thought for long. She was almost afraid she would change her mind. It seemed unfair, cruel almost, that having just lost Max she should have to lose Mira.

"I *need* you to come with me," Mira tried again, thinking she would die if Dr. Strauss really said no.

Eve felt seasick. "You have my number at home and at the office. You can call *anytime.*" She smiled, but she was really thinking that inside of a month Mira wouldn't need those numbers—she'd be deep in her therapy with Hannah Baughman.

"It won't be the same." Mira looked at her, hazel eyes sad, ready to cry again.

Eve looked away. She'd never thought it would be this hard.

The image of Max's face flashed in on her and made her feel dizzy, out of breath. The pain accelerated and forced her to run in her mind to keep pace. Her brain was an adding machine, summing up her thoughts with the terrible weight of emotional truth: she had lost her son; now she was losing a daughter. Max had needed her two weeks ago; Mira needed her now. Her body had forced her to let Max go; now, her mind forced her to let Mira go. She could help neither of them.

Mira seemed so young, so easily hurt, and yet Eve knew what a core of strength there was inside her: to have weathered all the abuse and still be whole, to have used her defenses to stay alive, to have projected the anger outward at last, instead of toward herself, to have killed metaphorically the one with whom she was angry instead of herself. Eve looked at her watch, moved from the window to the bed. "It's time to go." She closed the suitcase and snapped the locks.

Mira didn't say anything. She just ached inside. She would go through the motions of getting ready to leave—there was nothing else to do.

I'm not worried about Mira, Eve realized, as she watched Mira get up to go comb her hair in the mirror. *I'm sure Mira will be all right.*

You're the one who's not all right, she said to herself. *You're the one who's standing here pretending Mira belongs to you, you're the one who still hasn't cried for Max.*

The love that lets a child go is the hardest kind of love of all. She watched Mira fiddle with the buttons on her blouse, put her lipstick on very carefully, very slowly. *The kind of love Vivian never gave to Mira, the kind of love in my Mary Cassatt print.* She'd brought the reproduction back from the museum in July and hung it in her office. It seemed to her, finally, nearly understandable: that mother held the mirror up so that her daughter's face was reflected as a perfect whole, she thought, smiling as Mira combed her hair all over again. The daughter's study of her own face was a metaphor for learning about herself, for discovering who she is, what she wants; she reveals herself, a slow-blooming rose, petal by petal.

Eve could feel Mira looking at her in the mirror, but she was concentrating. It was very important that she make the right connections now, and she turned to the suitcase to check the locks again, stalling. The ideas shimmered in the air before her, nearly hers, nearly caught, but still possibly a mirage, still fragmented. She reached again with her mind. It was the mother who showed the girl *herself, her own face and outline, her own identity* in the small mirror. A mother had to know intuitively—as she knows the solid feel of her browbone, her cheekbone, her breastbone, the structure of her being—just how to get the mirror at the right angle so it reflects the child's face and nothing else—not even her own, especially not her own. And so they were linked—but not the same; tied—but still separate and different. It wasn't a painting about control, the way she'd seen it that day in the museum. It was a portrait of a mother giving her child the power to grow up and away by reflecting the child's own face. *That's it,* she thought, her bones snapping, recoiling from the effort of her stretch, the bright yellows and greens of the painting merging in her memory, the figures of the mother and child suddenly sharp, vivid, clear. Yes, she saw it now, just what it meant, those solid brush strokes, the silent leaping colors, the connections made and not made. *Ninety percent of mothering is figuring out how to guide your kid and still stay out of her way, and ninety percent of therapy is figuring out how to guide your patient and still stay out of her way.*

She sighed and a small part of her gave way, saying, *So what, so you're not perfect, so you're not a robot, so you care too much about this patient. Big deal. There are no perfect therapists or mothers.*

Mira smiled tremulously. "I'm ready. I guess."

Eve smiled back. Her feelings hadn't touched Mira, hadn't interfered with the therapy. What more could she ask of herself?

Mira sent Dr. Strauss one last desperate look. She hunched her shoulders together. She was sure she looked pathetic. "You're *positive* I have to go?"

Eve smiled. "You know what I think."

"And you can't come with me?"

"You don't need me to."

"I'm glad you're so sure."

"I know how strong you are."

Mira smiled and blinked hard against a sudden prickle of tears. "I want to say I love you but I guess that sounds silly."

Eve held herself very straight and kept smiling. She wouldn't have been able to say a word even if she'd known the right thing to say. The pain was fierce now; it was leaping inside her.

"I don't even really know you. I mean—who you are—except in your office, that is, but somehow I still feel close to you. As if you were really my friend, or my family." She stopped, embarrassed. "Is that dumb?"

Eve shook her head. Her smile was a Band-Aid across the pain. It was keeping it in.

"Would it be bad if I hugged you goodbye?" Mira's voice quivered.

Her words unlocked Eve's arms and they moved on their own. The softness of Mira's hair was against her chin, and then strong bones, shoulder to shoulder, hip to hip, knee to knee. They held each other hard. It was their first touch, it was their last touch. After a minute, Mira let go. She picked up her suitcase, tucked the pink cat under her arm, took one long last look around the room, and then walked quickly through the door, shutting it behind her.

Four faces, Eve thought, as she put her cheek against the

wet spot that Mira's tears had left on the shoulder of her blouse. *Four faces to carry under my heart. I put them behind me but they'll always be with me: Rose, Evan, Max, Mira.* And she put her hand up to her own face. With her fingertip she felt it, with her tongue she tasted it—liquid, salty, warm: the first tear in this drought of tears, a tear that fell on the hard cracked earth of her heart, a tear that would allow something new to push its way from seed to root to flower. She had begun to cry.

She sat down on the bed. It felt good; crying was practically better than sex, she thought, smiling in spite of herself. She went home to find Peter.

For a long time they just sat together in his writing room and didn't say anything, but after a while she got up, went to the bathroom, and put in her diaphragm. She called him downstairs, took his hand and led him to the room they'd made into a nursery the year before—a room with night-light and crib, with teddy bears and buntings. They undressed themselves and lay on the bright yellow carpet in the heat. Peter touched her and she cradled his face in her hands. Sunlight came through the window and onto the floor through the wooden slats of the crib. The shadow of the bars fell in a pattern across his shoulders: they seemed imprinted on his skin, the bare bones of fact. His body was damp, her face wet with tears. They opened to each other and she let herself be vulnerable for the first time. The tears and the sweat were one, the pain and the pleasure were one. Her husband moved over her, he was ready for her, ready to burrow where a life had been before, where she was empty now. Her pleasure couldn't mount against the great weight of the pain but she didn't care. She only wanted to connect with him. They were letting pain flood in and she didn't try to put up any defense against it— this was a mutual mourning, an undeadening, an unnumbing. They were uniting themselves against the loneliness and the despair, trying to regain what they had lost. It was a rite of acceptance. They were burying their child, they were making a bridge into a different future.

And when they'd finished, Peter rubbed the tears from Eve's face with his cheeks. He slid down to kiss her where her body had failed them, down to heal the wound with his lips, giving her what she had given him. And lying there on the floor with her husband, Eve began to forgive herself.

16

"COME *on,*" Mira said to her reflection in the train's wavy bathroom mirror, "quit crying and get it together." Mascara ringed her eyes and she tried to wipe it off but it was sticky. The skin under her eyes stung. The Kleenex tore. She gave up, went back down the aisle to her seat, and tried to read the magazine on her lap. She wished she could nap. It had been a long day.

Saying goodbye to the Rosses this morning had been terrible, almost as bad as her last session with Dr. Strauss. The past two weeks had given her time to think, to be quiet and alone, to be with good friends when she needed them most. She'd done a lot of watching, watching Michael with his family—the ways they were together and the ways they weren't. Every morning she and Michael had taken a long walk after breakfast along the water's edge. They'd picked up shells—cat's-paw and cowrie, sand dollars and starfish—for Mrs. Ross's collection. They didn't talk much on those walks, they just kept each other company. Mira remembered what Michael had said back in July about her secrets being too much for him. Now she made sure she didn't tell him anything that belonged in her therapy. Sometimes loving a person meant not telling him everything, she thought.

This morning Mrs. Ross had given her her best sand dollar

as they stood at the car saying goodbye, and now Mira slipped the sand dollar out of her pocket to look at it. It was perfect, without a crack or chip. The smell of the ocean came from its tiny beadlike holes. She put it back into her jacket, and the sand in the seam of her pocket went up under her fingernails.

Mrs. Ross had been great the entire time. She'd never pressured Mira to talk about what had happened. When Michael offered this morning to come in to the city and help Mira with her bags to the train, she'd almost caved in and said yes. But somehow she just couldn't. It was as if she'd promised Dr. Strauss she'd go alone.

While she was at Montauk she'd thought a lot about her last session with Dr. Strauss, about the separation she was supposed to be making from her mother. She guessed it was starting to happen—at least, she hadn't talked to Vivian since that night in the apartment—even though the guilt was gnawing inside her, stripping away her defenses like bark from a tree, right down to the soft tender rings. Even now, even when she knew better, part of her still wanted to get up and run back to her mother. There was so much love once. Where did the love go? she wondered. How could it get so mixed up, so wrong?

She put her head back on the seat and closed her eyes. I remember the love, she said, as if she were talking to Dr. Strauss, as if this were a therapy session or a letter, as if she carried a small part of the doctor inside her, the listening part. I remember how it was. And I'm still mad with you for making me go—even though I know you're right. It would be so easy just to stay and be loved by you.

The doors are shutting. The air brakes hiss. There's no escape now. There's no way to run back to what was, or what I'd like it to be. I want to be taken care of, I want you to take care of me—but I'm too old for that now. The conductor clips my ticket. Part of me wants to push past him and run home, and sometimes I still wish I could rewrite the past, rewrite my love or rewrite her love. But sometimes love is just a lure—I remember you said that. I trust you and I trust what you said. You were right. I have to go now. It's the only way. It's the most important thing I've ever done.

The station is sliding by. I'm leaving New York, I'm leaving my city, my sidewalks, my avenue. I try to picture how Grandma Charlotte's face will look when I get off the train at ten-thirty tonight. I try to imagine my new school, what it will be like to be put back one grade, how I won't know anyone. But Singapore will be there. And a new doctor. I wonder what she'll sound like. I wonder if she'll listen the way you do.

I open my eyes. You are gone. I am in a dark corridor now. The lights whiz by. The window beside me is a mirror. I can see my mother's face. And here is my face, too, a different face, a worthy face—my hair parted down the middle so that my scalp is a straight arrow to my chin, my face a long flat oval, my eyes not emerald but hazel. I am not a thin gray shadow. I am not a smudged imitation.

The train whistles. The mirror is gone. We are coming up from the tunnel, up into the train yard where boxcars stand and wait, up across the trestle that divides the East River, up over the skyline that trembles against a black mirror of water and sky, up past shadows, the tall brick tenements of the Bronx. I will be safe again. My life will be my life. I wrap my arms around myself. I am cutting our tight dark roots. Mother I say, I still love you I say. Mother I say, we were born in reverse. And so I am rocked, and so I am carried, and so I am borne, out into the new night.